Women in Nigerian and Indo-Anglian Fiction

A Comparative Study of Female Novelists

Women in Nigerian and Indo-Anglian Fiction

A Comparative Study of Female Novelists

Pratima Prasad

ATLANTIC

PUBLISHERS & DISTRIBUTORS (P) LTD

Published by
ATLANTIC
PUBLISHERS & DISTRIBUTORS (P) LTD
7/22, Ansari Road, Darya Ganj,
New Delhi-110002
Phones : +91-11-40775252, 23273880, 23275880, 23280451
Fax : +91-11-23285873
Web : www.atlanticbooks.com
E-mail : orders@atlanticbooks.com

Branch Office
5, Nallathambi Street, Wallajah Road,
Chennai-600002
Phones : +91-44-64611085, 32413319
E-mail : chennai@atlanticbooks.com

ISBN 978-81-269-1429-6

Printed in India at Nice Printing Press, A-33/3A, Site-IV, Industrial Area, Sahibabad, Ghaziabad, U.P.

Dedicated to

My father
Late Shri Radha Mohan Prasad
(1936-2007)
Bihar Administrative Service (Retd.)

Preface

The book presents an impartial and factual depiction of women's issues highlighted by Indian and Nigerian women writers in the post-Independence era. It pays special attention to women's perspectives and explores the options left to women in the given circumstances. The book critically analyses the works of Flora Nwapa, Buchi Emecheta, and Zaynab Alkali. It comprehensively outlines their attitudes, views and contributions towards women's emancipation. These writers belong to three major ethnic groups of Nigeria, namely the Igbos of the east, the Hausas of the north and the Yorubas in the west. Among these, the Igbos have made remarkable contributions in the field of literature in English. Temperamentally the Hausas are more conservative because of their adherence to Islam. However, they have begun to adopt western style of writing while retaining their own traditional poetic forms. The Yorubas too have adopted modern literary forms for their mythology and folklore. Like the Igbos, they have made considerable contribution towards Nigerian writings in English.

Along with Nwapa, Emecheta and Alkali, Indian women writers like Kamala Markandaya, Shashi Deshpande and Arundhati Roy have been discussed in detail. Kamala Markandaya is one of the prominent Indian women writers of Gandhi-Nehru era, Shashi Deshpande represents the writers of the late twentieth century, while Arundhati Roy belongs to the twenty-first century.

Image of women in Zaynab Alkali's novel *The Stillborn* presents an in-depth analysis of Nigerian society from a woman's point of view. Alkali is one of the most established literary figures of Nigeria. She has been very conscious of the fact that women in conservative societies are treated unequal to men which is now becoming increasingly unacceptable to them. Hence, in order to bring a balance in society and create some breathing space for women in the existing social system, Zaynab Alkali has created her masterpiece, *The Stillborn.* It has been critically analysed keeping in view the women's perspective as depicted by Alkali.

Arundhati Roy's *The God of Small Things* critically examines the role of caste and class in subjugating a helpless woman in Indian society. The complicated web of tradition and modernity which traps young women has been sensitively analysed in detail.

The works of Nwapa, Emecheta, Alkali, Markandaya, Deshpande and Roy are representative of the grievances and apprehensions of women. These authors have made a forceful commentary on the conditions of women, in their respective works. Their works have been compared and contrasted keeping in view women's perspective in the entire discussion.

The book highlights the contributions of the women writers of Nigeria and India in bringing to light the problems and predicaments of their own gender, thereby providing impetus for social change. It is an attempt to understand the psyche of both the genders regarding each other in the fast changing circumstances of twenty-first century. The reasons of mutual bias, prejudices, grievances, expectations and preconceived notions have been objectively and impartially studied.

The cultural similarities and identical nature of problems faced by women of African and Indian origin reflect the universal nature of women's problems and their persistence and continuation of hardships.

The book will be useful to students and teachers of Indian English literature, Nigerian literature and trans-continental studies. It is hoped that after going through this book, the reader will emerge as a more sensitive, considerate and helpful individual who is willing to make this world a better place to live in.

Pratima Prasad

Kusumnilay,
Road No. 14,
East Ashok Nagar,
Patna - 800 020

Acknowledgements

With gratitude, I thank Dr. Ila Sinha for her support and guidance. I thank Prof. Shaileshwar Sati Prasad for providing me valuable reference material without which this book could not have been completed.

I am thankful to Prof. S.M. Ashok, Head of the P.G. Department of English, Patna University, Patna. I would like to express my regards to Prof. Shiv Jatan Thakur, Prof. Shankar A. Dutta, Dr. Indibar Mukherjee and Dr. Mohiba Sami. I am also thankful to Mrs. Sushma Mishra, Head, Department of English, Patna Science College for her useful suggestions. I am also obliged to Prof. Arun Kamal and Dr. Sanjay Sinha.

I remember with all respect late Prof. S.D. Singh during whose tenure I completed my postgraduation (1994-96). I am grateful to my teachers—Prof. Vinod Sahay, Dr. Ratri Roy, Dr. Mamta Chaudhry and Dr. Anunaya Chaube.

I am grateful to late Dr. Farida Kalim, former Head of the Department of English, Magadh Mahila College, Patna. I also express my regards to Dr. Suman Prabha, Dr. Tara Sinha, Dr. Manju Sinha, Dr. Zaira Kalim, Mrs. Rashmi Zafar and Dr. Rekha Jha who illuminated the department during my graduation (1991-94).

I am thankful to Shri Himanshu Shekhar Jha and Mrs. Jha for their constant guidance and support during my initial years of college education. I am indebted to the teachers of Notre Dame Academy (NDA) Jamalpur and Patna for their guidance and support.

I acknowledge the support provided by Atlantic Publishers and Distributors (P) Ltd. in bringing out this book.

With all humility, I acknowledge the help and support extended to me by my mother Smt. Kusum Verma Prasad, elder brother Dr. Sangeet Kumar, elder sister Mrs. Divya Prasad Ambastha and my younger sister Dr. Jaya Prasad.

With all honesty, I must state that the contributions of my father late Shri Radha Mohan Prasad can neither be measured nor repaid. Thank you Papa.

Pratima Prasad

Contents

1 Introduction

The present work *Women in Nigerian and Indo-Anglian Fiction: A Comparative Study of Female Novelists* attempts an impartial and factual depiction of women's issues as highlighted by the Indian and Nigerian women writers such as Kamala Markandaya, Shashi Deshpande, Buchi Emecheta and Flora Nwapa with special emphasis on the first novels of Zaynab Alkali and Arundhati Roy.

India and the Federal Republic of Nigeria are countries of two different continents but share many historical, social and economic similarities. Both the countries have had a colonial past. Nigeria won freedom from British rule on October 1, 1960. However, real democracy was achieved only in 1999 after going through military rule from 1966 to 1975 and from 1983 to 1989. It is a West African nation, being the most populated in the whole of Africa. Its capital is Abuja.

Like India, Nigeria too has a rich history and culture. It is a country of ethnic diversity and plurality. There are about 250 ethnic groups of which the Yoruba. Fulani, Hausa and Igbo are the major tribes. Though the official language of Nigeria is English, the country, like India, has a number of native languages that are spoken by the different ethnic groups. Islam and Christianity are the two major religions of the country as in India. The Hausas of Nigeria tend to be Muslims while the Igbos are followers of Christianity. However, indigenous religious practices also continue to survive.

Like India, Nigeria too boasts of eminent literatures who have made a mark not just in their country but the world over. Wole Soyinka is a Nigerian who became the first African in history to win the Nobel Prize for Literature. Chinua Achebe is another name globally renowned. The two together have made valuable contribution to post-colonial literature in English. No less significant are writers and poets such as John Pepper Clark, Ben Okri who is the first Nigerian to win the Booker Prize in 1991, Buchi Emecheta, Helen Habila, Chimamanda Ngogi Alichie and Ken Saro Wiwa.

Nigerian literature is primarily a 'protest' literature. This means, almost all the Nigerian literary figures, whether male or female, have taken upon themselves the role of 'path finders' and 'motivators' for social and economic revival and also regeneration of their country. This attitude adopted by the literary world of Nigeria after independence from colonial rule was very apt and appropriate. For, a tired, exploited and exhausted nation does need energetic, intellectually sharp and farsighted leadership for nation building process.

Both India and Nigeria have withstood the colonial rule with fortitude and determination and extracted independence from foreign rule. They have done it with success. Nigerian literature has been at the forefront protesting against imposition of foreign influence and power over the country. At the same time, it has reacted sharply against internal rifts and misgivings among Nigerians themselves.

The civil war of 1967-70 gave scope for re-thinking and self-assessment. It compelled the intellectually enlightened people of Nigeria to mobilize and motivate the masses towards revival of their spirits in most positive manner. Those who made significant contribution in generating nationalistic fervour among Nigerians were the literary figures like Chinua Achebe, Wole Soyinka, Aminu Kano, John Pepper Clark, Christapher Okigbo, Onuora Nzekwn, Timothy Aluko, Elechi Amadi etc. However, Chinua Achebe has emerged as the strongest and the most successful ambassador of Nigerian literature and culture. He is regarded as the *Father of Modern African Literature*. During the civil war in 1967-70, Achebe who belongs to the Ibo tribe of eastern region (Biafra) tried to draw the attention of the whole world towards the plight of his people, their day to day hardships and the havoc caused in the lives of ordinary Nigerians due to the civil war. He wrote with utmost empathy and his worries, his concerns were well received. He tried to guide his people in those troubled years of social and political upheavals. Chinua Achebe is a socially committed literary figure and he has set a model for the rest to emulate.

Chinua Achebe has been awarded 2007 Man Booker International Prize for fiction. Achebe, 76, has authored almost 20 books and novels besides short stories, essays and also poetry. *Things Fall Apart* published in 1958, is considered to be his first and best work of literature. *Anthills of the Savannah* is yet another work internationally acclaimed, published almost 30 years later.

Talking about Chinua Achebe's contributions, novelist Nadine Gordimer, one of the three judges for the award, says, "Chinua Achebe's early work made him the father of modern African literature". Achebe's contributions and presence in Nigerian literary world can neither be ignored nor under-estimated. His relevance here in this research work is equally significant as almost all Nigerian female writers consciously or unconsciously seem to look up to Chinua Achebe for inspiration. No work on Nigerian literature can be regarded as complete without appropriate reference to this stalwart.

Literary figures the world over are considered to be 'the conscience keepers' of their respective societies. Buchi Emecheta, Flora Nwapa or Zaynab Alkali may not match Achebe's stature but they have been equally vigilant and vocal about assessing Nigerian society especially in the context of the women of their country. Like Achebe, this responsibility has been borne by Nigerian women writers too.

One very prominent and also significant aspect of Nigerian society and the world at large is that of the neglect of the female population. Enough attention has not been paid towards the genuine pain, problems and grievances of the women folk. What these Nigerian writers have done is to rectify this mistake. They have used their creative energies to highlight and emphasize issues that are crucial for the survival and well being of their gender.

Women writers, such as Flora Nwapa, Buchi Emecheta and Zaynab Alkali, coming from major ethnic groups of Nigeria, represent the values of their respective societies and the reactions towards the accepted social norms. The selection of these women novelists has been made taking into consideration their differing attitudes towards the role of women in the post-colonial era of Nigeria.

Florence Nwanzuruahu Nkiru Nwapa (1931-93) is a prominent Nigerian woman writer born in Oguta, East Central State of Nigeria. Being a sensitive human being, Nwapa felt deeply for her struggling nation and suffering women population. The chaos, the confusion on the political front and the plight of women on the social front motivated her to become a writer. She joined the literary world 'to protest' against exploitation, deprivation, poverty, and unrest felt all around. *Efuru* (1966), her most popular and first literary creation, has made her immortal. *Idu* (1970), *Never Again* (1975), *One Is Enough* (1981) and *Women Are Different* (1986) are her creative works dedicated to the cause of women. Although she wrote primarily about African women but she felt the universal similarity of the plight of women the world over. She has left behind collections of short stories and poems, namely, *This is Lagos and Other Stories*, *Cassava Song and Rice Song*, *Wives at War and Other Stories*. Nwapa has also written children's books, namely, *Mammy Wate*, *Journey to Space*, *The Miracle Kittens* and *The Adventures of Deke*.

The wide range of Nwapa's literary skill is a proof in itself of women's potentiality in creativity and sensitivity. Her sensitive soul could feel the pulse of every section of Nigerian society apart from her own tribal society. She belonged to the East Central State of Nigeria. She obtained a Bachelor of Arts degree from University College, Ibadan in 1957, and a Diploma in Education in 1958 from University of Edinburgh. She served as an Education officer in Calabar until 1959. She then accepted a teaching job at Queen's School in Enugu. Her subjects were English and Geography. She continued to work in both education and civil service in several positions, including Assistant Registrar, University of Lagos (1962-76), Minister of Health and Social Welfare, East Central State (1970-71) and Minister of Lands, Survey and Urban Development (1971-74).

Nwapa gained recognition with the publication of *Efuru* in 1966. She is the first African woman to publish her work in English. Nwapa, founded *Tana Press Ltd.* in 1974 and *Flora Nwapa and Co.* in the year 1977. She began to publish the rest of her creative works from these two publishing companies. She also promoted other writers through her publishing companies.

Nwapa continued her career as an educator throughout her life, teaching at colleges and universities around the world, including New York University, Trinity College, University of Michigan and University of Ilorin.

Flora Nwapa died at the age of 62 in 1993.

Nwapa is primarily concerned about marriage, causes of its failure and significance of children in an Igbo woman's life. Above all, 'barrenness' is the central theme of her literary creativity. The position of a woman in a marriage without children is the main issue in her works.

Questions that haunt Nwapa regarding women are:

- What is the purpose and utility of a woman in family and society?
- Is she accepted as an individual who happens to be a woman?
- Is she a woman first and nothing else?
- What is the actual position of a woman in Nigerian society?
- What do they do to unfortunate barren women?
- How do they survive?
- What are the options left for them in the given circumstances?
- Do they matter to their family and husband?

- Is their existence precariously dependent upon the mercy of their in-laws or family of their birth?
- What are the means through which barren women survive with self-respect and dignity intact, without any stigma upon their womanhood?

These are the vital questions that seem to haunt Nwapa's conscious mind and she appears to take upon herself the challenge of rehabilitating especially the barren women in society through her fictions. She desires to prepare ground for their social acceptance as human beings first and foremost. They must be allowed to survive without any sense of self-pity and guilt. The issue of lack of ability to give birth to a child should not be used to throw them out of family and social arena. They must not be made to feel the 'stigma of barrenness' and carry their irony of fate upon their shoulders in isolation and dejection. It should be treated as a flaw of nature and barren women as innocent victims of the irony of fate.

Usually, such women in Nigerian society lead rejected, demoralized, bonded labour-like life. They are under tremendous psychological and social pressure. Their very existence is treated as a burden on family, and its reputation. They become a 'curse' for their own self. According to Nwapa, education and financial self-reliance are remedies of most of the problems of women in Nigerian society. For achieving these, self-confidence is the basic criterian.

'Marriage' as an institution is under serious inspection by Nwapa. She examines this institution from the point of view of a barren woman. She also takes up the issue of economic aspect of women's lives. Are these issues co-related? The financial status of women within and outside marriage has been critically examined by Nwapa. According to her, women must become economically independent like 'Rose', 'Efuru', 'Amaka', in order to combat hardships of womanhood. Whether barren or fertile, women must be sound on economic front, that too on their own account. Their emotional or financial dependence upon men may cost them their very existence. Education is the medium through which women can become confident of themselves and attain self-reliance.

The traditional Igbo culture is used as the medium through which Nwapa highlights the contradictions in the lives of both the genders. She highlights the actual condition and situations in which women have to survive in the family and society at large. Women must become mother or else they are thrown out of the core group of their family unit. They are reduced to the status of necessary evils who cannot be wished off. They are made to toil like slaves to prove their utility before their family. *Efuru* and other novels highlight the irony of fate and how women combat it with grit and determination.

Nwapa does not allow much space to male characters in her novels. It could be a reaction against lack of space granted to female characters in the novels written by male writers. It is often alleged that they either treat female characters as decorative items or pathetic creatures. In other words, justice is not done to them even in fiction. Hence, at the unconscious level, this kind of retaliation might have happened. It is a literary warfare in Nigeria between the two genders on the issue of women and their relevance in society.

Female writers give minimum space to the opposite gender in their novels. They seem to follow the model and standards set by those they resent. Naturally, men are depicted only to function as mediums for family expansion and to head the family on formal occasions. They are failures as husbands or fathers. Brothers are better placed than husbands. Husbands are just tolerated. If a husband is unable to father a child, he becomes a cause of pain and embarrassment to his wife. She has to hide his incapability by adopting all sorts of traditional methods and techniques to bear children so that the family line does not stop abruptly. In return, the man gives his name to the children thus born. The reputation of the woman remains intact as ever. This hypocrisy of Nigerian society regarding child birth is highlighted by not only Nwapa but other female writers too. While barren women are boldly rejected, men are provided with enough cover up by family and society. Nwapa wants the same kind of thoughtfulness and sensitivity towards barren women too.

Efuru is dedicated to the cause of barren women in Nigerian society, especially the Igbo tribe. The repeated failure of the protagonist Efuru to become mother breaks her marriage. Her second marriage too ends up in divorce. Her only daughter dies by misfortune. Efuru returns to her parents to restart her life as a barren lady. Her other qualities do not prove enough to shield her from the stigma of a childless woman. She goes through a lot of psychological stress and strain before finally deciding to live by herself. She finds a purpose of her life in social work and succeeds in business to sustain herself and her social works. She emerges as a woman of substance. She gains recognition on her own account. She makes a name for herself by her sincerity for her own self and her commitment for her society. She sets an example for other women who live and die in depression due to bad luck and social ill will.

Idu her next novel is very similar to *Efuru*. Like Efuru, the central character Idu too is very beautiful and a successful business woman. She too is an excellent housewife and endowed with every goodness except that of motherhood. Both the women are ideal in every other sense. What they lack is children. They seem to idealize Igbo women and hence common women fail to identify with them. Idu finally bears a son to her husband but dies of shock on knowing about her husband's sudden death.

The characterization of Amaka in *One is Enough* is that of a rebel within the institution of marriage. The stigma of barrenness makes her suffer. Ultimately, she becomes defiant and abandons her husband who has twin sons from another woman. She becomes a successful business woman on her own initiative and mother of two sons from another man. She refuses to marry the father of her sons, but is a very caring mother to her sons. It seems her purpose of life has been met with and hence she rejects this man without any sense of moral binding or guilt. She behaves as matter-of-factly as men in these matters. She is too practical to remarry.

Nwapa gives equal freedom to both the genders for procreation outside the institution of marriage. She advocates separation or divorce if a marriage goes sour. For Nwapa, children are important and not the commitment to the institution of marriage. The sanctity of marriage holds no water when the very existence of the family is in danger of extinction. The sanctity of marriage has no meaning if it fails to bear children. For, the concepts such as legal or illegal types of liaison do not exist in Igbo family. What matters is the presence of children.

Women are different, declares Nwapa. The central character of this novel *Rose* is advanced in age and single. In Nigerian society this is not a welcome state for a woman. *Rose* is depicted as a tragic case rather than as a self-satisfied, successful individual like Efuru. Yemi Mojola pleads:

> Spinsterhood, just like marriage must be regarded as an acceptable way of life.
>
> (Mojola, 1988, p. 126)

Never Again deals with war and its impact upon society. The hype created by those who matter and the sufferings of the people in the name of patriotism and bravery have been depicted in this novel. The exploitation of men and material have been objected by Nwapa. She has depicted the psychological pressure felt by ordinary men to act bravely much beyond their capabilities.

Buchi Emecheta, another Nigerian female writer is more vocal and assertive in her own way regarding women and their conflict with masculine dominance. Most of her literary works are based upon her own experiences as 'a single parent and a black woman living in Britain.' Various shades of womanhood torment and torture her intellectually enlightened mind. Her first work *In the Ditch* (1972) depicts the struggle of an abandoned wife. In almost all her novels, Buchi Emecheta keeps pondering over the institution of marriage and family in the context of women and their perspective, just like Nwapa who is equally agitated and aggrieved over this issue. However, their presentation style differs. Nwapa is more somber than Emecheta in her outpouring against men. Making her stand clear Emecheta declares:

> Being a woman, and Africa born, I see things through an African woman's eyes. I chronicle the little happenings in the lives of the African women I know. I did not know that by doing so I was going to be called a feminist. But if I am now a feminist then I am an African feminist with a small "f". In my books, I write about families, because I still believe in families. I write about women who try hard to hold their family together until it becomes absolutely impossible. I have no sympathy for a woman who deserts her children, neither do I have sympathy for a woman who insists on staying in a marriage with a brute of a man, simply to be respectable.
>
> (Emecheta, 1998, p. 239)

Buchi Emecheta's second novel *Second Class Citizen* (1974) depicts the hardships of a woman who is left behind with small children to care for without any fault of hers.

Women and Nigerian society come face to face in Emecheta's *The Bride Price* (1976). The confrontation between society and women is best depicted by Emecheta in this fictional work.

The Slave Girl published in 1977 discusses the tendency to use and abuse women on whim. It also depicts the denial of basic human rights to women in general.

The Joys of Motherhood (1979) discusses the joy and agony of motherhood in a woman's life. Emecheta herself dislikes the rejection of children by women, but in her novel she shows the attitude of some women who feel cheated when their children ignore them in old age. Under such circumstances, motherhood is simply an emotional exploitation of women. Women are dumped in old age by their children and by their husbands in middle age. They are destined to be used and rejected. The bitterness in Emecheta's writings is perhaps due to these realities of Nigerian society including its insensitivity towards the older generation, especially the women.

Destination Biafra (1982) is based upon a larger issue that affected the whole of Nigerian society. This novel includes men and children too as it deals with the Civil War in Nigeria which affected not just women but everyone else. When the very fabric of a nation is under threat, family structure and gender clashes have no takers. Chaos and disorder make life unmanageable for one and all.

Emecheta seems to further widen her canvas by choosing to write about the colonial rule and its impact upon Nigerian society. In *The Rape of Shavi* (1983), Emecheta discusses the struggle of African society under foreign rule. Its struggle to protect cultural identity and the protest against economic and political exploitations are dealt with in this novel. She, however, never forgets her focal point, that is, women and their emancipation.

In her next novel *Gwendolen* (1989) she discusses the life of a West Indian young girl who has to survive in an alien culture of London. Her novel focuses upon the struggle of a young woman wanting to survive with dignity.

Kehinde published in 1994, deals with the problems of middle-aged Nigerian women who want to get assimilated in the Nigerian society after spending half of their lives in London. *The New Tribe* (2000) happens to be her latest work.

The autobiographical elements dominate Emecheta's works. Her central characters are reflections of her own life and struggle. The attempt to translate personal experiences into a sociological interpretation of African womanhood has proved problematic and has been challenged by other black women writers, most notably by Flora Nwapa, who did not believe in categorizing women as *Second Class Citizen*.

Unlike Emecheta, the other Nigerian women writers like Zaynab Alkali and, of course, Nwapa are less aggressive and critical of the opposite gender. What they ask for is that women must be treated in such a manner that they do not consider their life as a curse. They do not believe in rejecting either men and marriage or family and children. What they try to do in their fiction is to highlight the problems and make the implicit demand for improvement, so that neither the institution of marriage nor the association of family is rejected by women.

It is with this feeling that Zaynab Alkali has written *The Stillborn*. Through her creativity Zaynab Alkali tries to bring about a certain degree of adjustment between the two genders. Zaynab Alkali is one of the most important women writers in northern Nigeria. The northern Nigerian society is very traditional. The patriarchy is very strong and it is precisely due to this social set-up that Zaynab Alkali's novel *The Stillborn* has attracted so much of attention within the Nigerian literary circle and outside.

Like Nwapa, Zaynab Alkali too resents being labeled as 'a feminist'. Zaynab Alkali asserts she is merely a writer who just happens to write about women. **This fear of being labeled as feminist is common in almost all the female Nigerian writers. They take this term as an allegation of which Emecheta is both fearless and immune.** She is rather defiant towards public opinion and observations of critics towards her own views and creations of literary excellence, for she firmly stands by the realities at grassroot level. Her commitment towards her own gender and observations as a suffering woman herself are admirable.

Both Nwapa and Zaynab Alkali are ideologically closer. They seem to distance themselves from Emecheta's rhetorics and feel somehow embarrassed by her bold outpourings. Both Nwapa and Zaynab Alkali believe in bringing balance and harmony in family and society. They want to tone down the voice of resentment and wish for better understanding between the two genders within the family structure. Hence, their reconciliatory stands go against Emecheta's confrontationist attitudes. Highlighting this reservation towards Emecheta's 'so called feminism' Omolara Ogundipe observes:

> But many African women writers like to declare that they are not feminist, as if it were a crime to be a feminist.....

> Yet, nothing could be more feminist than the writings of these women writers in their concern for and deep understanding of the experiences and fates of women in society.
>
> *(Ogundipe, 1989, pp. 10-11)*

Alkali objects to women's aggressiveness towards men which is to a certain level irrational and prejudiced. She has always questioned feminism as a viable means, a platform broad enough, to champion women's cause. In an interview she remarks:

> Certain women have used this feminist issue to shout themselves hoarse about certain ideas.... (They) use the feminist movement to get back at them. So you have this feminist thing is one big cover where people give their own interpretation to what it is. Up till now, nobody has come up with a definite definition of what feminist movement is. So they are all deceptive.
>
> (Alkali in *Garba*, Issue 8)

It is due to this line of thinking that Alkali refuses to accept *The Stillborn* as a feminist text. She says,

> I remember somebody writing to me (Sic) from London, when I was writing *The Stillborn*, asking me to change the end so that Li doesn't go back to her husband. I told her that Li is not a feminist, and... as far as I am concerned, I wasn't creating a feminist character.
>
> (Alkali in *Garba*, Issue 8)

The difference between Nwapa and Zaynab Alkali on the one hand and Emecheta on the other is basically about the issue of rehabilitation of women in society, whether by revolt or by reconciliation. Both Nwapa and Zaynab Alkali believe in forgiveness and rehabilitation of women through personality development. However, all agree that education is the only medium through which self-reliance can be attained by women. Nwapa and Zaynab Alkali want women to educate themselves, groom themselves into refined, educated, cultured and economically sound persons. They want women to become financially self-reliant, emotionally stable and moderate in conduct.

Emecheta's women characters are also suffering souls but they become bold and rebellious out of pain and frustration. They make last ditch effort to survive against all odds. They want to retain marriage and family, but are rudely rebuked and rejected. In the process, voluntarily or involuntarily, they break the norms. They fail to reconcile with their tormentors and are unable to rehabilitate themselves due to the faults of others. They are victimized by society. Hence they revolt. Misfortune dominates Emecheta's female characters, while Zaynab Alkali and Nwapa's heroines come out of their personal grief and misfortune with their own inner strength of will and convictions. They are not hostile characters, hence they are able to retain their goodness of heart and purity of mind. They are essentially stronger women than those created by Emecheta who invariably lose the hope of better days and become equally hostile towards their sinners. The pain and silent sufferings go unnoticed and this ignorance of their pain provokes them to revolt against their society. Virtually no other option is left for her characters. There is a sense of bitterness in Emecheta's writings which are based upon her own hardships in life. She has observed society very minutely from an African woman's point of view. **Her observations regarding women and their struggle for survival have motivated Emecheta to drop diplomacy and do some tough talking.** Real life incidents have embittered Emecheta's imagination. Emecheta believes in presenting facts as she has seen around her.

Therefore, Zaynab Alkali's *The Stillborn* is very different from Emecheta's creations. Zaynab Alkali tries to keep the traditional fabrics of northern Nigerian society intact. Her characterization of Li is in keeping with the sentiments of the patriarchal social set-up. Zaynab Alkali avoids confrontation with her traditional society and makes Li return to Habu, her husband. Since women are considered the custodians of culture and tradition, Li has to abide by the rules. Naturally, she returns to Habu to make him feel wanted. Li also feels secure and complete in his association, as a woman, and also as a wife and mother. Her family is complete now with a daughter and a husband by her side. She is a self-satisfied individual who has a successful career and name of her own besides being wife and mother. However, she prefers to be known as Habu's wife.

Zaynab Alkali's *The Virtuous Woman*, published in 1986, her short stories collection *Cowwebs and other stories*, published in the year 1997, *The Descendants*, which came out in 2005, are all dedicated to the cause of women and their predicaments as mother, wife, sister, sister-in-law, fiancee, friend, colleagues etc. Every role a woman plays demands sacrifices and silence from her. She is destined to step aside as tradition demands the subjugation of the feminine gender.

This traditional approach has forced women to stay in deprivation for centuries. A sense of guilt grips them the moment they perceive elements of rebellion boiling within them. This sense of mental slavery and subjugation is one of the major reasons of backwardness among women. There need not be any compulsion for war of wits or whimsical reactions among the two genders for a respectable space for women in society. It is a psychological problem that can be solved by proper grooming and balanced approach towards life and society. And this is what seems to be the essence of Zaynab Alkali and Flora Nwapa's creativity. They are providing solutions of problems and issues raised by Emecheta. **Women must show tolerance, perseverance, education and confidence to make a place for themselves, instead of wasting time in lambasting men.** Almost all women writers feel that education is the only medium which can rehabilitate women.

The concerns of Nigerian women writers find an echo even in the works of Indian women writers such as Kamala Markandaya, Shashi Deshpande, Anita Desai and other. In fact, women occupy a central place in the novels of Kamala Markandaya too. She writes with a sense of moral binding, an obligation towards her own gender. Her writings reflect her sensitivity towards women when she weaves various female characters belonging to different class and status in her novels. Markandaya writes with a missionary zeal about the life and predicament of Indian women in general. The web of emotions, tradition, expectations of society in general and family in particular, all force women to behave more or less as puppets. Social rules regulate and modulate thinking and behaviour of women more effectively than the men. Kamala Markandaya takes upon herself the responsibility to generate awareness against the old age bias towards women and tries to induce rational thinking regarding problems faced by women. Problems faced by women become more complicated and delicate due to their sentimental nature.

Kamala Markandaya stands closer to Buchi Emecheta in presenting two alien cultures in confrontation with each other. Both focus on East-West encounter in almost all their novels. This encounter is the basis of most of their literary creations. However, while Emecheta is aggressive and extrovert, Markandaya is docile and amiable at the time of utmost crisis in the lives of her characters. Kamala Markandaya has deeper understanding of human limitations and compulsions than Emecheta who is in a state of agony and helplessness. Her anger and rejection of relationships is the result of her zeal to fight for women's right till the very end.

Markandaya exhibits equal skill in delineating western characters, both male and female. She dives into their mind and soul with equal ease and surety. She, like Emecheta, is familiar to both the East and the West, hence this confidence. However, she avoids going too deep into the problems and their causes, unlike Emecheta. Yet she tries her bit to eradicate misconceptions, suspicion, myth, fear, apprehension and mistrust which torment human mind regarding alien cultures on both sides. At the same time, she keeps her eyes fixed upon the plight of Indian women and does her bit to motivate people to treat women as their equals. She wants to convince people to adopt a humanistic approach towards women and their limitations as humans (if ever any).

Markandaya's liberated women characters like Roshan, Helen, Mira are, in fact, the medium through which she gives vent to her pent up anger over the plight of Indian women. If justice, equality and liberty are not possible for women in reality, let it be granted in fictions. Here, she is close to Emecheta, but her characters rebel only for a very short span of time and revert to their traditional roles after deriving the satisfaction of breaking the norms and challenging the society. This is done only to show that women have an element of revolt in them, but they prefer to obey the family and society for its secure future and not out of fear, as it is generally presumed by society.

Basically, what most of the Indian women writers want to convey is that Indian women are as practical as men and they do not appreciate a reckless life. In order to lead a dignified and meaningful life, they tolerate subjugation and humiliations within the four walls. In India, a liberated woman is not appreciated even by their own gender. Hence, they prefer to suffer as this is the price for a married status. Social standing of a battered woman is higher than that of a liberated woman, is the general opinion in India. It is due to this belief that even female writers avoid going to extremes in the depiction of gender clashes in their novels. They prefer to tread the middle path of balance and forgiveness. Like the Nigerian female writers, Indian women writers focus more on education and financial security of women than anything else. Only educated and self-reliant women can sustain themselves with dignity. Self-help is the motto of most of the women writers. The dependence on men for emotion or finance may cost them their very existence.

The novels of Kamala Markandaya like *Nectar in a Sieve* (1954), *Some Inner Fury* (1955), *A Handful of Rice* (1966), *Coffer Dams* (1969), *Two Virgins* (1973), *Pleasure City* (1982), all discuss East-West encounter along with gender clashes and conflicts between men and women on ideological and social levels.

It seems Markandaya's writing is more for her western readers than for the Indians. Hence, in order to suit the taste and temper of her readers overseas, she inserts some foreign characters. In this way, she tries to win acceptance and appreciation from Western literary circle. No doubt the western characters add colour and variety to her stories. Markandaya is less bothered about her readers back home. One wonders if her imagination would fail, were she asked to avoid her favourite scheme. The repetition of the same theme mars the curiosity and excitement, because the obvious tension is already perceived by her regular readers. It is only the treatment which is a bit different. The crux of the matter is the same: the bewilderment of the west upon the strangeness and complexity of human and social aspects of Indian society. The Western characters get perplexed, charmed, disillusioned or overwhelmed by the poverty, spiritualism, ignorance, illiteracy, strangeness and the unity in diversity. Basically, her novels are introductions to the western readers about India and Indianness.

The women characters of Kamala Markandaya are always very intelligent. They are worldly-wise and practical as well. They often maintain good relation with their husbands, are tolerant of the male egos and devoted too. They are the typical Indian housewives. *A Handful of Rice* is an apt an example of male-female relationship, where Ravi is an embodiment of the typical Indian man with an inflated ego, aggressive at home and submissive outside, while his wife is docile, subdued and non-interfering. Ira in *Nectar in a Sieve* and Premala of some *Inner Furry* are typical docile subservient Indian wives.

Gender clash occurs in Kamala Markandaya's novels at a subtle level. Markandaya never uses rhetorical language like Emecheta to highlight the plight of Indian women. She weaves stories to explain the pitiable situation of Indian women who lack opportunity and goodwill to evolve as well-groomed social beings. Tacitly, she raises the issue of overbearing presence of men in women's world. In the stoic silence of women, lies the key to their happy family and social life. In a patriarchal society, women feel it is futile to raise issues of human rights and compassion.

Markandaya, instead of raising controversial issues related to women's emancipation, very gently tries to prepare ground to gain support for women through her novels. She wants to spread awareness among the people and prick their conscience. She begins with the brighter and normal aspects of Indian women's lives. They grow up, get married and adjust automatically with their in-laws and thus their destination reached and future sealed. Individuality of a woman is considered in a peculiar manner in the Indian context. Their world revolves around their husbands and children. This is the story of almost every Indian girl from village to semi-urban society in India.

Markandaya draws contrast among her female characters with the help of western women like Helen of the *Coffer Dam* (1969). She has guts to stand against her husband on the ground of principles. Helen feels strongly for the Indian tribals. She opposes her husband who is both ruthless and mechanical in his conduct with the natives who are assisting him in the dam project. He is biased, perplexed and in a hurry to finish off the project as early as possible so that he may return to England. He feels homesick. He also feels that he is doing a thankless job. Clinton, her husband, wonders why and how can Helen feel so deeply for the strangers. He asks her how she manages to get along with the natives. She says, "It's nothing to do with age. I just think of them as human beings, that's all" (*Coffer Dam*, p. 48).

Here, Helen is shown engaged in intellectual discussion with Clinton and is firm in her opinion. An Indian wife would have obeyed the stern orders of her husband to stay away from the natives. Her personal opinions would not have mattered. In order to show her loyalty, she would have easily agreed and ordered her children to do the same. The reason behind such obedience is basically the fear that women, who are unaware of the socio-political situation outside, may end up making wrong decisions which may cause embarrassment and awkwardness to the male members of the family. The complications of outside world are best managed by the men of the family. This kind of compulsion or dependence, whatever one may call it, forces women to follow the dictates of the male members. Helen, a western woman who has adequate opportunity to know the realities of her own society and culture, is more confident and aware as a citizen and housewife than her Indian counterpart. Obviously, Helen is more confident and clear in her approach towards life and people. On the other hand, Indian women live in constant fear of rebuff and retaliation from within and outside.

Helen is a more socially committed individual than an average Indian woman. She is full of humanity and compassion. She realizes that innocent and illiterate tribals are being exploited and harassed by the local authorities and also by her husband's company. She reacts sharply when she is told that Mackendrick's and her bunglows were built upon the site of tribal hutments. They had been evacuated from the place. She gets irritated by their lack of will to retaliate and assert themselves. She asks Bashiam:

> Without protest. Just got up and walked away, like animals.
>
> (*Coffer Dam*, p. 48)

What Helen takes as meek subjugation is, in fact, the maturity of the tribals in assessing the whole situation and doing exactly what they would have been made to do even if they had put up resistance and protested against the decision. They would have suffered loss of life and humiliation, had they dared to oppose the government decision. They knew their enemies were beyond them. War and peace is possible only when the opponents are equals. Helen, being a foreigner having different cultural background, fails to measure the maturity of the tribals and the ground realities of Indian social system. She takes their limitations as their lack of awareness of their rights as humans.

Helen stands parallel to Indian women in her involvement outside marriage. Just like Ammu in *The God of Small Things* who gets involved with a low caste Velutha, her family servant, Helen in *Coffer Dam* gets involved with the crane man Bashiam. Both the ladies behave below their dignity and status. They opt to get involved with a man far below their standing.

Whether it is Arundhati Roy or Kamala Markandaya or even Shashi Deshpande, all use extra-marital relationships as a device to bring about balance and peace in women characters who are a frustrated and neglected lot within the institution of marriage.

It is often observed that after a very intense and serious extra-marital affairs, wives return to their husbands and resume their traditional role without any guilt. Likewise, Helen and Clinton realize that they are made for each other only after an extra-marital relationship. Bashiam, in fact, acts as a catalyst and brings the quarreling couple to a peaceful union with the realization and maturity that they lacked earlier. The tension at psychological level is resolved only after the lady in question has slept with another man. The tension keeps lingering till the wife sleeps with another man in Shashi Deshpande's *Roots and Shadows* too. Like Helen, Indu sleeps with Naren, her cousin and lover. The whole big joint family overlooks their flirtations intentionally. The sense of guilt does grip Rukmani of *Nectar in a Sieve*, because of her seeking medical and moral support from the British doctor Kenny, who happens to visit her village occasionally. She hides her psychological dependence upon Kenny from her husband. **The hypocrisy of Indian society is best exposed through these depictions. One cannot blame these women writers who are honest in the presentation of real Indian social life, which is apparently very orthodox and its traditional women very obedient and docile. Pretension is an important trait of Indian society.** The wife is suddenly shown taking note of the silent sufferings of her husband and his goodness. His devotion convinces her to come back to him. She returns to him without any guilt. It seems as if she is obliging her husband and children by not running away with another man.

Indian female writers seem to believe that invariably all women choose wrong men for marriage and end up having extra-marital affairs after they reach the middle age. It is hard to understand the psyche of the female writers. These things do happen in society but at a small scale. Women writers don't seem to realize the pressure which children of such families face in these situations. **It is their moral responsibility to discourage these trends through their literary creations.** But it appears, as if, just the opposite is happening. It seems children are made to realize that women must be allowed equal freedom and they should not feel bad about it. After all, mothers too are humans!

Shashi Deshpande, another woman writer of calibre, is also very honest in her depictions of Indian society and the characters are very realistic and natural. In her works, she highlights the ego clashes among the female characters residing under one roof. The gender clash does takes place but at subtle levels. The focus is always upon the intricacies of joint family system and the complications arising due to clashes of interests and egos between family members and outer influences. Shashi Deshpande cannot imagine any character in isolation. Talking to Holm Strom she explains, "But I can't see people in isolation, they are part of families" (Jain, 2003, p. 34). According to Jasbir Jain, "Beginning with *Roots and Shadows* right upto *Small Remedies*, Deshpande's novels show a concern with families and space" (Jain, 2003, p. 34).

'Roots' symbolize tradition and 'shadows' stand for the marginal culture. Shashi Deshpande, born in a Brahmin family in 1938, presently lives in Bangalore. She is different from Markandaya in many ways even though both identify themselves with average Indian women who live with all kinds of restrictions. They focus on women related issues, and have created masterpieces. The most remarkable thing to note about Shashi Deshpande is that she is not influenced by her Indian predecessors, rather she is deeply indebted to Jane Austen's style of writing. According to Jasbir Jain, "She is vociferous in her acknowledgement of Jane Austen's influence and refers to her on several occasions. By doing this she acknowledges her affinity with a woman writer who turned to realism in an age of romanticism" (Jain, 2003 p. 18).

Deshpande, according to Jain, is:

> silent about her predecessors. What kind of a tradition had she inherited as far as Indian women's writing in English was concerned when she published her first collection of stories in 1978?
>
> (Jain, 2003, p. 18)

Deshpande might not have appreciated Indian writers' handling of women's perspective or manner of presentation of facts related to women and society in general. However, her silence is a better option than vocal rejection of Indian literary stalwarts of her own gender:

> Deshpande values the realism of the novels of Jane Austen and a host of other women writers like Elizabeth Gaskell, Eliot, Margaret Drabble and Amy Tan, writers who alike reject the polarities and unidimensional portrayals, who deconstruct both romantic and heroic images of women.
>
> (Jain, 2003, p. 17)

The issue of 'women writing' or 'women writer' has been very irritating and provocating to almost all the female literary figures the world over. The tendency to categorize their works into a separate compartment of literary world has been rebuffed and rejected by all the important female writers. Even Deshpande registers her protest,

> the way I see the world is coloured by this fact of my being a woman, by the historical and social circumstances of women's lives. My themes, therefore, my characters and possibly, to a certain extent, even my language may be different from a man's.... Nevertheless, when I sit down to write I am just a writer — my gender ceases to matter to me. I am concerned with the

> same problems of language, narrative, structure and continuity....
>
> (Jain, 2003, p. 12)

Deshpande, takes this categorization as:

> ...a denial of the intellectual worth of the work and scales down everything to less than normal size.
>
> (Jain, 2003, p. 12)

Women writers the world over prefer to be addressed as "a writer who happens to be a woman." In her article "The Dilemma of the Women Writer 1985", Deshpande tries to find out as to how much importance is really given to the experience and feelings of a woman as a social being. Denial of a woman's right as a social being, as an individual having an identity of her own other than that of a 'wife' or a 'mother' has been investigated in almost all her works. *The Legacy* (1978) is a collection of short stories. Then came the novels: *The Dark Holds No Terrors* (1981), *If I die Today* (1982), *Come Up and Be Dead* (1983), *Roots and Shadows* (1983) and *That Long Silence* (1988) which fetched Deshpande the Sahitya Akademi Award. In the year 1993, came *The Binding Vine*, *A Matter of Time* in 1996. *Small Remedies* was published in the year 2000.

All her novels advocate women's individual identity in social and family spheres. Denial of rights and relevance of women in family and society has been taken as a cause of concern and worry by Deshpande. All her characters are very much Indian and restless to bring about a balance of power between the two genders in all spheres of life. Lack of concern for women, ignorance and intentional denial of proper place to them in family, in society and at personal level have motivated Deshpande to speak for average Indian women who come primarily from the middle class society. She is different from Markandaya in a sense that Markandaya is primarily concerned with the village women. Her focus is on the hardships of rural population, the socio-economic handicaps of rural women and men who have to struggle on all fronts at the same time with limited resources and defiance from the government machinery *A Nectar in a Sieve* and *Coffer Dam* highlight social issues. **Deshpande fights for individual space for educated middle class women who are forced to suffer for being educated and intellectual.**

Women writers writing along with and after Kamala Markandaya and her contemporaries like Ruth Prawer Jhabavala, Anita Desai, Nayantara Sahgal, Shashi Deshpande, etc. share and express the same concerns, albeit more uninhibitedly:

> There is no relationship that they have not analysed threadbare, no pain that they have not hinted and howled at in their narratives, no experience or feeling that they have not described graphically. Today there are no taboo topics and hushed issues in women's novels.
>
> (Jaya Prasad, 2006, p. 41)

A classic example of this trend is Arundhati Roy. In *The God of Small Things* she has shown all the squalor of Indian society in general and women's life in particular. Dealing with an innocuous affair between a lovely, divorced women and an untouchable man, the work becomes a masterpiece, because of its excellent treatment of class, caste and community angle. No work in recent times has brought to the surface the havoc wrecked on human lives, because of socio-political pressures as chillingly as Roy.

In fact, not just Indian but women all over the world have been devoting their creative energy to the cause of their gender using every opportunity, platform, forum and every genre of literature in the process. This is all the more true in the context of women writers from third world countries. Katrak rightly observes:

> Today, women writers work in a variety of literary genres—short story, drama, poetry, essay, life story/testimony, and the novel—that are often inspired by and rooted in a writer's own indigenous oral

> and folk tradition (as in Africa and the Caribbean), as well as literary traditions in other languages (in India).... Women writers share specific gender concerns in terms of how social and cultural factors appear from a female point of view. Their literary work imaginatively explore several conflicts between tradition (social, custom, religion) and modernization.
>
> (Katrak, 1998, p. 232)

2

Image of Women in Zaynab Alkali's Novel *The Stillborn*

The Stillborn (1984) is a novel with women at its centre. Women the world over are treated more or less in the same manner. They are treated as support system but not as equals. The novel reflects the author's belief that women should be allowed and encouraged to fulfill their potential if they are to make an effective contribution in nation-building.

Women are secondary to men, says patriarchy. It further dictates that women must accept and adjust to it. Nigerian society, being the follower of patriarchy, is no exception. Zaynab Alkali is not totally against the whole idea, but she pleads for better status and more rights to women for their personal growth and upliftment. She is hesitant to revolt against the tradition unlike Buchi Emacheta or Flora Nwapa, but feels strongly for more space to women within the existing system. Women must be educated, they must have control over their money which they earn and also have right to decide about motherhood. The timing and decision to bear children should be theirs and must not be dictated by their in-laws or husband.

Zaynab Alkali believes in maintaining the gender-harmony within the institution of marriage and society at large. She does not believe in demoralizing and blaming the men for anything and everything. Rather, she wants to convince them to modulate and rectify the mistakes of the past towards women. She is, in fact, still hopeful of positive change in the psyche of men who are showing signs of realization and attitudinal change for betterment of women. She strongly feels that there cannot be a sudden change in attitudes. It is a slow and gradual process. Nigerian society needs time and space to make adjustments to the demands of the modern age. Zaynab Alkali, through her novel *The Stillborn*, implores the society to understand the difficult situation in which women have to sustain themselves.

The Stillborn is not just a novel of literary excellence. It is a work of a sensitive soul with a purpose. The novelist pleads for justice and sense of realization from an otherwise immune society. Zaynab Alkali feels a sense of moral obligation towards her own gender. She wants to give voice to their viewpoints, because she can afford to take a stand on her own, whereas there are countless women in her society who are perishing under the oppressive and insensitive social structure of patriarchal society. The plight of women, their physical and mental discomforts are never taken into account. It is the intellectuals like **Zaynab Alkali, Buchi Emacheta, Flora Nwapa, Zulu Sofola, Ifeoma Okoye** and **Tess Onwueme** who are trying hard to change the traditional approach towards women in Africa.

Li is the central character of *The Stillborn*. The novel opens with Li returning home from her boarding school for summer vacation. Her family lives in a remote village of Nigeria. Li is filled with various contradictory emotions. At times she is thrilled to return home to her siblings, then suddenly she is saddened by the attitude of her parents. She is not very fond of them due to their stiffness and discipline with which they control and regulate the daily routine of their children. School-going children are usually very attached to their parents. Parents are emotional anchors for their children. But here, we find Li trembling with fear and discomfort at the thought of her parents:

> For a moment she thought of her parents and a dark shadow crossed her mind, threatening to dampen her happiness.
>
> (*The Stillborn*, p. 1)

This speaks a lot about parent-children relation in *The Stillborn.* The novel hints that every African family is not a very ideal happy family. There is often lack of warmth and commitment between parents and their children. They nurse contradictory ideas, feelings, hopes and expectations from each other. Li dislikes her parents, because they exercise excessive control over their children. She feels that the personal growth of children is being sacrificed at the whims of their parents. For children like Li, parents exist not as blessings of God but as necessary evils.

The children expect perfection on the part of their parents, though they themselves hardly meet the bare minimum expectations of their parents. Li is too biased to realise that in normal circumstances, parents are not as bad as they might seem to be. However, Li has some very strong reasons to feel offensive and resentful towards her guardians. She is defiant, cold and indifferent especially towards her father. At the same time she is very inquisitive about her mother.

Awa, her elder sister, presents a perfect picture of an ideal African girl. She is very traditional in her behaviour and attitudes towards life and family. Her sense of commitment and devotion towards her parents is an example for the rest. She is obedient, hard-working, fearful of her father and devoted to her mother. Above all, she is voiceless. That is, she hardly questions her parents about anything. She rarely thinks beyond her family. She is so groomed that her world revolves around her parents. The world outside her home doesn't exist for her. At least, she pretends so. Awa's younger siblings are fed-up with her idealistic approach which she never fails to exhibit before them:

> 'It is a rotten life'. Sule interjected. 'Don't talk like that, Sule', Awa warned. 'Yes, it is rotten life.' Sule insisted. 'Look at you, eighteen years old, still at home, single. Not allowed to go out at all except to the market, the riverside, the prayer house and the school. Even then you are always watched. I tell you, if this continues, ten

> years from now you'll still be right here performing the same chores; fetching water and teaching a group of dirty children. Not to talk of being bossed by a cruel headmaster at school and an irate father at home. The only difference will be, you'll be ten years older and much more frustrated.'
>
> (*The Stillborn*, pp. 3-4)

The above statement by Sule, Awa's brother, gives a graphic description of the traditional life of an eligible single girl. Her life is monitored by men around her for fear of deception. A young girl is never dependable and needs to be kept under strict surveillance, even if she becomes a puppet in the hands of her family and associates.

What Sule has observed is a bitter truth which Awa is purposely avoiding to acknowledge. At the same time, Awa's siblings don't realise that the young ladies must and should act in a responsible way, because family reputation is heavily dependent upon their personal behaviour in social life. What Awa is doing is not slavery, but she is simply leading a very pious and honest life of a traditional girl.

It is nice that Awa is a dutiful girl but then the line dividing obedience and slavery is very fine. When obedience of a child towards his elders is not followed by certain amount of freedom of speech and expression, it becomes slavery. Awa's case is more closer to slavery which has been noticed by her brother and younger sister Li. But, Awa herself is unable to comprehend. She is totally confused and feels insulted when Sule and Li point out to her about her predicament. What Awa takes as responsibility as the first born, her siblings take as exploitation and lack of far-sightedness on the part of their parents and above all Awa herself.

Awa stands for the continuation of the age-old traditional Nigerian culture. Awa is standing erect assimilating within herself all the vital elements of patriarchy and ethnic culture. She is being confronted by equally fresh and vibrant generation of Nigerians with western influence. Li and Sule represent the new flow of ideas and ideology coming with the modernization that has already made inroads in the remote areas of the Nigerian society. The psychology of Awa's siblings symbolizes the change in attitudes towards age-old tradition and social system. What is happening at the psychological level is transition from tradition to modernization in the younger generation of the Nigerian society. Li and Sule are mere representative of their generation. Awa is also being used to symbolize those who are young and full of life but too tradition bound to realise that everything that is old is not invariably gold. Respect towards one's own tradition must not blur one's vision. One must analyse critically the realities and make necessary rectifications so that no one is deprived of basic human rights. Awa is so tradition bound that her personality has stunted. She is psychologically trapped by her traditional values. Awa is a symbol of those women who are dumb dolls facilitating and furthering age-old system which demarcates women as lesser humans.

Awa's personality is in harmony with the old order. She seems to feel comfortable in the traditional set-up. Awa is fearful of her father's dominating and vindictive temperament. These traits of her father made a different impact upon Li and Sule. Both have become rebels. Awa prefers to obey rather than revolt and invite trouble. She wants to buy peace and somehow carry on with life. Above all, she is too conscious of her own age and her position of being the eldest girl of the family. The delicacies of being the eldest girl of the family prevent her from asserting herself even a bit. She is destined to follow the dotted lines even if she feels suffocated. This is the mould in which each and every girl of a patriarchal family is expected to adjust. They have few options. The family prestige and social pressures prevent girls from taking risks as there are innumerable pitfalls. Awa, being the eldest and mature is aware of these limitations.

Awa feels sorry for her parents because Li and Sule are not willing to consider their viewpoints. Being the eldest, Awa is afraid that Li and Sule may set bad examples for the rest of their siblings. They too may become cause of worry for their parents. Younger children may pick up bad habits and this may lead to lack of discipline and peace in the family. After all they too have some responsibility towards their parents and ancestors. They cannot allow people to laugh at their family and especially their parents. Awa is very thoughtful and committed to her family. Hence, she is forced to take a stand against her own well-wishers. Awa does not appreciate Li and Sule who want to open the gate of revolt and defiance against their parents on ideological grounds. Both the factions struggle to save their family from decaying and yet their paths to salvation are drastically different. Awa moves on the traditional road while Li and Sule are trying to build a highway. Both the parties are fearful of the dark future they foresee but the great relief is their faith in each other, inspite of differences on ideological grounds.

It is true that Awa is losing her age and opportunities of life. It is also true that her parents are not as honest towards her as she herself is. But then, there is no guarantee that if she revolts she will be getting all that Li claims. The world is a very complicated place to manoeuvre in. The unpredictabilities make people cautious and slow. It is precisely due to these limitations that Awa prefers to keep quiet and give some more time to her family before taking the final decision. She believes in maintaining family grace and interests against her own individuality.

Besides, Awa is very broad-minded and liberal as far as her younger brothers and sisters are concerned. She allows all these liberties and freedom which she dare not avail herself. She is very affectionate and caring. She is very sensitive and obedient towards her elders. She tries to avert crisis as much as possible. Her sense of commitment is admirable.

But her family-imposed restrictions, liabilities and limitations go against her personal growth and happiness. She is too aware of her handicaps. She is virtually chained down by her father. She is watched and monitored every second of her life. She just can't afford to extricate herself from the circumstances in which she has been put by her father. Actually, she is already trapped. The bitter truth of her life at the moment is that she will have to go on living like this endlessly. In order to save her self-esteem, she must go on doing her duty without any sign of resentment and bias towards her father. She feels that an adult girl's revolt invites many unhealthy reactions and situations. And such reactions and situations become a cause of shame and disgrace for the girl and her family. Therefore, Awa will have to forgo her personal growth for the future and reputation of her family.

Awa is an embodiment of obedience, sacrifice and compromise in the name of tradition and duty. The depiction of Awa is that of a very traditional and mature person. She is very cool temperamentally. She is aware of the limitations of being the eldest girl of the family. Her father makes most of her predicament. Her father is a very shrewd fellow. He tries to keep her mind under his grip by trying to force her to think and do things that would serve his purpose. Even her thought process is being monitored. People try to penetrate into the minds of young people and handle them for selfish ends. This strategy ensures complete control of the elderly people over the individuality and psyche of the young and energetic human resource.

It is for fear of losing power over the young and vibrant sources of energy, that senior people with ulterior motives try to manipulate them. Some guardians are so obsessed with a sense of power of guardianship that they stretch it too long and a bit too far. Usually, the daughters have to bear the strain of such sick mentalities of the elderly people. They use women to display their authority before others. The presence of women is crucial for display of influence and power.

On the family front, the gender game starts with marginalizing the mother in front of her children and relatives. This is done with the explicit motive of hijacking the rights of a mother over her children. At the same time, efforts are made right from the beginning to magnify and establish the contributions of a father in family welfare. The father figure is allowed to dominate the lives of wife and children in such a way that there is no scope for discussions and mutual adjustments, rather it demands immediate compliance.

The characters of Li and Awa present contrasts before the readers. The changing mind of the masculine gender of the Nigerian society is represented by Sule. While Baba stands for continuation of patriarchy, Mama symbolizes abject subjugation of the feminine gender of which Awa is the new torch-bearer. Grandma is the rebel who has broken all rules of tradition, yet has survived to scorn at the hypocrisies of masculine gender. Each character in *The Stillborn* is representative of a particular approach towards tradition and society. Faku, Li's best friend, symbolizes disillusionment and her husband Garba symbolizes deceit. Habu stands for lack of commitment. The school master is an example of the failure of male ego to mould itself with the changing times. Grandfather is the symbol of time.

What one notices in *The Stillborn* is lack of stability in mutual relationships within the family and marriage. Parents and children are supposed to share a strong bond of emotions, but this is lacking here mainly due to lack of communication between them. Mental distance between the guardians and their children is breaking the family. Li and Sule are too eager to get away as soon as possible.

The relationship between their parents is also very formal and full of mutual bias. They fight at night and during the day lead very reserved and detached life from each other and their children. They interact with their children only to order them or seek explanations. Their dictatorial style of functioning is drifting them away emotionally from their children. The formal environment at an informal place like home is really strange. Li and Sule are mature people who are quick to guess this and have become sarcastic towards their parents. They have lost all respect for their father who rules over them with an iron hand.

Li feels suffocated in this environment. Her life at the hostel is more relaxed and comfortable. The officiousness at home is killing the joys of holidays. Besides, the stagnation in Awa's life is so apparent and obvious that Li and Sule begin to feel uncomfortable:

> After a few weeks at home, Li began to find the atmosphere in her father's compound suffocating. She felt trapped and unhappy. Already, she missed the kind of life she had lived at the primary boarding school, free and gay. At home the little ones were too young to understand the restrictions and the older ones too dull to react. They all seemed to accept the situation as natural except, of course, Sule, her senior brother who suffered the silence with her. Restless and dissatisfied at home, the two got the worst treatment.
>
> (*The Stillborn*, p. 3)

'Older ones too dull to react' include the dullest of all—Awa, the eldest but the most passive member of this family. For her, this is her family, her home where she must not complain of constraints and feel happy and contented with whatever freedom she has. The idea of restrictions and limitations do not bother her as these concepts are unfamiliar to her. Awa identifies herself with her parents, her family and cannot think of her life in isolation:

> Li and Sule minded very much the rules they considered stupid and unnecessarily rigid. They abhorred the don'ts' that heavily out numbered the do's'.
>
> (*The Stillborn*, p. 3)

Li and Sule on the other hand are more receptive of the changing moods of modernization and westerns influence of the world outside their village. Exposure to new culture and the attractions of urban life is making Li and Sule restless and impatient. It is not that they are totally wrong. They are rational in their approach inspite of the fact that they have lost patience and hope of any positive change in the attitudes of their parents who have distanced themselves from their children for no apparent reasons:

> 'It's worse than a prison', Li complained one day as she sat with her brothers and sisters in the cooking hut.
>
> (*The Stillborn,* p. 3)

Sule and Li join hands against their father. They wage a cold war against their father. Awa, on the other hand, is a source of relief for her guardians. Awa follows the dictates of her parents with religious devotion. What exactly is going on in her mind is a mystery.

Apparently, she prefers to obey her parents and extend a helping hand to her own people rather than roaming around looking for a suitable match. She is more thoughtful and understands that her family reputation will be adversely affected if she becomes desperate for marriage. Usually, the eldest child is very much aware of family limitations, compulsions, social commitments and obligations towards extended family, friends and neighbourhood. These factors make a child mature much before his/her age.

Awa is going through this very stage of mental growth when she has taken upon herself all the possible responsibilities of her family while her parents are very aloof, detached and silent over these vital issues. They think that by keeping Awa involved in household jobs, they are able to manage her life quite well. But Awa is watched and monitored not only by her parents but by Sule and Li too. Poor Awa! She has to prove herself right to both the factions. She has no relief. Even her thoughts are being watched. People try to peep into her mind to find out the contradictions in her personality. Awa is being attacked by two different attitudes. One is very vibrant, lively, full of hope and challenging. The other is cold, silent, hard, defiant and rigid, unwilling to lose power so easily. Awa decides in favour of the old system with which she is more familiar. She is unwilling to take risk.

Awa feels it is safer to stand by tradition. Atleast, she cannot be blamed if anything goes wrong. She lacks confidence to take decisions on her own. She has to follow the dictates of her parents. She has, in fact, accepted the subjugation of women by men, hence her actions are in conformity with the ethnic tradition. What is holding Awa back is her fear that Li and Sule may not be able to out-wit their father. And also, her fear of the new culture which is totally unfamiliar to her. Its uncertainty and uniqueness frighten her.

Awa is not mature enough to realise that everything that tradition stands for is not very conducive for women. Women are not able to think beyond family and children. Their mother's life has made Li conscious about her own. But Awa can't feel the silent suffering of her mother. She takes her life as normal. Baba's misconducts and humiliating statements have made their mother a silent spectator of their lives. She is not allowed to interfere between the father and the children. Awa is going to follow her.

Their mother is a non-entity. She has to just move around once in the morning to see that the house functions according to the rules laid down. No other role is assigned to her. Her primary duty being mothering a dozen children. The rest of the responsibilities lie on Awa. She has to bear the burden of bringing them up. Her mother must keep herself confined to her hut attending to the needs of the youngest one. Baba being the supreme authority, the most painful part of their mother's life is to tolerate her husband's irrational allegations and humiliations because of children's mischiefs and mistakes:

> Whatever faults the children committed, especially Li and Sule, Baba would punish them and afterwards lash at their mother with words. Only the other day he had said to her, 'A heathen woman can only have heathen children. Why I married you is what I can never understand. There were many believing women in my village, but I had to end up marrying from a heathen village. And even after I have civilized you, you still behave like heathens. Of course, the lion cub takes after its mother'.
>
> (*The Stillborn,* p. 13)

Men feel it is they who are carrying upon themselves the burden of civilization. Baba too claims he has civilized his wife. It is nothing but gender bias and frustration at not being able to manage the small world that he has created with his wife. His ego clash with Li and Sule infuriates him and he makes his wife his victim. She has to act as a shock absorber. Sule, being a man himself, is unwilling to allow his father to dominate him anymore. Li is confronted by Awa and father is confronted by Sule.

The gender clash turns inwards. Each time Baba tries to control his children, Sule and Li try to challenge him:

> What about you Li? Were you at the dance? 'I was, Father'. Again Li was forestalled—this time by Sule's deep voice which jolted everybody. Li looked up in surprise. Sule was shielding her. Awa looked from Li to Sule and back, obviously confused.
>
> 'I had to go', Sule was still speaking. 'All my friends were there. I could not sleep'.
>
> (*The Stillborn*, p. 23)

Sule is a representative of the attitudinal change that is visible in the younger generation of otherwise traditional society of Nigeria. Sule strongly feels that his father is stretching himself a bit too far. Above all, Sule is becoming conscious of himself and wants to assert himself as the adult son of the family. He feels he has a right to avail himself of the life as his young age is also slipping away like that of Awa's. The restrictions are posing a challenge to his individuality as a man. His integrity and pride is being overlooked by their father before the younger brothers and sisters which is unacceptable to Sule. His father cannot treat him like a five-year old. He is an adult and must not be restricted from venturing into adult life anymore:

> What worried him now was, what was he to do with this man-child? He was a man now and it wasn't just his age, but what

> he stood for. He could beat Awa easily if she erred, no matter how old she was, but not Sule, his firstborn male child. And to beat a man for going out to dance at night was outrageous. He decided to give him a chance to apologise. That way both could salvage their pride.
>
> (*The Stillborn*, p. 23)

This is how Li's father tries to discipline and control Sule, his first born male child. Poor Awa! She can be beaten up easily. She will not retaliate. For, she is a girl who has no right to retaliate and she is very mild-mannered and obedient. Her tenderness and gentleness is no match to her father's rusticity and toughness. But Sule is just the opposite. He is not a girl but a full grown man ready to take on life on his own. He is willing to take risk and meet challenges from old and new generations. His father is just a symbol of every hurdle that he will have to handle once he proceeds towards modernity with a sense of independence and objectivity towards men and women.

Sule is not as biased towards women as his father is. He is kind, considerate, sympathetic, humane and above all realistic in his approach toward women as well as men and situations at home and outside. He is aware of the fact that he must take the initiative to change the situations at home. Otherwise, his brothers and sisters may end up dancing to the dictates of their father who is obsessed with himself and his authority over them:

> Silence. He fixed Sule with a hard stare and with his eyes begged him to apologise, but Sule stared back, a new kind of look creeping into his eyes. It was a defiant look as if he was challenging his father to a duel.
>
> (*The Stillborn*, p. 23)

Baba is facing challenge from the most unexpected quarters. Sule, for whom he is guarding his kingdom, is about to revolt. It is for his male child that he has been following the tradition so faithfully. He is puzzled. He feels threatened and helpless. His efforts are going in vain. He was expecting to transfer his legacy to Sule. But Sule is busy shaking the roots of tradition. He is absolutely fed-up with the existing order and is waiting to get away from this heritage. Sule's disenchantment is sensed by Baba. He is emotionally shaken and he falls silent. Sule's inner fury has got expression here.

Sule is frustrated and angry not only for Li or himself. He is furious with Baba for Awa. Her example is a torment to his conscience. Being the eldest son, he feels responsible for his elder sister Awa and is very worried about her future. Baba's indifference and Mama's silence are puzzling and torturous to him. He tries to make Awa aware of her situation, as he feels Baba is intentionally delaying Awa's settlement:

> What kind of life is this anyway? And you, big sister, so content with it.... 'Look at you, eighteen years old, still at home, single. Not allowed to go out at all except to the market, the riverside, the prayer house and the school. Even then you are always watched. I tell you, if this continues, ten years from now you'll still be right here performing the same chores; fetching water and teaching a group of dirty children. Not to talk of being bossed by a cruel headmaster at school and an irate father at home. The only difference will be, you'll be ten years older and much more frustrated.'
>
> (*The Stillborn*, pp. 3-4)

One does not find any ego or gender bias in Sule who is representing his generation of people. He is more humane and sincere towards women as a whole. He is witness to the harshness with which his father has been treating his mother. His mother is marginalized in her own home and family. She is totally overpowered by her husband who is too authoritarian to let a mother do her duty towards her own children. Mother-child relationship has been challenged by the father. He is being cruel by depriving his wife her legitimate rights over them. She is made to maintain a safe distance with her own children. Her husband watches her interactions with her children. Sule can feel the cunningness of his father who wants to have full and absolute control over the lives of his children to such an extent that even the mother is made to stay away emotionally and physically from her children. It is the father and only his instructions, orders, presence and influence, both direct and indirect, upon everyone. Sule is intelligent and shrewd. He is filled with repulsion towards his father, because of his cunningness and over-possessiveness. He is not going to surrender his individuality before his father. He will oppose him and his faulty thinking.

Sule gets full support from Li, his younger sister. Both brother and sister are trying to establish gender equality and regain their lost identity from the rubbles of the decaying tradition of patriarchy. Li and Sule are representatives of the changing times. They are the symbols of modernization and western influence upon the Nigerian society. Both are intellectually enlightened persons who have to fight on two fronts. At one front, they have to fight for their individuality and at the other, they have to fight against orthodox thinking of their people who are rigid and apprehensive about freshness of ideas and new approaches to life. The progressive people in every society have to take upon themselves this responsibility. This is what Sule and Li are trying to do. They want to change the suffocating atmosphere at home. They want attitudinal change towards life and its way of expression. They want to take risk, make changes, adopt new thinking and replace the age-old ideas, values and systems which have become useless, irrelevant and a liability for the younger generation.

One fine day, Sule leaves the village of his ancestors. But not before the final clash of egos and bitter showdown between the father and the son. Sule denies knowing the goldsmith's daughter, whereas her family insists that she is carrying his baby. Finally, Baba disowns him and turns him out of his house. However, Baba is forced to accept Sule's illegitimate son as his own blood. Bala is the name of Sule's first born from an illegitimate relationship. What happens to the girl in question is not known.

Sule refuse to marry the girl and Li feels sorry for both. She can't leave her brother with his troubles and at the same time she is unable to persuade him to agree for marriage. Sule decides to move out of the place and start his life afresh. He moves out of his village, leaving his chequered past, gloomy present and unforgiving people behind.

Kaka, who loves his grandson Sule more than his son Baba, cries his heart out over this episode. But since he is not relevant now, his opinions also have no takers. His son Baba, especially, would not allow anyone other than himself to control or influence his children. Sule, being the eldest, son must remain under his father's grip. His grandfather must not interfere. His days are over. Kaka has become a non-entity. All he can do is to grumble and cry like a woman in pain. His authority has been ceased and hijacked by his son. Now Baba is the master of the house and Kaka only a dependent.

> Kaka wept for two days. 'Cursed be me', he wailed, 'that I should live to see the day a man-child is disowned for proving his manhood.'
>
> Two months ago, the family of the blacksmith had brought them Sule's child, and now Kaka seemed to live only for his great-grandson.
>
> (*The Stillborn*, p. 59)

The clash of egos begins within the inner group of male members and the power to control and dictate terms is automatically transferred to the one who is next in line.

Baba has snatched power from Kaka and Sule has tried to do the same to Baba. But Baba is strong at present preventing Sule from hijacking the authority to decide the future of one and all within his compound. Sule has been outwitted due to his own weakness of character. Had he been strong emotionally and morally, he could have easily asserted himself.

But his inability to prove maturity of mind and strength in character loses a winning battle. Kaka laments his defeat as he had seen Sule as his answer to Baba's dominance and defiance to him. Both Kaka and Sule are pushed to the margin due to their own weaknesses.

Kaka has found another Sule in Bala (son of Sule). He is resentful of Baba for disowning Sule. He doesn't care whether what Sule did was ethically wrong and unfair to the girl and her family. All he cared for was his grandson and his presence. His loss of morality is not an issue for him. It is an issue for his son who is a fool and whose sense of justice is depriving the family its first male grand-child. He dislikes his son for his uprightness and high moral values.

Baba, on the other hand, is another example of emotional turmoil. He is as scornful of his own parents as his own children are of him. Baba hates Kaka because of his step-mother who is a constant reminder of family disgrace and gender clash within the four walls. She has been a woman of loose virtue. Kaka has been a weak master of a defiant woman. He and his son have been unable to control her various unethical ways of seeking admirers of her beauty and vulgarities of adulthood. She has publicly and privately brought shame to the family. Her greedy appetite and shameless conduct have filled Baba with contempt for Kaka, grandma and women folk in general. He has developed a strong dislike for the purely ethnic culture and its provisions for free mixing of young boys and girls. These customs and their misuse by grandma have been a source of embarrassment for Baba and Kaka.

Everyone is unanimous regarding the decision of Baba to isolate grandma. Baba has ordered his wife and children to stay away from her influence. She is just being tolerated. This is one of the reasons why Baba keeps strict discipline in the family. He fears that his wife and children might get infected by vulgarities of the old lady.

Both Baba and Kaka failed to control a woman of loose character mainly because her seekers prevented them from asserting themselves as husband and son of the woman concerned. She proved to be stronger than her husband and son, because of the clash of interest among them. She entertained her seekers and they defended her before her husband and son. Both father and son were outwitted by this woman and for a very long period. These experiences have had a very negative influence upon Baba who goes to another extreme to prove his point. He becomes inhumane, irrational and an over dominating guardian of his family. He overreacts and out of frustrations of the past overexerts himself in the present. This chain reaction is being watched minutely by the grandma herself and she makes fun of their frustration and helplessness. She mocks at Kaka and Baba even more and instigates her grandchildren to challenge and revolt against Baba. She sometimes even threatens to expose them before their father if they do not supply her with money and other items of her requirements. She is very cunning and is as much manipulative as her step-son.

Whereas Kaka has proved himself weak before his wife, Baba wants to show him how a woman ought to be controlled. However, he has great misconception. It is not men who control a woman and her chastity. Neither traditional, nor a modern society can make or break the character of a lady. Usually it is she who makes or breaks herself in normal circumstances. It is her own conscience and uprightness which keep her firm and her integrity intact. It is surely foolhardy to assume that a husband or some other male relative can keep a woman on the right track.

Baba is overestimating himself and underestimating his wife and daughters. It is their inner goodness of character and not his discipline which is preventing them from following the example of the grandma. Whereas Baba keeps a vigilant eye on women-folk, he was over sure of his own son, his own gender. He just forgets to keep vigil on his growing son in his obsession to keep the ladies of the house under strict observation. Now, Baba is defenceless. He has no answer to his son's characterlessness. Since he himself and his father were of good character, how come Sule became a shame for the family. He should have been equally dependable and upright, not taking any undue interest in any woman. But he goes his own way and comes back with an illegitimate son. Sule gives a rude shock to the family, tradition and belief that men are more dependable than women. Sule challenges him and his belief in his authority as the head of the family. It is his own gender that brought shame to the family and not the female of the household.

Awa's future is already sealed. She has been pushed into a situation which is beyond her control. She has to follow the dictates of her parents, especially the all domineering father. She has realized the futility of Li's insistence and hence makes fun of her younger sister. She is unable to assess the seriousness of Li's determination to challenge her father in all possible ways. Since Li has time on her side, she can afford to take chance while Awa's case is just the opposite. If she fails in her attempt to extricate herself from this situation, she might lose both, i.e. her own reputation and her family. Hence, she insists that she has no complaints and is happy to serve her family.

Li is right when she insists that Awa's life is caged. She has no freedom. She is forced to interact only with the apparently harsh, ruthless and stoic schoolmaster. Awa visits the village school where she teaches some dirty village children. It might be a way of thrusting upon her the schoolmaster. On one hand, she is not allowed to meet and talk to anyone other than the family. On the other hand, she is allowed to visit the village school as a teacher where she can interact with this man. In fact, it is a very shrewd way of forcing Awa to accept what is given to her without any option. Decisions are made on her behalf without bothering to know her opinions and expectations regarding her own life and marriage.

Awa is not shrewd enough to see through the game. She never questions herself why she is allowed to go to school, whereas she is watched otherwise. May be her father and the schoolmaster might have reached some understanding. For Awa, everything happens naturally. Awa tries to hide her affair with the schoolmaster till Li finds out by chance. Awa has made maximum use of the given opportunity. She has made a fool of herself by hiding her feelings from Li and Sule, because these two could have helped her in critically assessing the whole situation before arriving at a logical conclusion. Single-handedly she manages the whole thing foolishly, falling into the trap. Now, indeed her future is sealed finally. She will have to continue to live as usual managing two households on her shoulders and derive contentment out of it.

Baba has masterminded Awa's settlement taking all possible precautions. He has prevented Awa from asserting her independence. Even after marriage, her activities can still be controlled and channelised towards family welfare giving her no reprieve from manual labour and mental pressure to meet the expectations of father and her husband at the same time. As usual, the mother will remain a silent spectator not allowed to interfere. Without women like mother and Awa, society can't continue with patriarchy. Women like Awa are so psychologically dependent upon tradition for their safety and survival that they make things all the more difficult for those who want to bring a positive change within the system.

Li, Sule and grandma all are rebels of different types and degrees. Li wants the right to live as a normal human being without abnormal stress upon her womanhood. Sule believes in equality of opportunity and control over one's own life. The grandma is the real threat to the whole social structure posing serious challenge to patriarchy by completely subjugating and crushing male ego under her feet by throwing tradition to winds. She has violated almost all the rules laid down by men and yet survived, mocking sarcastically upon the system. Male hypocrisies are no match to her vulgarities and obscenities and wickedness. She learned the tricks and applied them all against those whom she served and availed and finally rejected.

This rejection is mutual, because grandma is no more young enough for new seekers. But she has succeeded in retaining her place in the family of her husband by her wickedness and rusticities. She is so indecent that Baba, her stepson, avoids her like plague and her husband is a defenceless prey who has no use for her. She is exactly what the male world has made her—a married prostitute.

Thus, Baba is surrounded by all sorts of women. He is scared of his stepmother who may take Awa under her bad influence and push her into the dirty game. Then, he is fearful of his wife, who may instigate Awa against him and his plan. He wants to dominate in Awa's life and does not want Awa to get closer to her mother. He derives sadistic pleasure in snatching away his children from their mother. But the more he asserts the greater is the pull which the children feel towards their suffering mother. Physical barrier is no hindrance. They obey Baba for family peace and not because they like him or favour him. Even Awa, who is so much in his grip, is suffocating under his thumb. Baba wants to decide her future according to his convenience and planning. Even Awa is not taken for granted. What if Awa selects someone else? She will then refuse to marry the schoolmaster. She might even reject the man and revolt openly against her father.

The problem with Baba is that he is too biased against women. Moreover, a strange sense of power is misleading his sense of judgement. He is unnecessarily fearful of disobedience from wife and children. In order to keep them in discipline he keeps asserting himself in every aspect of family life. Awa, being the eldest, has to bear the strain of maintaining family grace by doing exactly what is expected of her.

It is generally believed that girls are usually emotional and make foolish decisions due to whims and immaturity. They react on impulse. They get swayed by exteriors which may prove to be mere illusions. In other words, they are brainless creatures. Hence, Awa is watched and observed not only for her own sake but for the sake of her seekers. She must not be allowed to do anything that may go against their plan.

Is Awa so naive and innocent? Traditionally groomed girls are more mature and calculative than modern girls. Awa is very cool about everything. Her priorities are clear in her mind. She is not obeying Baba, rather she is following her instincts. She wants to stay back in the village and continue with her school teaching, because her primary concern and target is marriage. And the schoolmaster has shrewdly influenced her to stay on. Awa is taking Li and Sule for granted, not bothering to relieve them of their worries about her future. Li and Sule fear that Awa may end up remaining single if she is not made conscious of her future. She must not wait for her siblings to come of age to manage the household, rather she must find a boy and settle down. Even after marriage, she will be able to help them and advise them. They all will be there for each other.

Li is not totally wrong. But she is being taken for a ride by Awa. Awa has done exactly what Li and Sule are suggesting but without informing them. She has found a man who is willing to marry her and settle down in the village itself with Awa. Her requirements of marriage are being met with. She will get married indeed but to a widower who is not much older than her. His first wife died after a year of their marriage.

Awa has selected this tough and distasteful school teacher Fiama as her future husband and they are waiting for the right moment to get married. This is both shocking and beyond comprehension for Li, Sule and the rest of the children. They fail to find justification for her selection. It is sheer desperation on the part of Awa. She thinks she is in love but no girl can select such a man for marriage. It shows Awa's desperate effort to somehow settle down in life. Li and Sule can very well understand the seriousness of the situation and they accept her decision as the end result of Baba's restrictions on Awa.

Awa's decision to accept what is offered to her is a very traditional stand on her part. She has made all the right moves at the right moments. Ideally, she should have been the happiest. But the irony of human life is its unpredictability. Misfortune and hardships can knock at the doors of anybody and everybody. Awa's precautions, Baba's calculations all fail before the designs of destiny. The complications of human life can extract moments to torture and torment its victims. No way of living, no culture, no tradition, no ideology is sure way to happiness. Neither modern life is the best way to salvation nor tradition is all secure. There are many pitfalls. Happiness cannot be guaranteed by anyone.

Even if a person is humble, traditional, god-fearing and law abiding, do misfortune and hardships spare him? But then, these can be reduced and controlled to a certain extent by the various support systems and formal and informal pressure groups that operate in society. The human life, irrespective of gender, depends heavily upon these mechanisms of social control and support to overcome various types of crisis in life. Awa and Li, Sule and Habu, Faku and all others face different types of problems, very unique and specific, which they overcome after initial shock and pain.

Awa marries the most approachable, available and manageable person in the vicinity. She was very sure of her selection, yet her marriage proves to be a flop. Her husband Fiama turns out to be a drunkard. He is an escapist. He marries her only to leave her with poverty, children and hardships of various nature to cope with. An eighteen year old girl turns into middle aged woman burdened with liabilities within one or two years of marriage. She is left alone to feed her children and watch her husband's personality disintegrate and break into pieces due to failure in career. He is mentally a weak man. He lacks strength to stand up against odds in his professional world. He is too demoralized to make efforts to overcome the crisis.

Fiama has been demoted to junior section in his own school where he was appointed as the headmaster. His demotion has come as a rude shock and he is unable to swallow the insult. Humiliated, he falls in bad company. He begins to drink. His detoriations drags him away from his wife and children. Fiama's ego is so hurt that he forgets his responsibilities towards his own family. He feels ashamed before his old friends, associates and tries to avoid them and his own family. He does not realise that the end of career is not the end of life. He should have tried his luck elsewhere in order to sustain his family. He should have behaved like a mature person who has taken upon himself the responsibility of a woman for life. Marriage is a serious commitment and it demands a degree of subjugation of one's own whims and fancies for the well-being of the family. The life and future of many people are affected if a marriage runs into a crisis. One cannot play havoc with one's own life, because the lives of wife/husband and children might be shattered as a result.

Awa symbolizes tradition. It is stable and continuous. Culture and tradition are related to geography and people. Awa's characterization is symbolic of Nigerian rural culture, its continuity and stability. The refusal of Awa to move out of the native village, is symbolic of continuation of ethnic culture and tradition inspite of the threats of westernization on the Nigerian rural society as well. Awa's firmness of personality and religious devotion with which she follows her tradition is indicative of the fact that women play important role in sustaining the traditional culture even today.

The challenges of modern age are breaking the confidence of some men who are neither able to manage their personal life nor professional life, as is the case of Awa's husband. But Awa is not shaken. She holds on to tradition and sustains its old flavour with strong faith in it. It is she, a woman, who is keeping tradition alive and not her man. Men, in fact, have failed either to protect the merits of culture or eradicate the demerits of tradition. They have failed to meet the expectations of their time and requirements of their age.

However, just as tradition and culture are difficult to change, so is Awa. She is rigid and unwilling to adopt something new. Her obsession with her traditional way of life prevents her from moving out of her native place so that her husband can have reprieve. He is now trapped in fast changing circumstances within the village. Fiama's inabilities to modify according to the demands of western pattern of education system has made him useless and insignificant. He has lost prestige and importance in the village circle. Loss of social prestige has made him very self-conscious. In order to forget his humiliations, he has begun to drink. He comes home only to extract money from Awa for drinking. The money he earns from the school goes to his drinks and bad circle of friends. Li enquires:

> 'What changed your man, big sister? He
> used to be the best there was in the village.

> I hope our father's house was not the cause. It is an unlucky family,...'
>
> (*The Stillborn*, p. 87)

Li is overwhelmed by the domestic problems back home. Awa is still there acting as an axis around which the whole family revolves. Awa and Fiama tried to make adjustment with the sudden and drastic change that came like a strong wind and blew away their family peace and harmony. Explaining her situation Awa describes in detail how things became bad to worse:

> I don't know, Li, I think many things helped to change my man. The village itself changed and he changed with it. The government took over the mission school just as we had hoped. A secondary school was added to it. But it wasn't my man they made head over the school. They said he wasn't educated enough to head such a big school, so a stranger was brought to take his place. This time a brown man. He wasn't even white, Li. Not the white people we are used to in the village. My man was pushed into the junior classes to teach. Those of us that could barely read were asked to work anywhere in the school except the classrooms. The men have no choice. Most of them have grown too stiff in the waist to till their ancestors lands, so, they were content to sweep the offices and run errands, jobs their women and small children do at home.
>
> (*The Stillborn*, p. 87)

Awa can see the reasons and their effects upon her family life and yet she is unable to prevent her husband from degenerating into a lesser human. His personal grievances, ego and social standing are more important than his wife and children. Their existence and survival are lesser issues. They are secondary to him, primary being his self-esteem and bruised ego. Like a faithful wife Awa tries her best to cope with the situation:

> I had a choice Li, the children and the old people at home, so I left. I didn't have to stay and be humiliated by other people's children. My husband had to stay. We needed the money. He stayed, but it wasn't to feed the children. You know now where his money goes. I wouldn't have known how to cope without Mama. We live on the proceeds of her farm. The woman would go to the farm at cockcrow and won't come back until the chickens have gone to roost!
>
> (*The Stillborn*, p. 87)

Awa's ethnic bias towards the new school head who happens to be a brown man is indicative of her frustrations and helplessness. She is willing to accept the superiority of a white man but not that of a brown man. We find that clash of interest gives rise to all kinds of deviation in thinking and attitudes of people irrespective of gender and race. What matters most is survival and if the source of sustenance is hit hard, people forget rationality and sentimentalize even purely commercial issues. In the present case, there are other factors too. Lack of sufficient academic qualifications to deserve better post in the changed system is the main reason for her husband's demotion which even Awa understands but refuses to acknowledge. Awa's inclination in favour of her husband is quite natural but the racial bias and criticism of administration is just a cover up for her husband's weakness of merit.

Even Awa's ego is inflated like that of her husband. She too is sentimental and instead of adopting a practical approach towards the changed circumstances, she decides to stay at home. Her decision cannot be appreciated, however positive her attitude is towards her own decision. She is indeed making good use of her time by managing the house and children. But, what about the financial aspect of their life? Her mother has to work very hard to keep the house running. At this advanced stage of life when she should be looked after and taken care of by her grown up children, she has to till the land to feed her daughters and grandchildren. Awa herself admits this to Li. Their mother has begun from where she was forcibly removed. After the death of her dominating husband, she has picked up the broken pieces of her shattered home.

Her life, her children's lives have been spoiled due to excessive discipline and overindulgence. Too much of instructions or restrictions mislead and confuse the thinking faculty and people take wrong decisions on impulse. Baba's harshness has made most of the children take hasty and wrong decisions just to get out of his grip. Awa married the schoolmaster out of fear of being left spinster without caring to assess his personality type. She is now struggling to feed herself and her children. Li has made the same mistake by selecting Habu. Now she is cooling her heels back home. Both Dan Fiama and Habu have been bad choices. Mother was never consulted when Baba was alive. Mother sat in the arena watching quietly the ego-clash between father and her children. They fought and won their freedom but lost many other things. The mother could do nothing. The children could not reach out to her for fear of humiliation and bad blood from Baba. They were too protective and sympathetic towards her to allow Baba to drag her into the duel.

Now, when Baba is no more, they are surviving the crisis by the strength of mother's love and affection which lay hidden in her heart for her loved ones. She is still a silent character of the novel, yet the most important female who symbolizes the contributions of women in the human world. She is non-demanding, dutiful, and self-sacrificing, tolerating injustice silently for the sake of her children. Their survival is more important than her own comforts. She does not expect anything in return. In fact, it is she who is the giver from the beginning till the end, from giving birth to her children to providing bread for her grandchildren. She is there to provide protection and shelter. She never demands anything in return neither loyalty nor obedience. The contribution of women to the society is immense. It is impossible to repay the debt:

> Li listened silently, feeling guilty. She had done nothing herself but add to the growing number of mouths....
>
> (*The Stillborn*, p. 87)

Women of younger generation are so engrossed in their own life that they forget the hardships which their mothers face for them. In fact, younger women and men too tend to negate the contributions of their elders and ignore their problems saying, they have grown old anyway. The insensitivity of young women towards elders of the family must also be taken into consideration while addressing gender issues on larger platforms.

It is precisely due to a sense of guilt of adding financial strain upon her old mother that Li feels uncomfortable. Li is sensitive and reasonable yet her own condition does not allow her to do much. The irony of Li's life is that her own sister Awa is mortgaging Li's future to Alhaji Bature for maintaining her family. Her mother's farm is not yielding enough to meet the requirements of her large family. Awa giving birth to a child every year has swelled the family size.

Dan Fiama is a worthless man who burdens his wife and in-laws with his progenies without bothering to own up his responsibilities as a father. Earlier Awa was used by her father to run his house, now Dan Fiama, her husband, is using her to groom and feed his innumerable kids.

> 'Big sister', she had commented. 'This place looks like the house of the chief.' 'Of course it does', Awa had answered mockingly. 'It is the house of the chief alcoholic.'
>
> (*The Stillborn*, p. 86)

Awa, in order to feed her man and his kids tries to thrust upon her married sister yet another man. She tries to convince Li to dissolve her marriage with Habu and remarry her seeker who is helping Awa on her behalf. It is a sheer bargain of Li's physical beauty against family needs. Li is shaken:

> 'Big sister, you cannot mean that'. 'It is true, Li', Awa looked at her pleadingly. 'I cannot help it when he comes well-stocked with food and the children are hungry, I haven't the heart. And if it gives him pleasure to feed us for your sake, why should I refuse him?'
>
> (*The Stillborn*, p. 87)

Awa tries to convince her on humanitarian grounds to agree. But Li asserts herself and refuse to cooperate. Li is still committed to Habu, her husband and is waiting for him to reclaim her. She is unwilling to break her marriage even if informally she and Habu are leading separate lives. Re-marriage for Li is an unthinkable proposition. Her emotional bonding with Habu is much stronger than her hardships. She expects to return to him one day. How, she is yet to know. Habu and his brother have been trying to convince her to return home. It is her self-respect which is preventing her from going back.

Awa has always helped the wrong people by blindly following the tradition. In fact, she is cooperating with ambitious people who make use of conventional ways for their ulterior motives. She becomes a medium to fulfill such motives. She thinks that by following in the footsteps of her ancestors she will be safe. But she is not aware of the fact that her submissive nature is adding extra burden upon her parental family. Instead of holding on to her job, she abandons it because of demotion. She now expects Li to break her marriage in order to re-marry a notorious rich man Alhaji Bature who is in no way a proper match for her but is providing financial help to the family. Li is being expected to return the favour although Alhaji Bature has made her life difficult in the village. His supporters and connivers irritate and tease Li whenever she ventures out of her home under compulsions. She is being harassed and heckled by his men while Awa is being supplied with all possible help to sustain her family. Alhaji Bature keeps pressurizing Li to surrender to his whims. He has developed an unhealthy fancy for her and wants Li to surrender her integrity before him. Her personal opinion hardly matters either to him or to Awa. In fact, her elder sister is enthused with the task of convincing Li to agree to the arrangement. Li's predicament is that her seven years daughter from Habu is being taken care of by Awa. Hence, Awa is in a position to exert pressure upon Li. Her problems do not end here. Li has to face many more during her stay in her village.

It is her own gender which is forcing her to kneel down before men. It is disgusting to see how people connive with each other to extract desired results from their victims. But then, it is not that they succeed all the time. Li is made of a different metal. Her priorities are rightly placed even if she is not as traditional and conventional as an average Nigerian village maiden. Li is progressive but certainly not a revolutionary in negative sense of the term. She can't abandon one marital tie to form another and so on. She is a woman of integrity.

Awa, being an average village woman, is not intellectually sharp enough to draw the line. She does not want to understand either. What matter to her are the daily requirements of her family. In order to meet them she is ready to make or break marriages too. Her marriage is, however, safe. Hence, she did not care what Li thinks about her. There is a certain degree of stability in Awa's life. Her husband is around even if he is an escapist. His presence in the village makes her safe and socially stable. Li is neither safe nor stable in life. Her ties with her husband are almost broken. Her daughter stays with Awa. Li, herself, is struggling to get a job in school after completing her training in school teaching. Right now she is going through a very lean phase of her life. She needs moral support from her people. Instead of giving her peaceful and congenial environment back home, Awa is busy taxing her patience.

However, Li is a woman of strong will and clear perceptions. She will not give in. She will work hard and make a place for herself and her daughter. She will work hard to make herself self-reliant and take her daughter away.

But, the constant worries of being left behind by Habu and its repercussions on the family reputation is forcing Li to re-think over her decision to wait for him. Her failing confidence in Habu and her own self is primarily due to external reasons rather than internal. Li is breaking down due to the pressures from outside. The indirect allegations, teasing and taunting go on endlessly within her hearing distance. She feels humiliated.

She tells Kaka about the gossips and her worries. She also says, she is tired of waiting. Li has always been closer to the ancient one—her grandfather. She has begun to interact more and more with Kaka, her grandfather, who is always ready to console her and guide her. Her troubled mind gets reprieve and direction from Kaka. When Li overhears gossip about herself and gets disturbed she runs to Kaka for advice:

> They have to talk, child, he said simply. They have to talk about someone or something and just now our family is ripe for gossip. But do not keep it locked up in your heart. It will swell you up. Bad words are nothing but wasted air. Tomorrow the gossip will shift to another family.
>
> (*The Stillborn*, p. 62)

Her grandfather is quick to understand that Li is in a haste to get out of the depressing scenario. But, he does not want her to take any drastic step to get rid of the mental torture that she is going through as an abandoned wife. He scolds her for her weakness of mind. He very intelligently turns the discussion towards the family:

> 'You are tired of us!' Grandfather's voice cut her thoughts short.
>
> (*The Stillborn*, p. 63)

He prevents Li from taking the ultimate decision. In his eyes, Habu is still a better choice for her even if they are informally separated. According to him, there is still hope left. Kaka is also aware of the problems Li is facing from the villagers. But he is confident that things would change soon. Li must have patience and faith in herself. The struggle of Li as a married young woman is very realistic and also very typical. She is facing problems at home also. Even her elder sister Awa becomes nervous and fearful for Li:

> One night Awa begged her to go back to the city, to her husband. 'The village is laughing behind our backs once more. Take heart and go back to your husband. No one needs know he did not send for you.
>
> (*The Stillborn*, p. 83)

Li is disgusted at this proposal of her elder sister. How could Awa not understand her situations? She too is a woman, her own sister:

> It is not done, daughter of my mother. The day a woman begins to woo a man has not yet come and if, it has, it will not begin with me.
>
> (*The Stillborn*, p. 83)

Li has regained her confidence which was shaken by the village men and women in the market place. She has regained her equilibrium and begins to reassess and analyse her life. She will not pursue Habu. He will have to come and reclaim her. Awa's request to cultivate him on her own initiatives is unacceptable to Li. She is as firm in her convictions as ever.

However, what Li considers her confidence is rather her over-confidence. She is becoming cynical by adopting strange ways. She has begun to dress extravagantly and begun to frequent cultural dances and festivals. Obviously, the flow of suitors increase and she is overwhelmed by her popularity. But, it is not what women of dignity aspire. These kinds of activities and admirations are short lived and drag women into muddy circles. Li is losing grip over her own life. She is declining fast.

Gradually, women of her village begin to ridicule her and call her names. Li realizes soon that she is overreacting. Self-realization fill her with shame. She has been a cause of embarrassment for her family. She realizes her days were over in the village. She then decides to go back to the city and make an independent life for herself. Leaving her two years old daughter behind, she begins her journey again. Her only treasure and support is her class seven certificate. Li has taken another bold decision.

Her strategies are as aggressive as was her father's oppressiveness. And she continues to oppose the unfair and unjust influence of men over her life. The ego-clash, the clash of power and gender clash go on till Li is able to overcome hurdles and achieve her goals. She becomes self-reliant and makes a place in society inspite of Habu's rejection and Baba's contempt. Li's inner strength, her convictions and hard work lead her to success. She becomes 'the man of the house' by becoming self-reliant and resolves all the problems which Awa and her mother fail to do. Li is readily accepted as the guardian in her father's family in the absence of the eldest son Sule. Li has proved the merit of the feminine gender ultimately.

She is back in the village after five years. Her daughter is now seven years old. Situations at home have changed. Now, there is hardly any tension in the family regarding discipline as Baba is no more in a position to enforce it. He is unwell. Sule has already been driven out of the family by Baba. Humiliated and rejected he fled from the village. Everyone is silently and eagerly hoping to hear about him but in vain. Awa is managing the family as predicted by Sule. The only difference is that she is married to a very irresponsible and emotionally disturbed man, Dan Fiama. He has now given himself to drinking. Her best friend Faku is married to Garba and lives in the city. All are somehow managing their lives. None of them are as happy as they had expected themselves to be. All had dreams and chosen different paths to fulfill those dreams. All of them have failed. They have tried to be happy but failed due to various factors beyond human control.

Li is the most mobile character of the novel. She gets an opportunity to visit Faku in her city and realises that even Faku's dreams are shattered. She is struggling hard to survive.

> Li was looking forward to seeing Faku, whom she had not seen for almost six

> years. She wondered how Faku would look after all these years. Fat? Modern looking? Rich and sophisticated? Li had learnt, from Faku's mother in the village, that Garba had another woman with six children. How did they all live?
>
> (*The Stillborn*, p. 76)

Li is obviously very happy to visit Faku, her best friend. Both have had similar dreams of city-life. Li has failed to realize her dreams due to Habu. He has changed drastically. The city life has adversely affected their mutual harmony and faith in their future together. At present, Li is trying hard to rebuild her life with Habu who has begun to behave strangely with her. But she is consoled by the traditional approach that adjustment are difficult during the initial years of marriage. Li is expected to be more adjusting, flexible, compromising and forthcoming and not to expect anything from Habu. It is expected of her to make the marriage succeed. This is the traditional approach adopted by society. And Li is no exception even if it has been a choice marriage. Habu must be tolerated. Li must not question him or nag him unnecessarily. This, Li is made to realise.

Withstanding these hard realities of married life, Li happens to meet Faku in the city of Kano on her way to visit the ailing Baba. The journey to Kano takes two hours only. Even though Habu and Li fight with each other, he feels worried for her and instructs her to spend the night at Faku's place before proceeding to the native village. Her pregnant stage is a matter of concern for all. Hence, Garba, Faku's husband and a common friend of Li and Habu is informed about her visit. Naturally, they are waiting for her Li's expectations regarding her friend's life in the city are much higher than the harsh realities:

> She stood still at the entrance and stared at the gaunt-looking woman before her. For a brief second, she thought she was in the wrong room. The gaunt woman rose slowly from the mat where she was sitting

> and advanced doubtfully towards Li, she too, was obviously unsure.
>
> (*The Stillborn*, p. 77)

Time has changed both the ladies. The impact of mental and physical strains have changed their appearances to such an extent that they are unable to recognize each other instantaneously.

> She could not believe this was reality. How could this near-stranger be her friend Faku? Famished in body and no doubt famished in soul?
>
> (*The Stillborn*, p. 77)

Li has realized that Faku too is a tormented soul. Her expectations from Garba remains unfulfilled. Her friend has been going through rough weathers since her marriage. What Li feared about Faku has come true. Living with co-wife is a difficult proposition and Faku being immature earlier, couldn't forsee the pitfalls that lay ahead. She was, in fact, in favour of co-existence six years back. But now, Li knew marriage of Faku had not been a success. Li, her best friend, has been with Faku all through. She has been witness to the tragedies faced by Faku's family one after another. Today again, Li lands at Faku's place to share her pains.

Right from the beginning Faku was very conscious of her family image which is still so tarnished in the eyes of the villagers. This stubbornness of the villagers had made Faku defiant and rebellious. She will have what she wants at all cost. Marriage was the most challenging mission of her life in such adverse and hostile surroundings. Li had sensed this quite early that Faku might go to any extent to get married. Faku did not listen to Li's advice to think twice before falling for Garba, a stranger. Faku decided to live as co-wife. She had her own reasons to defend her stand:

> Faku, however, thought quite differently. What was this love the rest were cracking their heads about? When a man cared for his family, fed and clothed them properly,

> what was it if it wasn't love? She would like to be Garba's only wife. What woman wouldn't? But if the man could afford to feed a dozen other wives, who was she to object? For her, polygamy wasn't the point at all. The point was that once she married, living alone with her mother was over. They would no longer have to work their fingers sore to feed themselves or mend the leaking roof, but someone else would be responsible. She did not seem to have taken in Garba's gibe about women slaving for men. All she thought of was that Garba was obviously wealthy and wise as a tortoise.
>
> (*The Stillborn*, p. 47)

Faku is standing with Awa supporting and nurturing patriarchy for her own reasons. The demerits of polygamy has become merits for Faku especially. Her personal problem of getting married is being resolved. Hence, she finds no problem with it. She is more interested in grabbing the man than bother about the co-wives and the rest. Garba is rich, she thinks.

At last, she will have a man in her family. Her mother and Faku will have no worry. He will be providing food and clothing to them. Faku is seen exploiting the tradition as much as men in her favour. The traditional duty of a man to maintain his wife and children is the main motive behind marriage. If this aspect of marriage is not fulfilled, only then Faku will have to worry. She can tolerate co-wives willingly but not singlehood and malice of the whole village. Faku is too immature to realise the torture and exploitation women as co-wives go through. The basic requirements of life and their fulfillment is the main worry of Faku. There is no place for sentimental and emotional outpourings which her friends indulge themselves in. Survival is more important for her than sentiments. She takes polygamy very casually. But her casual approach towards polygamy costs her heavily.

Li is again witness to her friend's most serious crisis in her life. Faku is literally perishing under the pressure of poverty, polygamy, isolation, hostility and blank future under her husband's roof.

Faku, in a haste to get married, had opted for a man who was of her mother's age group. Li had felt awkward and resented the idea. She feared Faku is making a wrong selection. But Faku was determined. And hence Faku and Garba got married soon. His shady background, his exploitative tendencies towards women and his fascination for town life, all had no effect upon Faku. She was too immature then to see the devastating effects these tendencies of Garba would have on her.

After six years, Li's apprehensions and fears regarding Faku's marriage have come true. Both avoid talking about the present. They have grown mature with experience and have gathered enough facts about each other without any extra efforts:

> The house was filled with tiny feet, running in and out of the outer room, but no feet came into Faku's room. She looked round the tiny outer room. There wasn't much in it, two old arm-chairs, a small wooden table, some tattered mats and a half-filled glass cupboard.
>
> (*The Stillborn*, p. 77)

Faku is a loser altogether. The financial reasons for which she decided to marry Garba prove false. He is not as rich as he had pretended before Faku and the rest. Now, her bare needs are also not being met with. She and her only son somehow survive with the little that his first wife allows to be given to Faku. Faku's co-mate, i.e. Garba's first wife is very cunning and assertive. She exercises absolute control over Garba and the household. Faku is just an appendix to his establishment and she has no role or right as co-wife. She is confined to her room and is totally isolated and rejected member of the family. But, Faku is not willing to leave the place. She is married to Garba and will stay with the family, however difficult the situations are. Li understands the cool headedness with which Faku is retaliating against the machinations of Garba's first wife. Both the wives fight for their claims over the man and his earnings. One is aggressive while the other is submissive but persistent.

However, Li can guess. Faku will have to escape from there if she has to survive. She may die due to her insistence to stay on. Her compulsions are again the same. Even after six years of marriage, the question of economic crisis is unresolved.

Garba is not rich enough to provide for her and her son. He already has a wife and twelve children to feed and maintain. Faku has made a fool of herself. She has selected a wrong man who is too aged, financially weak and unreliable. He has dumped her practically. All her calculations have failed her.

At last, Faku realises that it is futile to waste her time any longer. She will have to take a bold decision to walk out of marriage or die uncared. She decides to leave Garba and his house for good. She decides to find a new way to salvation. Instead of seeking shelter from Garba, she will explore other options. There must be some way to sustain and survive. She gives herself another chance.

The role of another woman in Li's life is also very significant. She almost breaks Li's marriage. But it is her inherent goodness that makes her stick to her marriage vow. She remains loyal to her husband. Li doesn't understand that essentially she is as traditional as Awa whom she has been criticising all through. Li, too, cannot imagine marrying again. It is only due to anger and humiliations that she had once contemplated another marriage. But Kaka rebukes her and she prefers to concentrate upon her career rather than re-marriage or divorce from Habu. Kaka is optimistic as he has been in touch with her in-laws. Kaka dislikes women failing under the influence of loose men.

While Li struggles to keep herself and her family intact, Habu is found enjoying life with another woman in the city. Li narrates to her sister how Habu came under the influence of a city maiden and her charming ways:

> She came from the south. They worked in the same office. It was when Habu was new in the city and was a bit awkward, but she showed him round, cooked for him and was generally helpful.
>
> (*The Stillborn*, p. 91)

Habu and the lady in question came so close that she found herself carrying his child. But the relationship was unacceptable to her family. She looses her baby. They had injured body and bruised souls as a result. They paid for their miscalculations. Habu didn't realize that friendliness and helping attitude towards women do not demand lack of loyalty to the wedded wife. Li innocently waits for him while he comfortably flirts with another woman playing novice to the urban ways of life, fooling both the women and playing with their sentiments. Habu could have sought the help of his male colleagues instead of accepting the help of a young woman and that too for a quite long time. The poor woman does not know that the man is two timing her.

The desperation of young women to get married is common in every society. Young ladies become victims of their desire to get married. Invariably, they end up selecting wrong people. Be it Awa, Li, Faku or the urban lady, their men cheat them. But then marriage is the most important aspect of any civilized society. Men and women with normal mind and body do get married. The institution of marriage and family forms the strongest pillar of civilized world. There was nothing wrong in their eagerness to get married but due to fear and apprehensions, they hurried into it and suffered endlessly. However, their faith in religion and tradition saves them ultimately, because essentially they are women of high moral values. Even their wayward husbands realise this. They respect these women mainly because of their sense of commitment towards their men irrespective of their demerits and weaknesses. Their honesty and firmness of personality in the absence of their men makes them extra-ordinary. Habu becomes invalid after accident. It is Li who forgives him although he had lost hope of any forgiveness.

The most pathetic is the case of the other women in Habu's life. She stands nowhere. She is ruined for ever. She has lost her reputation, her future is darkened and she is left to repent all through. It is often seen that young women who move in public life become very confident of themselves. They start taking men too casually. But the fact is that women ought to be very cautious and thoughtful in selecting their associations and workplace. One wrong decision spoils the whole of future. Women cannot and should not imitate men and their carefree life style. The cordiality at workplace does not guarantee reliability.

Extending help is no crime. It should not be treated as a sin either by society or family but there has to be a limit and discretion also in every relationship. Civil conduct demands honesty in thought and deed from both the parties. Too much of indulgence is an unwelcome tendency. People who forget this are the most irritating elements within the social circle and right minded people dislike them. Habu should have been discreet in seeking help while his female friend ought to have resisted overindulging in the name of friendliness.

Habu was morally responsible towards Li and his responsibility towards her was more crucial, as it was a self negotiated marriage much against public opinion, because of his checkered family background. Li had boldly stood by him and accepted him as her husband. But he forgot her obligations and discarded her for the other women. When finally Habu is forced to accept Li under family pressure, he ill-treats her by his rudeness and long absence. He begins two-timing her and his urban associate, not knowing how to resolve the triangle. Li is thoroughly unaware of the existence of the second woman in Habu's life. She is confused, agitated and isolated.

Li finds a sympathiser in her landlady who is of her mother's age group. She is kind and forthcoming. She consoles her and provides moral support. Hajiya, the landlady, is in the know of the fact that Habu is cheating her. She feels sorry for Li and treats her with compassion. Li is taken to a fortune teller and through his help she tries to drive the message home that Habu is having another home and wife. But Li is too innocent to realise that Habu is now interested in the other woman. On hearing about her father's grave illness Li returns home. Li remains practically abandoned till she moves towards self-reliance by becoming a highly qualified teacher. She returns to her husband as a successful and accomplished woman.

Li neither rejects Habu nor her ambition to make a place for herself and maintain her family on her own rightful earnings. She is no more as aggressive and hyper-sensitive as she used to be. She has become cool and composed. The struggles of her life and those of Awa and Faku have made her mature. The story of the struggle of Hajiya has greatly influenced her thinking. She has become forgiving and reconciled to her fate. She accepts Habu with his handicaps. In the meanwhile, Habu has become an object of pity and mercy. He is no more capable of attracting any other lady and is hopelessly dependent upon his family's goodwill and support. They have been coaxing Li to come and look after him mainly because he has become a liability rather than support. Habu has lost their respect and goodwill due to his lack of commitment to Li and, of course his associations with the urban woman. Li's stand is vindicated.

Compared to the Nigerian society, Indian rural women are more bold and aggressive temperamentally. They are fiercely feminist and do not tolerate wife-beaters. Instead, they get their husbands beaten up by their male relatives or admirers if they feel agitated. Indian rural women do have admirers and many a times, they run away from their home full of children, husband and extended family. They don't care even about their children. The boldness and indifference towards their traditional role of mother and wife is posing a serious threat to social peace and stability.

Marriage in rural India too is becoming unstable and volatile. It is a myth that patriarchy is still strong. Externally, its facade is being maintained but internally women do assert within their family life. Men and women both indulge in relations outside marriage. The complications are such that people prefer to keep quiet. Indian village society is no more very honest from marital point of view. Many values are being broken down. Many norms are being shaken and many incidents take place that kill the faith of people in tradition and as well as kinship ties.

Women in Indian society have started showing peculiar traits, especially the upper class and lower class women, while the middle class women are worst affected and also most secure too. The upper class and lower class women have started using their feminine attributes as a tool and as a weapon to counter male dominance. They have also begun to use male as the pawn and as mediums to outwit their own rivals. The middle class women on the other hand, counter male dominance with their tolerance. Once the initial years of marriage are over, their fears of being left alone are over too. Usually, middle class men don't beat their wives nor torture them to provoke extreme reactions from their women. Normally, they are reasonable, tolerant, adjusting and respectful towards their women and treat their women with respect. They see to it that family differences don't go out of control. They make compromises and sacrifices for their children. Children of middle class homes are a great binding force and they are so conscious and indulging that it becomes practically impossible for a middle class husband or wife to break away from family. In upper class and lower class homes, on the other hand, children hardly matter either to mother or father. Individual life is more important. Both the classes are highly influenced by money and hold all other things to ransom. Sense of responsibility and moral bindings are missing in both the classes.

The role of children is very limited and conditional in upper and lower classes of Indian society. They hardly have any say. They are the ones who suffer the most. Broken homes break them psychologically. Children in upper class are compensated with excess flow of money and the lower class children become orphan and dependent upon social goodwill. It is neighbours and relatives who arrange job and sustain them till they are completely independent. These children become too mature with experiences. The harsh realities of life make these children worldly wise too soon. They, in most cases, fall in bad company and become matter of concern for the whole neighbourhood. Thus, when a home is broken, a fraction of our society is also shaken. Society cannot afford to ignore these break-ups. The children of broken homes become social liabilities and irritants for local authorities as well.

Morality can neither be snatched forcibly nor can be imposed from above. It is ingrained and is reflected in the personality of the individual concerned. It has nothing to do either with gender or age, culture or tradition. However, normally, women are more cautious, fearful and alert, because of their own conscience. They keep reminding themselves about their womanhood and are thus over-conscious about their security and image. They are basically tradition-loving and enjoy their role of home makers and do not nurse much complain or bias towards their family or society. Essentially, they are devoted to their family and committed to their religion and faith. What they feel strongly is that inspite of their immense contribution to society, they are not being given proper share in education, health, economy and social lives.

Except the grandma, all the female characters of *The Stillborn* have proved to be strong women having very rational mind with strong family values. They have fought back against adversities of life and won. They do not complain but find ways to move on in life. Instead of wasting time in slogan shouting and emotional outpourings before male relatives, neighbours and society in general, they struggle, make errors, rectify them and work harder to give shape and meaning to their lives without reducing themselves into prostitutes or kepts.

Zaynab Alkali tries to prove through her female characters that there is enough scope for improvements, adjustments and modifications within the framework of traditional social set-up. What is needed is flexibility, reliability and confidence in the ability of women. Women are too gentle at heart to inflict injury to the male egos and hence they should not be haunted by their men. The women are more content to forgive their men on their own initiative and feel obliged too. As long as these tendencies to forgive, defend and protect their loved ones, who are sometimes offenders, are present in women, offending men need not worry. Li exhibits this tendency the best when Sule is found guilty in blacksmith daughter's case. Instead of confronting Sule and pressurizing him to own up his sin, she help him to escape to the town. She acts against ethics and leaves the girl in question in distress and shame. As long as these trends continue, women cannot claim for justice on moral grounds. Such acts raise questions of ethics.

The cry for justice also demands neutrality and impartiality from women as well. They are over eager for reconciliations with male members even at the cost of basic human rights. They become very benign and forgiving when they have to judge a male member's conduct. But that is just to win back male members' goodwill and support rather than anything else. Li is more forgiving towards her brother and husband than towards the two women whose lives have been deshaped by these men. She hardly bothers to provide any relief to them as she holds these women more responsible for their plight than the men.

The gender bias against women is not just confined to men. It is women themselves who nurture, polish and relish these attitudes depending upon their interests involved. If it suits their needs they support the bias with their active participation in drilling the idea of subjugation among women. And if it hurts them on individual level, they put the blame on the men and society for the precarious conditions of women at large. Their dual stand towards their own gender is making life miserable for innumerable women the world over.

3

Portrayal of Women in Arundhati Roy's Novel *The God of Small Things*

The novel *The God of Small Things* is a forceful commentary on the decaying morality of Indian society. In this novel, Arundhati Roy writes about the problems faced by a traditional society which is going through a period of transition. The women of India are also going through changes on psychological and social levels. They have been granted certain rights for which women of previous generations struggled without success.

The hurdles, the pitfalls are many and yet there is a zeal to add meaning to their existence. It creates a kind of tension on social and intellectual levels among women and also with the opposite gender. Complications in personal lives of women and the impact upon people around them especially the children, the elderly and other dependents have acquired serious dimensions.

Arundhati Roy is honest and bold in her expressions. She writes with conviction and faith in herself. Her writing is primarily based upon her experiences and observations which cannot be challenged.

The God of Small Things is woven around the socio-political fabric of Kerala. The hold of casteless Christianity upon those people who are equally impressed with egalitarian Marxist ideology is constantly challenged by the age-old Brahminical thinking of the upper caste Hindu society. In the whole of Kerala, right from the upper class influential people to the lowest ladder, people are busy trying to grapple with these contradictions. Rigidity on the ideological level and flexibility on the practical level creates problems and confusions. Yet the inherent homogeneity of Indian society has made it possible for various factions to co-exist inspite of all the differences and grievances.

Many sacrifices are made to keep the secular temper of Indian society intact by the minority communities as well. They suffer silently on personal levels to make sure that communal harmony is not disturbed because of their over-assertiveness or aggressiveness. Ammu of *The God of Small Things* had to suffer on many fronts yet she could not assert herself mainly due to her gender and religious delicacies. Her assertiveness would have disturbed the caste-harmony of her village and local political equations.

The novel is a biographical sketch of Ammu, Rahel, Estha and Velutha. Arundhati Roy brings to light the vices of Indian society. It is said that her novel *The God of Small Things* is her own story, the story of her parents, especially that of her mother. She has made some changes to suit the story line in order to produce a work of fiction. For example, according to her mother, the Velutha episode never happened in her life. She never had any extra-marital affairs, or any formal divorce from her husband. They simply separated and did not bother to seek divorce. However, the natural flow and spontaneity of language and thought process is unaffected by these minor changes.

What is most admirable about Arundhati Roy is that she depicts the irony and trauma of a broken family in the *The God of Small Things* with a deep sense of hurt and empathy. The novel brings to light the plight of a divorcee who is considerably young with two kids who are twins.

Indian society rarely gives a second chance to women. Those who are unfortunate in their marriage are made to suffer all the more. The novelist also brings to notice certain vital issues related to humanity. The right to lead life according to one's own choice, to survive with dignity and integrity has always been unthinkable for a divorcee and a widow in rural and semi-rural societies of India. In fact, divorce is an unheard of proposition in rural Indian society (except in Muslim and Christian communities).

The cold-bloodedness with which the basic rights of marginalized citizens are crushed in rural India is frightening. Class and caste conflicts, ideological differences, religious intolerance and disharmony on linguistic levels, all these disappear as soon as there comes to light an issue related to women's emancipation and plight. The whole society gets worked up and emotionally charged fearing threat to religious sentiments and tradition.

Ammu is a representative of such women whose marital life is unhappy. Such women are thrown out of marriage. The reasons could be many, both moral as well as immoral. But the blame falls on the 'weaker' gender invariably, because it is very convenient and the victim is an easy prey to both social criticism and family bias. Ammu is subjected to humiliations primarily because she chose her own path much against tradition. Through Ammu's life history Arundhati Roy tries to highlight the hypocrisy of Indian society.

Women in ancient India too were accorded secondary status as is evident from texts like the Manu Smriti but they did not experience such suffocating environment as the one that they encountered during the Medieval period. The idea of *Purdah* prevalent among the victorious Muslims greatly suited the whims of men of the defeated Hindu community and they went to illogical levels to force it upon their own women. Later on, religious conflicts, political instability, social disharmony, mistrust and mutual suspicion created an environment not conducive for the well-being of women in general. Modern Indian society is not different so far as the position of women in rural India is concerned.

Some sections of Indian society still believe in keeping women under pressure and resent granting them normal environment for growth and personality development. The aggressiveness of the conservatives create problems for single women especially divorcees and widows. Ammu is made to suffer due to the inflated male ego and insensitivity of her own gender. Bias towards women make people commit serious mistakes which can hardly be compensated. Mahatma Gandhi once said:

> A man should learn to give place to woman. A country or a community in which women are not honoured cannot be considered civilized.

But, till date we have failed both as a nation and also as a community in granting equal status to women as expected by Gandhi. Women like Ammu suffer all kinds of mental and social harassments in the land of Mahatma. Ammu is forced by circumstances to lead a single life without any substantial support from the family of her origin or her in-laws. She is an outcaste for both the families. Ammu belongs to no one. They cannot identify with her as she belongs to them only partially.

The novel begins with the present state of Ammu at her parent's house where she has to adjust to the whims of her brother. He too is a divorcee. His wife has left him for better options even though he had been a very sensitive and caring husband. Ammu has to adjust with her haughty and violent father and assertive and sarcastic elder brother. Ammu has to help her brother and mother in their pickle factory. She is a sincere worker yet her contributions are taken for granted.

The most important characters in the novel are the twin children, Estha and Rahel. They call their mother Ammu. Ammu tries hard to fill the void created by absence of their father.

Ammu has been forced to seek divorce from her husband due to his beatings and immoral ways. The most important reason has been the weakness on the part of her husband to protect his wife from the lust of his boss. He became violent when she refused to oblige. She tried her best to save her marriage but could not bring herself to compromise on moral grounds. She is basically very religious and morally upright lady. Her physical beauty becomes the cause of worry for her. She could not digest the fact that her own husband wanted her to entertain his superior. She was shocked and shattered. She was filled with shame and hatred. She refused to oblige.

Differences on mental and moral levels compelled them to part ways.

In any society, a wife expects her husband to act as a shield for her and her children. He must exhibit at least moral courage and inclination to work hard to provide all kinds of support to his family during any crisis. A husband must provide all necessary help, support and protection from whatever is evil, immoral, unethical, unjust and unfair. A woman expects not only financial security from her marriage but also social, psychological and moral support. Ammu's husband has failed her on moral grounds. In fact, he even tried to push her into unethical ways with his own consent and convenience much against her wishes. An understanding had been reached at between her husband and her seeker behind her back. She was being treated as a luxury item to be sold and procured for entertainment and relaxation. It is quite obvious and understandable that Ammu is furious and becomes very violent and aggressive against the whole arrangement. She is shocked, shattered and digusted. She then decides to walk out of this hellish situation as early as possible. Divorce, thus, becomes the obvious destination of Ammu's marriage. She returns to her parents at Kerala with shattered dreams, shocking memories and new hopes.

The sudden change of events in the otherwise peaceful life of Ammu, compel her to seek solace from her parents. Her expectations and eagerness to reach home and get warmth and shield of parental affection and protection soon get evaporated with the heat of stoic silence with which she is received by her people. She realizes that she is heading for a long and lonely journey with her children.

Chacko, Ammu's elder brother is very possessive about his family legacy and refuses to share his property with his sister. Ammu on the other hand, being a divorcee, is in desperate need of financial and social support from her own people. Chacko's attitude is typical of any ordinary Indian family where married daughters are not allowed any space in their parental establishment for fear of complications in personal and social lives.

Ammu is a divorcee. Hence her problem are all the more serious. Chacko is too alert to let Ammu assert herself and hence cold war between the two begins right after her return. Chacko is very ruthless, insensitive and calculative. His attitude towards his younger sister is not at all justified. Chacko and her parents prefer to ignore her repeated pleas for financial help. Ultimately, she takes a job as a receptionist at an ordinary hotel. Due to illness this job too slips out of her hands. She is jobless and again dependent upon her unfriendly family members. She is forced to send away her emotional and moral support, her son Estha, to her ex-husband due to family pressure. She hopes to bring him back as soon as she gets a new job. But before anything positive happens in their life, Ammu dies under mysterious circumstances in another town. She had gone there to appear in an interview for a job but the news of her demise reaches her daughter Rahel who is the narrator of this story. She is writing about her mother. She writes with passion and pain, with dedication and caution.

The cause of Ammu's death is traced to the death of Velutha in police custody. Ammu, unable to cope with social harassment and emotional void in her personal life, had sought respite in an untouchable man called 'Velutha'—*The God of Small Things*. Velutha, son of her old family servant, plays an important role in the life of Ammu. Velutha is very skilled in mending things, especially machines related to domestic use. He is a trusted servant of the family and is treated with favour compared to the other servants. The faith and reliability of Velutha gets tainted when he gets emotionally involved with Ammu. This news spreads like wild fire in the whole of Ayemenem. When the family comes to know of their involvement (which is both physical and emotional), they oppose it vehemently. But Ammu and Velutha refuse to retrace their steps. They meet regularly at mid-night by the river to satisfy their carnal desires.

The shamelessness and defiance of Ammu and Velutha is tolerated till people hoped the two would realise their mistake and retrace their steps. Finally, the man is eliminated with the help and connivance of police. The police tortures him mercilessly before killing him. Even a false case is registered against him before his death in police custody. Due to serious injuries at the hands of police *The God of Small Things* dies a very painful death. On hearing about his arrest Ammu approaches the police to set the record straight but the police, knowing the main reason behind Velutha's death, refuse to register her protest and humiliates her for bringing bad name to her family.

Velutha has been implicated in a false case of abduction and murder of Sophie Mol, the grand daughter of the family. Since the family is influential, Baby Kochamma the grand-aunt of Rahel and Estha, uses the opportunity to punish Velutha and Ammu who have been till then throwing ethics to winds.

The pent up anger against Ammu and Velutha come out spontaneously and forcefully because of the emotional jolt of Sophie Mol's sudden death. Ammu is held responsible because Sophie had gone by the river with her cousins Estha and Rahel. The boat in which they were crossing the river had drifted towards deep waters. While Estha and Rahel escape unhurt, Sophie is drowned in the swollen river. Her body is found the next day. Baby Kochamma seizes this opportunity to get rid of Velutha by implicating him in Sophie's death. She uses Estha and Rahel as puppets in her game plan. Here one finds Ammu totally defenceless. She is unable to either plead innocence on behalf of her children nor seek legal actions to defend Velutha. Tension is so much that "though Ammu, Estha and Rahel were allowed to attend the funeral, they were made to stand separately, not with the rest of the family. Nobody wanted to look at them." (*The God of Small Things*, p. 5)

Margaret Kochamma's grief and bitterness at her daughter's death coils inside her like an angry spring. She says nothing but slaps Estha, whenever she can, during her stay in Ayemenem before returning to England. Ammu is unable to defend her son out of guilt and helplessness. Ammu is finally compelled to send Estha away to mitigate tension in her parents' home.

Estha's father, by now, has left his job as tea-estate manager and moved to Calcutta. He has re-married and works for a company that makes carbon black. He has stopped drinking and suffers only occasional relapses. Rahel did not see her brother for years since the day he left for Calcutta.

Rahel grows up, marries and seeks divorce. She returns to India to meet her brother Estha who has come back after twenty-three years:

> And now, twenty-three years later, their father had re-returned Estha. He had sent him back to Ayemenem with a suitcase and a letter.
>
> (*The God of Small Things*, p. 9)

Rahel decides to write down the story of her mother and of Velutha who was not only their mother's lover but also a very good and sensitive friend of the fatherless twins. When Rahel and Estha meet, what hangs heavily upon their memory is the death of Velutha. They remember vividly how they were forced to implicate Velutha in a crime he had never committed. Rahel and her brother Estha are not able to forgive themselves for being tools in the hands of fate and family to destroy the only support they had in their lives in the name of Velutha.

The novel is a commentary on the life of not only Ammu but also upon countless women like her who fail to give proper shape to their lives due to lack of sympathy, goodwill of their own gender especially and other pressures caused by loneliness and lack of timely help by friends and relatives. Their hopes and aspirations are shattered by the untimely demise of their loved ones.

The psychological pressure of implicating an innocent man in a false case, the death of Velutha, the way he dies, the trauma their mother goes through after his death and her final exit from this world at thirty-one, all create havoc in the lives of her two children:

> Edges, Borders, Boundaries, Brinks and Limits have appeared like a team of trolls on their separate horizons. Short creatures with long shadows, patrolling the Blurry End. Gentle half-moons have gathered

> under their eyes and they are as old as Ammu when she died. Thirty One.
>
> Not old
>
> Not young
>
> But a viable die-able age.
>
> (*The God of Small Things*, p. 3)

Estha feels he is guilty of Sophie Mol's death, Velutha's death and eventually his mother's end. He could not protect her or assert himself against all the manipulations of facts and events as he was too young to do anything. He wanted to grow up and take up her responsibilities but destiny had its say. He lost his mission of life:

> Slowly, over the years, Estha withdrew from the world....
>
> (*The God of Small Things*, p. 12)

Something in him dies with Velutha. But before that the shock of loss of Mol affects him deeply. Her death crystallizes his sense of guilt and remorse to such an extent that he becomes almost silent. Baby Kochamma has been instrumental in bringing about this by forcing Estha to give statements against Velutha, an innocent victim of circumstances. Velutha is killed due to Ammu's fatal attractions towards an untouchable servant. Her weakness of character has killed Velutha and forced Estha to lie before the police in order to save family interests. Estha neither could stop his mother and Velutha from immorality nor protest against Baby Kochamma's pressure to give wrong statements to police regarding Sophie's death.

He is finally broken by his mother's death. The helplessness of Estha as a child kills his zeal to achieve success in life, to add meaning to his own existence. The agony of being the cause of all that has happened in the past erodes him emotionally. He becomes an introvert and rarely talks to anyone:

> A barely noticeable quietening. As though he had simply run out of conversation and

> had nothing left to say. Yet Estha's silence was never awkward. Never intrusive. Never noisy. It wasn't accusing, protesting silence as much as a sort of aestivation, a dormancy, the psychological equivalent of what lungfish do to get themselves through the dry season, except that in Estha's case the dry season looked as though it would last for ever.
>
> (*The God of Small Things*, p. 10)

The rash temperament and irrational approaches of Ammu and Baby Kochamma towards each other, Chacko and Mammachi's detachments towards her daughter's crisis, all fall heavily upon Estha's humble shoulders. He is forced to make false statements much against his conscience. The whimsical acts of elders are the cause of Estha's sufferings and predicaments. It is Ammu's family which is responsible for the present crisis in Estha's life.

Essentially, Estha has been a quiet, obedient, sensitive and thinking child. He has always tried to be a worthy and caring son. He loved his mother more than anyone. When Ammu is being humiliated at the police station by the Inspector Thomas Mathew, both Estha and Rahel guess that something unfair has been said to her. They had then wanted to know what 'Veshya' and 'illegitimate' meant. But Ammu's stiffness and hot tears prevent them from asking. They silently suffer with their lonely mother. The inspector had said: "the police knew all that they needed to know and that the Kottayam Police didn't take statements from Veshyas or their illegitimate children." (*The God of Small Things*, p. 8)

The socio-political atmosphere at local level force the local authorities to take sides which is reflected here in Inspector Thomas Mathew's reactions. They too get influenced by bias, prejudices, greed, lust and temptations. They begin to have vested interests in local issues. In the process, these official functionaries inflict injustice and humiliation on innocent victims of circumstances:

> It was the first time they'd seen their mother cry. She wasn't sobbing. Her face was set like stone, but the tears welled up in her eyes and ran down her rigid cheeks. It made the twins sick with fear. Ammu's tears made everything that had so far seemed unreal, real.
>
> (*The God of Small Things*, p. 8)

Estha is the only support Ammu and Rahel can bank upon in the future and at the present. Estha tries to share her pains as much as possible. He is always by her side trying to instill hope and courage to overcome the present crisis. He mediates between his emotionally disturbed mother and other people to balance the situation as much as possible. When the bus conductor questions her about tickets, Ammu is off. She is lost in her sorrow and cannot interact properly with him. It is Estha who answers him:

> He took the money out of Ammu's purse. The conductor gave him the tickets. Estha folded them carefully and put them in his pocket. Then he put his little arms around his rigid, weeping mother.
>
> (*The God of Small Things*, p. 9)

Exactly, two week later Estha is forcibly separated from his mother and sister. He is sent to Calcutta to return only after twenty-three years.

The description of the events and their impact upon the main characters is very realistic and natural. The depiction of the perpetrators of crime is neutral and unbiased. The writer has tried to present facts without any bitterness and ill will. She hints at their sin in the most decent manner. She is, however, very clear in her objective. Her purpose is to expose the culprits and prick the conscience of the readers regarding women like Ammu and her children. Those who are less fortunate in their personal lives need help and concerns of their kith and kin and associates to overcome their crisis. It is highly unfair and uncivil to push them to the wall.

The way Ammu and her children are treated by their relatives is highly objectionable and regrettable. Social humiliation and family pressure force Ammu to make all the wrong moves. Ammu is made a tool to destroy her own life and that of Estha, Rahel and Velutha too. Her impulsive nature, her reactionary steps, her lack of morality all lead to her loss of reputation and loss of sympathy for herself and her children.

The novel is dedicated to the cause of humanity. It is a novel which highlights the irony and predicaments of a woman who is extraordinarily attractive and morally upright initially. She dares to refuse to comply to the unjustified, unreasonable and immoral demands of her husband. But, she is forced by circumstances to fall for a man who is much below her status although she cannot own him socially and legally due to social restrictions. A servant cannot marry his master's daughter. Despite being aware of their predicament the shameless conduct of Ammu and Velutha is reason enough for their indictment and lack of goodwill. Even if Velutha had been of any other caste or religion, objections would have been raised even then. It is not a question of caste but of ethics and morality. They have been guilty of committing moral sins which deserves serious objection.

However, the way Ammu was provoked and harassed by her own people highlights the traditional approach of Indian society towards their married daughters. People dislike their married daughters putting financial strain upon their parents. Here, Ammu is divorced with two children and has become a permanent fixture of her parents' household. This is what is irritating for Ammu's parents and her aunt. Even her brother makes her feel unwanted. All these things put a lot of mental pressure upon her and her kids. She fails to discipline her impulses and takes those very steps which she had objected to when asked by her husband. Her weakness of character leads to her destruction.

What has happened to Ammu is nothing new or unexpected. She has paid the price for breaking the established norms of society. She might have escaped this fate had she learned to put up with her social and economic constraints and yet stuck to her family vocation, accepting whatever came her way till her children grew up to support her both socially and financially.

For a woman her dignity is in her chastity. Respectability is earned not granted. A woman must keep herself away from all kinds of evil doings. Once she becomes a mother, she is looked up to as woman of strong character and high moral values. Her commitment toward her family, husband and children, legacy and tradition all depend heavily upon her personal conduct. A woman generally does not like to break this image of a sincere mother and committed housewife. Respect at personal and social level is earned by sticking to right moral values and balanced conduct in personal as well as public life. And those who fail on this ground whether male or female are subject to criticism and rejection from the society at large.

The ego clash between Ammu and Chacko is one of the reasons of her downfall. Being an Indian, she should have enough sense to understand the emotional dependence of her parents upon her brother. They were naturally more attached to their son than her. Indian people depend heavily upon their male heirs for sustenance and continuation of tradition and legacies. The emotional bond between son and his parents are too strong to be objected and resented. Ammu should have accepted it rather than resenting and creating pathetic scenes for herself and her children. Highlighting her candidature for parental attention and care when they were so stiff and rigid made her situation all the more pathetic. She should have been more mature and handled the whole situation graciously. It is the Hindu influence that has penetrated into the Indian Christian society. Her family has been behaving as a typical Hindu patriarchal family. Christianity does not disown/ disinherit daughters to such an extent.

Ammu is essentially a Syrian Christian (of Kerala). But she somehow forgets Kerala. She remembers only her Syrian Christian origin. Her mental world is busy striving hard for equal treatment from her parents and her yearning for sympathetic hearing from her brother. Her Christian values are harshly challenged by her family's 'Hindu' rigidity of mind. They are 'Hindu' in their approach regarding Ammu. The insensitivity, the irritations, the bias, the reservations which they exhibit towards her and her kids are typical of any Hindu family. Daughters are not to be allowed much space and facilities in middle class families. Even upper class families do not appreciate interference or presence of their married daughter in their establishment. Even other communities have begun to imitate the majority community's way of thinking, they unconsciously get influenced by the traditional Hindu way of life. The more Ammu asked for kindness the more rigid they become towards her. Her marriage with a Hindu become a permanent bone of contention between them. They are unwilling to forgive her for going outside community and causing embarrassment to the family. They are taking revenge now. Punishing her for her marriage. Ammu is left with no one to console her and guide her.

Ammu's unreasonable ways make people dislike her. Her brother too tolerates her barely. Her brother is a great flirt; she blindly imitates him by getting involved with Velutha. She is an angry woman who is also very whimsical. She fails to realise that first of all she is a woman. Nature has made her different from her brother. Being born a woman means a lot. Womanhood demands dignity, grace and value based life-style. Those who refuse to accept these basic rules of nature are bound to commit mistakes and pay the price. Ammu also fails to realise that her family being traditional would not immediately grant her all the rights she wants to exercise. She expects tolerance from everyone while she herself is quite intolerant and sharp tongued. Her sharpness of tongue spreads bad blood among her people and they lose even the slightest bit of sympathy they have for their rebel. They become all the more resentful and intolerant with passage of time and by the time Ammu dies, they have lost all interest and sympathy for her. Only her brother turns up to collect her body. He comes with a sense of propriety and duty rather than with any sympathy for his deceased sister. Her rudeness, her sarcasm, her rebellious temper, her unreasonable acts make her both unpopular and unacceptable.

Ammu's restlessness and her desire to escape from the hard realities of her own life and her own society, and her repeated attempts to escape from her loneliness lead her to her doom. Besides, the insensitivities of her own people, the corrupt police, the rigid social set-up—all create a very complex web of circumstances in which Ammu gets trapped.

India is basically a predominantly Hindu society with a secular temper. Here, caste system plays a very important role in individuals' life. Other communities have unconsciously imbibed the upper caste Hindu psychology which is very traditional and inflexible in nature. Since most of the converts come from the majority community, their fore-fathers have carried their caste bias into their new faith. The concept of purity and impurity dominate the whole psychology of Indian people.

Ammu did not care about these things. What makes her fearful is her 'single' status and uncertain future. She did try to stick to her family and give shape to her life but her people reject her time and again. She becomes desperate day by day. Finally, she seeks emotional support from a man who is no match to her family. Here too, her brother and aunt outwit her and she is again left alone.

On the other hand, Velutha is a silent, defiant and obstinate man, who lacks maturity, thoughtfulness and loyalty towards his caring masters. Ammu's family always treated him with favour. His conscience should not have allowed him to get influenced by Ammu's unethical ways. Obviously, the Syrian Christian family's pride is greatly hurt as their trusted man has ditched them. His actions show that their goodness of heart made him bold. He misunderstood their temperament and underestimated their potentialities to harm him if their family prestige and dignity were so nastily challenged. Ammu has made herself a medium through which Velutha tries to challenge their superiority although he has no grievance or reason to complain. It is a simple case of breach of faith on the part of Ammu as well as Velutha. Ammu is revengeful and Velutha lacks circumspection.

Velutha and Ammu make things difficult for their families with each passing day. Public pressure is building up upon both the families to discipline the culprits. Ammu's family feels embarrassed and insulted when she seeks refuge in an untouchable man who happens to be their servant. His being their employee is more shameful than his being untouchable. Taken together, these two factors infuriate the whole village. Resentment turns into rage and the whole society gangs up to punish the two law breakers for their misadventure. The woman is finally locked up in her room while the man is killed. His crime being lack of propriety.

Velutha is brainwashed by Ammu who is too impulsive and reckless in her conduct. It is Ammu who has dragged him to his death. She has been desperate for a man's protective shield. She compels Velutha to provide all kinds of emotional and moral support to her and her kids. Velutha, unable to strike a balance between his duty and his status, falls prey to her seductive ways and loses his life.

The greatest irony of Velutha's life is that his own father, out of fear and a sense of guilt, shame and subjugation, informs Ammu's family about his whereabouts and gets him arrested. The caste politics plays a vital role in the whole drama. His father is pressurized to give information about his son else his whole caste might suffer. Threatening and also warning from all sides compel the old man to sacrifice his son to buy peace for his castemen. He is made to realise by his own caste people that they don't want to suffer on account his son's follies. He must own his mistakes and take the punishments. He is made aware of the gravity of the situation. As soon as Velutha is arrested, the tension melts. Everything comes to normal.

Velutha never opens his month against his masters. He maintains the decorum outwardly and yet dies unrepentant. His inner strength to stand up for what he feels is his right never dies out till the very end. Actually, he identifies his pains and his rejection, by upper caste and class with that of

Ammu's. She is rejected because she is a divorcee while he is rejected because he is an untouchable. She needs a man in her life and he is willing to give psychological support to the family which is struggling for its existence. He strongly feels responsible towards Ammu and her children. He realizes that they are heavily dependent upon him for all kinds of support. A sense of unity of feeling is found here between Ammu and Velutha. Both lack moral strength and right sense of judgement. What they have failed to realise is that more than their different backgrounds, it is their way of interaction which is highly objectionable and unethical. It is feared by the people that if these two are not punished, it might send wrong signal to the rest of the society. It might set a bad example before the people. Lack of social commitment in Ammu and Velutha fill people with anger and contempt. They should have shown guts to challenge the society in the daylight, opted for court marriage or visited the Church. But what they did and how they did tell a lot about the inherent weakness of their respective personalities.

However, Velutha takes a belated step to rectify his mistakes. He decides to accept his relations with Ammu in public and seek support from his party men and caste people. But Chacko outsmarts him and manipulates facts and favours against him. Velutha's resources are no match to an influential Syrian Christian family. Ammu is confined to her own room and not allowed to come out till Velutha is eliminated.

Velutha has failed due to more than one reason, caste bias being one of them. Anger towards him is mainly due to his breach of trust. His illicit relationship with the daughter of his master is highly objectionable. It is taken as a challenge and provocation to the upper caste people. He is alleged taking advantage of the pitiable condition of Ammu as a separated, rejected and resented woman of her family. He is blamed for enticing her. Had he been honest towards his masters, he should have expressed his helplessness before her and sought excuse from her. He could have informed his master and left the job instead of encouraging her and bringing bad name to the family of his employers. What Velutha did cannot be justified. He made himself defenceless. In fact, both he and Ammu forced people to take tough stand in order to defend the grace and dignity of a respectable family.

Even if they had succeeded in legalizing their relationship, it would never have gained social acceptance and assimilation within the village. His party leader Comrade Pillai and Chacko discuss this delicate issue:

> 'That Paravan is going to cause trouble for you', he said. 'Take it from me...get him a job somewhere else. Send him off.'
>
> Chacko was puzzled at the turn the conversation had taken. He had only intended to find out what was happening, where things stood. He had expected to encounter antagonism, even confrontation, and instead was being offered sly, misguided collusion.
>
> (*The God of Small Things*, p. 278)

Chacko is apprehensive about the fall-out of Velutha-Ammu scandal. He is very careful and judicious in selection of words and expression. He fears that this affair can threaten the very existence of his family. Being a minority, he has to be defensive and at the same time, try his best to defuse the tension as decently as possible. What if Velutha's community becomes aggressive and united? Poor Chacko is paying for his arrogance and insensitivity towards his sister. She has shaken the roots of her legacy and family prestige of which Chacko, Mammachi and Pappachi are so proud. Their daughter, out of revenge, desperation and depression stooped to nasty levels. Ammu has forced her family to plead for support from outsiders in defusing the crisis. The family gets desired amount of help mainly due to the fear that if they allow mercy to them, it may send wrong signals to notorious people in society. Even though Velutha is basically a good human being whose conduct has always been appreciated in the past, yet his involvement with Ammu is highly regrettable.

Even Velutha's caste people resent the Velutha-Ammu equation. They also resent his favoured position in his master's household. He is their most dependable servant. His special status among the rest of the workers is taken adversely. His caste-people feel that since he is involved with his master's divorced daughter, he is treated differently. This is what Comrade Pillai is hinting at. Other workers come to Comrade Pillai with complaints. Comrade Pillai does not disclose its specific nature but cautions Chacko against further problems:

> 'Nothing specifically as such', Comrade K.N.M. Pillai said. 'But see, Comrade, any benefits that you give him, naturally others are resenting it. They see it as a partiality. After all, whatever job he does, carpenter or electrician or whatever it is, for them he is just a Paravan. It is a conditioning they have from birth. This I myself have told them is wrong. But frankly speaking, Comrade, change is one thing. Acceptance is another. You should be cautious. Better for him you send him off....'
>
> (*The God of Small Things*, p. 279)

Comrade Pillai, a communist, who is expected not to believe in caste and religious hierarchy, is trying to convince Chacko to recognize the caste factor as a reality. His being a Christian doesn't matter. What matters is his acceptance of the social norm wherein most people show respect to the caste system. Those who are untouchable must be treated differently and should not be encouraged beyond a point. Even the minorities must ditto the caste system if they have to survive in the Indian society. They dare not encourage the subjugated castes and invite ill-will of the majority community. Caste is here to stay. Chacko must not try to break the rules by treating Velutha as rest of the workers. Velutha is a Paravan first, that is, an untouchable who has right to live, right to work but no right to raise his stature in social ladder either through diligence or otherwise. He must die a Paravan. The stagnation in personal and social life is his fate and no change is acceptable to the Hindu society in this regard. The society cannot and will not allow even other religious community to pull him up. The sentiments of the majority must be respected at all costs. Let the humanity go to hell!

Chacko needs Velutha to run his pickle factory. He is a great support to him. But Pillai wants him out due to pressures from other workers. They don't want to be ordered around by a Paravan, an untouchable. He is just unacceptable to them as an equal. Christian values of brotherhood, equality etc. are unacceptable to them. Chacko must keep his Oxford education to himself. He must accept Indian ways of social interaction. With the help of an untouchable, he cannot run his factory and earn money. Others including Pillai, politician and rival businessman too do not allow this to continue. Velutha cannot continue any more. He must go.

Ammu's involvement with Velutha is the basic cause of resentment. As long as they were not involved, Velutha was successfully countering the political game of others to disturb the workers of the factory. Pillai could not instigate the workers of pickle factory against the establishment, that is, Chacko. But due to Ammu's involvement with Velutha, people get a chance to bounce back with new found energy and crush Velutha for ever. The caste politics comes to the forefront. Pillai and others pressurize Chacko to literally surrender Velutha in compliance to social dictates.

The villagers' sentiment has been hurt. An untouchable, however meritorious, cannot rise the social ladder. An untouchable cannot cast his eyes upon his master's daughter who comes from an upper caste convert family. Whether Chacko likes it or not, he must respect Hindu sentiments and forgo his claims on Velutha and leave him defenceless.

Comrade Pillai is just the spokesperson of those who are opposing Chacko's secular style of functioning which is taken as a challenge to the majority sentiments. People are watching the two men negotiating the matter:

> Men were made to wait outside. The door
> was left ajar. When Comrade Pillai spoke

> next, he spoke in Malayalam and made sure it was loud enough for his audience outside.
>
> (*The God of Small Things*, p. 280)

Chacko is desperate to save his factory while Pillai is determined to hijack it from both its owner and its manager. He wants to get rid of both by making use of the scandal. The shrewdness of Pillai and the revolt of the workers force Chacko to close down the factory. What led to its closure can be best explained in the words of Rahel:

> Nobody ever learned the precise nature of the role that Comrade Pillai played in the events that followed. Even Chacko-who knew that the fervent, high-pitched speeches about Rights of Untouchables ('Caste is class, Comrades') delivered by Comrade Pillai during Marxist Party siege of Paradise Pickles, were pharisaic—never learned the whole story.
>
> (*The God of Small Things*, p. 281)

Velutha makes a last desperate attempt to protect himself, Ammu and his two lovable, adorable little friends from the cruel holds of Baby Kochamma and the rest, but he fails miserably. He is ditched by his caste men, his family and above all his destiny. Rahel says:

> Velutha's last visit to Comrade Pillai—after his confrontation with Mammachi and Baby Kochamma—and what had passed between them, remained a secret. The last betrayal that sent Velutha across the river, swimming against the current, in the dark and rain, well in time for his blind date with history.
>
> (*The God of Small Things*, p. 282)

This is the final stage reached by Velutha, thanks to the inhuman and insensitive social set up of village India. Here, life of an untouchable is of no value.

Pillai, the theorist, the politician, ditches Velutha, a low caste labourer, to further his own interests:

> To be fair to Comrade Pillai, he did not plan the course of events that followed. He merely slipped his ready fingers into History's waiting glove. It was not entirely his fault that he lived in a society where a man's death could be more profitable than his life had ever been.
>
> (*The God of Small Things*, p. 281)

Ammu's failure to get help and sympathy from her family lead to her death too. The life of a divorcee is worse than that of a widow or an abandoned wife. The later, because of her misfortune, gets the sympathy and support from her immediate family, relatives, friends and the society. Social pressure compels relatives and well wishers to guard a widow or an abandoned wife's interests. But a divorcee is taken as a very liberated woman who must have been the cause of the failure of her marriage. Broken homes are looked at with suspicion and prejudice. The image of a woman takes a beating as soon as the news of a her divorce reaches her acquaintances. The natural reaction is that of despair and anger. The woman in question is looked down upon as a home breaker who is not willing to follow the established patterns of life in a civilized society. She loses the goodwill of not only her immediate relatives and close friends but the whole society.

People want that the institution of marriage must be maintained at all cost, even at the cost of morality and humanity. The woman is expected to tolerate ill-treatment and still maintain a pleasant exterior. No one seems to entertain the idea of supporting a divorced woman, either financially or socially for fear of being misunderstood by one and all. The divorced woman is painted as the main culprit who breaks her own home and moves around independently disturbing the peace of society. Every other woman feels threatened by her single status and looks at her with suspicion. People presume that a divorced woman has no moral or religious obligations towards her ex-husband and in-laws. This means she is totally free to indulge in unethical ways to sustain herself. This one sided biased view that floats around in society makes the life of an innocent but divorced woman too difficult. The bias also gives great scope to those who move around to trap these unprotected young women who are in great need of help, both moral and social, to sustain themselves and their children. The vested interests take undue advantage of these women who are compelled by circumstances to survive on their own. It is the public bias and lack of honesty on the part of immediate family and the relatives which push such women into multiple problems. While trying to avoid unwanted suggestions, favours and disfavours, such woman and her children undergo tremendous mental stress and strain.

Ammu is just an example of such helpless women. Till her end Ammu is trying hard to earn enough through rightful means to sustain herself and her children. But the insensitivity of Chacko, Mammachi, Pappachi, Baby Koachamma force her and finally provoke her to take the most reckless decision of throwing herself upon Velutha. Only an unstable mind could take such a decision. She behaves in strange ways and finally it is discovered that she has lost her sense of reasoning which ultimately leads to her untimely death:

> On the days that the radio played Ammu's songs, everyone was a little wary of her. They sensed somehow that she lived in the penumbral shadows between two worlds, just beyond the grasp of their power. That a woman that they had already damned, now had little left to lose, and could therefore be dangerous. So on the days that radio played Ammu's songs, people avoided her, made little loops around her, because everybody agreed that it was best to just Let Her Be.
>
> (*The God of Small Things*, p. 45)

Ammu struggles with her own self and the world outside. Her people know why she has become like this. But they do not feel either guilty or try to rectify their conduct towards her.

They simply refuse to include her as their own. They watch her coldly. Ammu is drifting towards insanity. The cold war between Ammu and her hostile family is making her desperate, rash and reckless. Her conduct at mid-night is testimony to her unstable state of mind:

> On days like this, there was something restless and untamed about her. As though she had temporarily set aside the morality of motherhood and divorcehood. Even her walk changed from a safe mother-walk to another wilder sort of walk. She wore flowers in her hair and carried magic secrets in her eyes. She spoke to no one. She spent hours on the riverbank with her little plastic transistor shaped like a tangerine. She smoked cigarettes and had midnight swims.
>
> (*The God of Small Things*, p. 44)

Ammu is gradually and steadily losing her hold over her emotions and her sense of reasoning is also failing her. She behaves strangely and instills fear and apprehension among her people. No one can gather what has made her so unpredictable and defiant towards life and people. Ammu's hurt ego refuses to ask for help and support anymore. She has stopped waiting for a helping hand. She plans to extract help and support from someone who can never refuse her. She makes all the mental planning for her future with an element of revenge hidden in her abnormality of conduct and attitude:

> An unmixable mix.
>
> The infinite tenderness of motherhood and the reckless rage of a suicide bomber. It was this that grow inside her, and eventually led her to love by the night the man her children loved by day. To use by night the boat that her children used by day. The boat that Estha sat on, and Rahel found.
>
> (*The God of Small Things*, p. 44)

Ammu is beginning to take revenge. Her anger turns into sarcasm and fury and she plucks the forbidden apple not to eat it but just to show to her family how vicious and humiliating she can be. She is throwing all the ethics and morality to winds. Family legacy, family prestige and reputation all are at her mercy. She does everything possible to spoil them all. She creates history to tarnish everything that seems bright and promising in the Ayemenem House. Their pride, their sense of superiority, their blue blood, affluence, exclusivity, everything is dashed to the ground by one nasty move of Ammu. She will have her revenge. Velutha is her target, her destination, her doom. She has become immune to everything. During the day, the world will have its say, by night she creates her own world, own rules and her own style of functioning.

Mutual contempt and stiffness do not allow any scope for reconciliation and rectification. The trap is ready for one and all. The good and happy days are about to be over but no one is sensitive enough to realise this fact. They are too busy and too blind to see through the game of destiny and intervene to change the course of events. Everyone is contributing towards the fatal end without realizing the gravity of the situation. Ammu is taking society for granted. Her children are taking childhood for granted and Baby Koachamma is taking Ammu for granted. All pay heavily for mismanaging their lives, situations and Ammu. Mutual dislike, and extreme reactions destroy many lives. When Baby Koachamma, who herself is spinster, rejected Ammu and disliked her twins, little did she know she is rejecting the future of Ayemenem House, their pride, their property, their people, their lives. All have gone. Only Baby Koachamma, her cunningness and her sins stay behind with her during her old age. But surprisingly she is unrepentant. In fact, she too has become abnormal and hence fails to realise what she has done to her niece and the two innocent children. Baby Koachamma's role has been very annoying and depressing. Although she cannot be wholly blamed for what she has done, but she is indeed responsible for causing unrepairable damage to Estha, Rahel, Ammu and

Velutha. She is unkind, ruthless, inhuman and vindictive towards Ammu and Velutha.

What Baby Koachamma has done to Ammu is counter-revenge initiated by Ammu essentially. At least this is what she feels. The relationship between the two most important single women of *The God of Small Things* is very tense right from the beginning. Their ideologies never being the same, they have always been poles apart. Instead of sympathizing and helping each other in distress, they prefer to ignore and (if possible) hurt each other. The role of Baby Koachamma is especially very objectionable and regrettable. The loneliness of her life has made her into a manipulative, puritan and sadist lady who derives strange kind of satisfaction in humiliating Ammu and her children before others. She has become very orthodox in her bid to make herself useful and relevant to rest of the family. She behaves like a barking dog rather than a sane and mature old lady with all the tenderness of a mother. Cool headedly she pursues Ammu to her death, leaving Estha and Rahel to lament and suffer silently. Baby Koachamma feeds upon their agony till the end.

Rahel is right when she says Baby Koachamma, ex-nun, and incumbent baby grand aunt is not having any illusion about herself either. Baby aunt strongly feels that even though her people love her, yet she too is a dependent, a parasite who has no right to be there. But since she is unmarried, her position is better than that of Ammu and the kids. She never hides her bias against them and their Ammu:

> Baby Koachamma disliked the twins, for she considered them doomed, fatherless waifs. Worse still, they were half-Hindu Hybrids whom no self-respecting Syrian Christian would ever marry.
>
> (*The God of Small Things*, p. 45)

She paints very shabby pictures of their gloomy future and pathetic present. Their innocence, their happiness, all prove irritating to her. She keeps reminding them to behave in a certain manner as they are in need of social and financial support.

Baby Koachamma dislikes Ammu for her refusal to accept her fate, her loneliness and her rejection by her family due to her marriage outside community:

> Baby Koachamma resented Ammu because she saw her quarrelling with a fate that she, Baby Koachamma herself, felt had graciously accepted. The fate of the wretched man-less woman. The sad, Father Mulligan-less Baby Koachamma. She had managed to persuade herself over the years that her unconsummated love for Father Mulligan had been entirely due to her restraint and her determination to do the right thing.
>
> (*The God of Small Things*, p. 45)

Baby Koachamma, like every normal girl wanted to get married and have a home and husband. She falls in love with a young priest who happens to share a very warm relationship with her father. Father Mulligan, visits her house and Baby Koachamma develops a liking for him. She wants to marry him but he refuses politely, even though he too has liked her secretly. Baby Koachamma joins the convent to pursue him further. But she fails to reach him as she finds him surrounded by other senior nuns who indulge in religious discussions with him after the Church hours. She is disappointed.

Naturally she becomes restless and unhappy in the convent. Very quickly she realizes the futility of her endeavour. The senior sisters have virtually monopolized the priests and bishops with their Biblical doubts. They are proving to be very tough competitors to Baby Koachamma. Baby Koachamma's life in the convent is very dull and uneventful. She begins to feel homesick and contrives to return home by cleverly informing her parents about her life in the convent and pleads to be called back. Her mother gets her hints from her letters and her father, Reverend Ipe goes to Madras to withdraw his daughter from the convent. Though she returns home, she decides that she would not reconvert and that for the rest of her days she would remain a Roman Catholic. Soon enough, her father realises that his daughter will never get a husband because she has developed a 'reputation'. He then decides to give her education to make positive use of her time. She is sent to America to pursue a course of study. She returns after two years from Rochester with a diploma in Ornamental Gardening. Her emotional attachment to Father Mulligan, however, remains the same. Baby Koachamma spends her afternoons in her garden. Her life revolves around her parents and brother's family. She loves her Ayemenem home and its people until she is forced by circumstances to rush to protect her family's reputation which is being threatened by her niece Ammu.

Right from the beginning Baby Koachamma:

> Subscribed wholeheartedly to the commonly held view that a married daughter had no position in her parent's home. As for a divorced daughter—according to Baby Koachamma, she had no position anywhere at all. And as for a divorced daughter from a love marriage, well, words could not describe Baby Koachamma's outrage. As for a divorced daughter from a intercommunity love marriage—Baby Koachamma chose to remain quiveringly silent on the subject.
>
> (*The God of Small Things*, p. 46)

Baby Koachamma has no decency left in her for her niece and her fatherless twins. She loses no opportunity to express her repulsion and annoyance towards Ammu and her children. Poor children! They can hardly understand or retaliate against their grand aunt.

Baby Koachamma's rudeness compels Ammu to become aggressive and defensive towards her innocent children. She is their Mama and Baba both. Ammu feels hurt when her family victimizes her children. She warns her children not to try win favours or love from those who dislike them or misbehave with them. But the natural innocence of the children becomes a cause of embarrassment for Ammu time and again. They are children and they behave normally with one and all, practically unaware of the cold war that goes on continuously between their mother and her relatives. Ammu feels utterly helpless and exhausted fighting on all fronts. She feels irritated at times:

> Ammu loved her children (of course), but their wide-eyed vulnerability, and their willingness to love people who didn't really love them, exasperated her and sometimes made her want to hurt them—just as an education, a protection.
>
> (*The God of Small Things*, p. 43)

The mental stress, the emotional void all boil within a lovely, intelligent and suffering lady. She understands with perfect accuracy the intensity of pain which is inflicted upon her and her innocent children. She bears them all bravely and silently until finally she decides to take revenge. Her revenge is as devastating as her silence has been chilling and piercing.

A full fledged war ensues between the rest of the family and Ammu. The relationship between Ammu and Baby Koachamma has always been sour and the aunt takes the Velutha episode as an opportunity to outwit Ammu finally. Since Baby Koachamma had advised Ammu to accept her fate and lead a single life with all possible grace and dignity, she resents Ammu's relation with Velutha all the more. Her dislike degenerates into hatred and contempt. She is virtually ashamed of Ammu's lack of discretion. Baby Koachamma can no longer stay immune to all these. She takes the whole matter into her own hands and tries to solve the crisis before her nephew's return home from Cochin. She outsmarts everybody in fabrication of facts before the local police to suit her motives. Her intention is to use the local authorities in her own way to get Velutha away from their life.

Baby Koachamma goes to the local police station to complain about the missing kids and puts the blame upon the loyal and trusted servant who has recently turned hostile due to some reasons:

> We told him that if he did not leave Ayemenem quietly we would call the police. He started off by saying that my niece had consented, can you imagine? He asked us what proof we had of what we were accusing him of. He said that according to the Labour Laws we had no grounds on which to dismiss him. He was very calm. "The days are gone," he told us, "When you can kick us around like dogs....". By now Baby Koachamma sounded utterly convincing. Injured. Incredulous.
>
> (*The God of Small Things*, p. 260)

She manipulates facts and defames a man who happens to be innocent victim of Ammu's fatal attraction. She is equally vicious towards both Ammu and Velutha. Baby Koachamma targets Velutha to chasten Ammu. She wants to teach a lesson to Ammu by harming Velutha.

Inspector Thomas Mathew believes every word she speaks. For, he has no reason to doubt her. She is an elderly lady coming from a very respectable family. They are in serious trouble and need his help. Her bitterness, coated in despair, helplessness, fear, shock and apprehension, weaves a perfect trap in which Inspector Thomas Mathew falls unknowingly:

> 'You people', Inspector Thomas Mathew said, 'first you spoil these people, carry them about on your head like trophies, then when they misbehave you come running to us for help'.
>
> (*The God of Small Things*, p. 261)

The Inspector here, appears too simple for Baby Koachamma. She outsmarts an experienced police officer with her dramatic display of innocence and fear of being a woman confronted by an aggressive young man. Her display of shock is so apt and convincing:

> She had known the Paravan since he was a child, Baby Koachamma said. He had been educated by her family, in the untouchables' school started by her father, Punnyan Kunju (Mr. Thomas Mathew must know who he was? Yes, of course).... He was trained to be a carpenter by her family, the house he lived in was given to his grandfather by her family. He owed everything to her family.
>
> (*The God of Small Things*, p. 261)

In this way, Baby Koachamma drills in Inspector's mind, the background of Velutha and the number of obligations and favours that their family bestowed upon their untouchable servant and his family. The ungratefulness of Velutha is tacitly highlighted before the authorities concerned to bias them against him fully and completely. She just doesn't want to take any chance. She is playing her cards well in time with perfect accuracy.

Indeed, the poor Inspector is no match to Baby Koachamma's scheming mind. She weaves schemes as fast as the situation changes with each passing hour. The shrewdness, the confidence and the act to demonstrate the exact amount of pain on account of emotional jolt that an elderly woman experiences is so convincing that the whole of police station is filled with sympathy towards the Ayemenem House. How could such good people be betrayed by a Paravan? The caste-bias begins to act in the veins of the police men. Velutha is loosing ground everywhere. Baby Koachamma is too quick and accurate in her assessment of the situation and manipulation of the facts. While Ammu, who can challenge her, is locked up in her room, her kids are used by her aunt to destroy the only support she has:

> Inspector Thomas Mathew gave her a cup of police tea. When she was feeling better, he helped her to set down all she had told him in her FIR. He assured Baby Koachamma of the full cooperation of the

> Kottayam Police. The rascal would be caught before the day was out, he said. A Paravan with a pair of two-egg twins, hounded by history—he knew there weren't many places for him to hide.
>
> (*The God of Small Things*, p. 261)

The stage is set for the final scene. Once Velutha is caught, there is no escape. The Inspector, however, is measuring all the eventualities in his mind. Trying to assess if Velutha is getting support from some unforeseen quarters or he is all alone in his fight with his masters. Inspector must consult Comrade K.N.M. Pillai before taking any action. He has come to know that Velutha might have Naxalite connections besides being an untouchable. Both the facts are sensitive issues and can cause trouble in his career if things go wrong. What the Inspector does not know is Baby Koachamma's manipulation of facts and incidents. She has made sure that however careful the Inspector be, he is bound to commit mistake. Even Comrade Pillai can guess how facts have been manipulated but he prefers to keep his secret:

> They were not friends, Comrade Pillai and Inspector Thomas Mathew, and they didn't trust each other. But they understood each other perfectly. They were both men whom childhood had abandoned without a trace. Men without curiosity. Without doubt. Both in their own way truly, terrifyingly adult. They looked out at the world and never wondered how it worked, because they knew. They worked it. They were mechanics who serviced different parts of the same machine.
>
> (*The God of Small Things*, p. 262)

What is to be noticed here is that Baby Koachamma, Comrade Pillai, Inspector and Chacko all are trapped in the scandal created by Ammu's desperation and defiance. They all try to exploit the situation to their own benefit and crush the innocents to death. Velutha's caste-status forbids any possible support from others in this hour of crisis. The caste-class factor plays an important role in his defeat. He is left defenceless and crushed by one and all inspite of being innocent. All try to put their burden upon him to relieve themselves of any allegation and responsibility regarding the FIR and its fall outs. Baby Koachamma, despite being a woman has outwitted all the rest in exploiting the situation most. However, her lies are exposed before the Inspector. Now the situation changes drastically against her and the local police. Inspector realizes very late that he has put himself in trouble:

> The Kottayam police had acted on the basis of an FIR filed by her. The Paravan had been caught. Unfortunately he had been badly injured in the encounter and in all likelihood would not live through the night. But now the children said that they had gone of their own volition. Their boat had capsized and the English child had drowned by accident. Which left the police saddled with the Death in Custody of a technically innocent man. True, he was a Paravan, True, he had misbehaved. But there were troubled times and technically, as per the law, he was an innocent man. There was no case.
>
> (*The God of Small Things*, p. 314)

Obviously, the Inspector's eagerness to help Baby Koachamma without confirmation of facts lead him to trouble. He is annoyed at Baby Koachamma's shrewdness. She has now implicated the local police into her own schemes of things. They will have to act in haste to guard themselves against any possible fallout on account of various implications of death of an untouchable in police custody, that too an innocent untouchable. Naturally, the police feels cheated. They need Baby Koachamma's help in solving the riddle. She must get desired statements from the kids to set the records straight.

What worries Inspector most is Comrade Pillai's shrewd political motives in the changed situation:

> He was aware that Comrade K.N.M. Pillai would not pass up this opportunity. He kicked himself for acting so impulsively.
>
> (*The God of Small Things*, p. 315)

It is Baby Koachamma who is directly or indirectly taking the services of different factions of society to get her job done. She not only implicates Velutha, she drags the local police, politician and the family's youngest members into her manipulations. She compels them to stand by her and get things done the way she wants. Velutha must not be allowed to escape. Ammu must not be allowed to stay in Ayemenem any longer. Her plans are ready and the first phase of her planning is already being executed.

Intra and Inter-gender clash and ego-problem against the low caste are the root cause here. She resents Ammu who too is a single woman of her own family. She dislikes Velutha who comes from stronger gender but weaker caste and class. Baby Koachamma succeeds in subjugating him with the help of various factions of society who believe in maintaining the traditional way of looking at things. Velutha and Ammu clash with the established norms of society. They inadvertently challenge the status-quo. They are challenging the society and hence it stands united against the law beakers to uphold the ethics. Society is left with no other option because Baby Koachamma has closed all the other amicable routes much earlier by brainwashing the Inspector against Velutha and Ammu.

Baby Koachamma is more farsighted than many. She has acted with vengeance and determination. She wants to show Ammu her zeal with which she guards her family name and grace. The two ladies fight with each other in Ayemenem House and try to counter each other with all their might. Baby Koachamma succeeds, because she has led a very disciplined life and accepted her fate with grace. She does not get desperate to grab anybody to get married and settle down.

Ammu by misfortune has failed twice. Both the men with whom she got involved have proved to be weak contenders who have failed to support her. The first one left her, the second cannot own her. She invariably selects wrong persons. Velutha can never legalise his relationship with Ammu. The social approval to such relationship is unthinkable in Indian context. It is exactly due to their own miscalculations and shamelessness that they lose the battle. Instead of sympathizing, people become scornful and allergic to Ammu and Velutha. Their illicit relationship destroys Ayemenem House for ever. What Baby Koachamma did is equally unethical and inhuman. In her bid to punish her own blood, she squeezes the blood out of an innocent man who was literally trapped by Ammu in her fit to seek revenge on her own people.

Baby Koachamma's manipulative mind can only be matched by Comrade Pillai who feeds upon the field tilled and fertilized by Baby Koachamma. He is ready to harvest the ready crops without any sense of guilt and remorse. He has ditched Velutha, misled the Inspector and tacitly supported Baby Koachamma to extract favours from Chacko in his pickle factory. Comrade Pillai has always wanted to grab the management of the factory but Chacko and Velutha did not allow him to interfere. Now that Velutha is humiliated and about to die in police custody, Comrade Pillai will have to convince Chacko. In the changed circumstances it won't be difficult. Chacko, Baby Koachamma and the rest did not attach any importance to Ammu's existence. They have been ignoring Ammu and this has taken a nasty turn. They somehow, have failed utterly to guard their own interests:

> In their blind hatred towards Ammu they have virtually sacrificed Estha, Velutha and Rahel. Ammu is also finished. In her bid to counter Baby Koachamma's machination, Ammu becomes a medium of all that goes wrong in their lives. What led to their final disaster is Ammu's retaliation against Baby Koachamma's

> cruel moves. Baby Koachamma underestimates Ammu. Ammu in her desperation to protect Velutha, visits the police station to give correct version of the story rejecting the false allegations labeled upon Velutha. She has become bold out of desperation. Baby Koachamma has been of the opinion that Ammu would never accept her relationship with Velutha in public. Out of bitterness and a sense of moral binding toward Velutha, Ammu accepts her relationship boldly and firmly. She takes along her children to the police station to support her statements. All of a sudden her children have become important as witness. Baby Koachamma has complicated the issue to a dangerous level. By the time Ammu get there Velutha is already dead and his body removed. Baby Koachamma is naturally terrified. Ammu can be equally vicious. But Baby Koachamma hadn't taken into account the Unsafe Edge in Ammu. The Unmixable Mix-the infinite tenderness of motherhood, the reckless rage of a suicide bomber.
>
> (*The God of Small Things*, p. 321)

Ammu is rebuffed by the Inspector because he might get into trouble by the revealation of fact. Even though Ammu is right, she cannot do anything about the whole thing. She has lost her only support. She is shattered, unguarded and defenceless. After Velutha, it is her turn. Baby Koachamma now concentrates upon Ammu to get her out of Ayemenem House as soon as possible. Ammu has now become a living threat. K.N.M. Pillai is waiting to get hold of Ammu and use her politically. Both the Inspector and Baby Koachamma harass Ammu no end. They do everything possible to break her down emotionally. While the Inspector threatens her physically, Baby Koachamma harasses her emotionally. She instigates Chacko to get her thrown out of Ayemenem House as soon as possible. Estha is sent to Calcutta while Rahel is held back at Ayemenem and Ammu just told to move out.

It is Baby Koachamma, the master planner of events, who is destined to receive Estha back after twenty-three years. It was she who was instrumental in sending him away. She has not changed. She is as insensitive as ever, as immune as ever. But Estha has changed. He is full of repentance, remrose and deep in sorrow. He cannot forgive himself while Baby Koachamma never has any sense of guilt. In fact, she seems to enjoy his being in pain:

> She was delighted that Estha had not spoken to Rahel. That he had looked at her and walked straight past. Into the rain. As he did with everyone else.
>
> She was eighty-three. Her eyes spread like butter behind her thick glasses.
>
> 'I told you, didn't I?' She said to Rahel. 'What did you expect? Special treatment? He's lost his mind, I'm telling you! He doesn't recognize people any more! What did you think?'
>
> (*The God of Small Things*, pp. 20-21)

Baby Koachamma has survived her rivals. She is eighty-three and as energetic as ever to play her dirty tricks again. She, somehow, feels happy to see the outcome of her machinations. She derives sadistic pleasures out of Estha's helplessness and troubled soul. However, Rahel watches them with stoic silence. Baby Koachamma fails to disturb her mental equilibrium. Rahel has indeed survived to tell the story of her mother Ammu.

Ammu's life has been a long story of struggle, bias and hardships due to lack of sympathy and kindness. Her parents never treat her with affection. Their parental affections are reserved only for Chacko. Right from the beginning, Ammu struggles for their attention and concerns:

> As a child, she had learned very quickly to disregard the father Bear Mother Bear stories she was given to read. In her version, Father Bear beat Mother Bear with brass vases. Mother Bear suffered those beatings with mute resignation.
>
> (*The God of Small Things*, p. 180)

Her Syrian Christian family suffers from gender bias. Her father ill-treats his wife and daughter for being a burden, a liability for life-time. It seems he dislikes them for being born as women. Ammu has to guard herself and her mother from her father's ruthless beatings and madness. His strange behaviour have been a cause of constant worry and fear for mother and daughter:

> As she grew older, Ammu learned to live with this cold, calculative cruelty. She developed a lofty sense of injustice and the mulish, reckless streak that develops in someone. Small who has been bullied all their lives by someone Big. She did exactly nothing to avoid quarrels and confrontations. In fact, it could be argued that she sought them out, perhaps even enjoyed them.
>
> (*The God of Small Things*, p. 182)

Ammu becomes defiant, immune and indifferent towards family quarrel and difference of opinion due to Pappachi's bias and cruelty. Ammu had been denied education ever since her father retired from his job in Delhi and returned to Ayemenem. Pappachi insists that a college education is an unnecessary expense for a girl, so Ammu has no choice but to leave Delhi and return to her native Ayemenem with her parents. There is very little for her to do. She begins to wait for her marriage proposals. She expects to be married off like normal girls, while helping her mother with the household works. Her father, however, has never saved enough for her marriage. Naturally, they fail to arrange a suitable match for Ammu.

> Two years went by. Her eighteenth birthday came and went. Unnoticed, or at least unremarked upon by her parents. Ammu grew desperate. All day she dreamed of escaping from Ayemenem and the clutches of her ill-tempered father and bitter, long-suffering mother. She hatched several wretched little plans. Eventually, one worked. Pappachi agreed to let her spend the summer with a distant aunt who lived in Calcutta.
>
> There, at someone else's wedding reception, Ammu met her future husband.
>
> (*The God of Small Things*, pp. 38-39)

Right from the beginning Ammu has been facing problems regarding herself from her father. He resented educating her, he never saved enough to marry her off timely and above all he is biased towards her due to her gender. She is his girl child. Hence, her existence must not be acknowledged. She must be ignored. Ammu is left with no choice. She has to think about her own future much against her wishes. She will have to find someone suitable to marry and settle down in life. The family is gradually beginning to push her towards her doom step by step.

Without bothering much about her future and consequence of her decision, Ammu consents to marry the first man who proposes to her:

> He was on vacation from his job in Assam where he worked as an assistant manager of a tea estate. His family were once-wealthy Zamindars who had migrated to Calcutta from East Bengal after partition.
>
> (*The God of Small Things*, p. 39)

In the given circumstance, Ammu did the right thing to accept the proposal. It is a pity that both Ammu and her husband Baba fail to live up to each other's expectations. There should not have been any problem but then the future has things unexpectedly good or bad in store for its recipients. So is the case with Ammu. When there is no hope for Ammu, Baba brings hope for her. She can afford to avoid her insensitive family and begin her life afresh. But then, her marital tie breaks after initial years of happiness due to outside interference. She is beautiful and her husband careless. His drinking, beatings, his lies all puzzle her and finally when he asks her to entertain Mr. Hollick, his boss, it becomes clear that Ammu will not be able to save her marriage.

Ammu returns to Ayemenem to restart her life with her parents. She narrates her story to her father. But:

> Pappachi would not believe her story—not because he thought well of her husband, but simply because he didn't believe that an Englishman, any Englishman, would covert another man's wife.
>
> (*The God of Small Things*, p. 42)

Pappachi's reaction is strange and Ammu feels helpless. She cannot convince her father against his bias towards his own daughter and a strange sense of obligation, affinity and faith towards Mr Hollicks who happens to be an Englishman. For Pappachi, they are the perfection incarnate.

It is Chacko who understands his father's psyche much better than his sister Ammu. Chacko says that the more correct way of explaining Pappachi would be by addressing him as Anglophile instead of calling him by strange names:

> They were a family of Anglophiles. Pointed in the wrong direction, trapped outside their own history, and unable to retrace their steps, because their footprints had been swept away. He explained to them that history was like an old house at night. With all the lamps lit. And ancestors whispering inside.
>
> (*The God of Small Things*, p. 52)

Pappachi is trapped in his own world of dreams where he finds everything belonging to the western culture pure and pious. His daughter's experience has no value for him. He rejects her statements, her sufferings and her too. She lives in his house as a rejected and abandoned offspring. He admires everything that reminds him of old world charm and rejects everything that is current and real, happenings around him. He has always been a very insensitive self-obsessed man. He has never taken any interest in his wife and daughter's well-being. He has always concentrated upon Chacko, his son.

Pappachi is seventeen years older than Mammachi and the feeling that she is still young while he is an old man frustrates him. He has always been a jealous man resenting his wife and her existence, her excellence as a housewife and as a student of music. He has always disliked people appreciating her. He has always tried to prove his superiority over her and now even after retirement, he decides to continue with his arrogance and snobbery even though his wife is struggling hard to sustain the family financially with the help of her small pickle industry. Her pickles have become popular in the local market and she is always busy meeting the demands. She works very hard. Ammu helps her but Pappachi and Baby Koachamma are unaffected and unimpressed. It is strange that Pappachi never bothers to take any interest in his wife's endeavours. At such an advanced age, Mammachi is working so hard for her family but his negative attitudes towards her remains unchanged:

> He had always been a jealous man, so he greatly resented the attention his wife was suddenly getting. He slouched around the compound in his immaculately tailored suits, weaving sullen circles around mounds of red chilies and freshly powdered yellow turmeric, watching Mammachi supervise the buying, the weighing, the salting and drying, of limes and tender mangoes. Every night he beat her with a brass flower vase. The beatings weren't new. What was new was only the frequency with which they took place. One night Pappachi broke the bow of

> Mammachi's violin and threw it in the river.
>
> (*The God of Small Things*, p. 48)

Pappachi stands for tradition. Traditionally a wife must be subdued by her husband both socially and psychologically. Whenever he finds Mammachi getting more attention than he can digest, he beats her in isolation. Children are not allowed to interfere. They have watched their father thrash Mammachi mercilessly and endlessly. He ill-treats his wife but behaves in just the opposite manner in public view. He is very decent towards women outside his family. His grace, dignity and his mannerism cause jealousy among women towards his wife. This contradiction in his conduct and his hypocrisy is maintained at the cost of Mammachi's sense of commitment and reverence towards her husband. She never resents. She tolerates him and his ill-treatment with servility.

Pappachi has always had his say in his house. With his son always away, no one is there to persuade him against his style of disciplining his wife and daughter. It seems he has never had any problem with his sister Baby Koachamma. It is only Ammu and his wife who irritate him and provoke him to violence:

> On one such night, Ammu, aged nine, hiding with her mother in the hedge, watched Pappachi's natty silhouette in the lit windows as he flitted from room to room. Not content with having beaten his wife and daughter (Chacko was away at school), he tore down curtains, kicked furniture and smashed a table lamp.
>
> (*The God of Small Things*, p. 181)

Pappachi, not satisfied with his beatings, wants to punish them even further. He wants to hurt them to the level of insanity. A wife and a daughter must not do anything that might attract the attention of outsiders. Mammachi's gentleness, her music earn appreciation from his friends and relatives. Ammu too is bold and beautiful. Their friendliness irritate Pappachi no end. His frustrations come out violently when he can't withstand anymore the goodwill and praise of his wife by others. He derives sadistic pleasure and infinite peace in completely destroying their dreams and their cherished objects:

> While Ammu watched, the Imperial Entomologist shred her new gumboots with her mother's pinking shears. It took ten minutes for her beloved gumboots to be completely shredded. When the last strip of rubber had rippled to the floor, her father looked at her with cold, flat eyes, and rocked and rocked and rocked. Surrounded by a sea of twisting, rubber snakes.
>
> (*The God of Small Things*, p. 181)

Pappachi is a frustrated man. He is not satisfied with his life and his career. He has always wanted to gain recognition at national level but his career graph somehow has stagnated due to bad luck or sabotage. All he can do best is beat his wife and daughter who are directly under his influence and control. He can sabotage them. That can nurse his bruised ego to a certain degree.

Pappachi is punished for his ill-treatment by divine justice. His discovery and research about a particular species of moth is hijacked by his junior whom he has always disliked:

> The real blow came twelve years later, as a consequence of a radical taxonomic reshuffle, lepidopterists decided that Pappachi's moth was in fact a separate species and genus hitherto unknown to science. By then of course, Pappachi had retired and moved to Ayemenem. It was too late for him to assert his claim to the discovery. His moth was named after the Acting Director of the Department of Entomology, a junior officer whom Pappachi had always disliked.
>
> (*The God of Small Things*, p. 49)

The setback that he receives in his career frustrates him no end. He is deeply hurt, much more deeply and intensely than he has been hurting his wife and daughter all through his life. Mammachi and Ammu too suffer silently for the man who makes them cry. His failure is a matter of concern for them too. They can't hate him for his lack of compassion towards them. They feel that their suffering is somehow related to his failure at the professional level. In addition, faulty grooming, misplaced values and gender-bias running in veins through generations have made him a monster incarnate.

Pappachi has never seen his wife's even small achievements in a positive light. He has always throttled her at the slightest provocation. A small praise of his wife by others would be provocation enough to stop him from allowing Mammachi some moments of relief and relaxation from domesticity:

> It was during those few months they spent in Vienna that Mammachi took her first lessons on the violin. The lessons were abruptly discontinued when Mammachi's teacher, Launsky-Tieffenthal, made the mistake of telling Pappachi that his wife was exceptionally talented and, in his opinion, potentially concert class.
>
> (*The God of Small Things*, p. 50)

His over possessiveness, his pride as the man of the house, his ego as a superior gender and his sense of power over his wife all make him obstinate, rude, and demanding in nature. He has been the only man in the family for so many years due to his father's death long back and his son's preoccupations with his own self. Pappachi takes all possible precautions to ward off any problem which women of the house might create. The women of his family must not ignore him or disobey him. He dislikes anyone who shift his or her attention away from him. His wife's talent getting noticed by her violin teacher is enough to evoke irritation in him. He himself wants to be admired and praised but dislikes this to happen to Mammachi and Ammu. His wife and daughter need not get any scope of social interaction without his consent and presence. Somehow he feels threatened and provoked. His main purpose is that his wife must not become fearless and confident of herself. Social interaction and approval might fill her with confidence and this might make her defiant towards her husband. His misconduct makes his wife very fearful and insecure under the roof of her husband.

However, inspite of all his evil doings, Mammachi is a devoted wife. Her world revolves around Pappachi and his children especially Chacko, her only son. Though Chacko is not too fond of his parents, his very presence fills them with pride and confidence. They seem to agree only on one aspect of their married life and that is Chacko's presence as their heir. They both bank upon him for everything. Chacko is both their weakness as well as their strength. They hate Ammu as much as they love Chacko. So is the case with Baby Koachamma. She hates Ammu for everything but she likes Chacko more dearly. He is to carry her father's name ahead. He is the son of her dear brother who has never been rude to her. She loves her brother and has won over Mammachi's sympathy with silent acceptance of her spinsterhood.

Everyone feels blessed because of Chacko. He is the cause and also the source of their happiness. Only Ammu feels and acts differently. Her hurt ego, her bruised soul and her unheard prayers since childhood have made her hate Chacko and Pappachi most. Like a traditional girl she wants emotional, moral, social and also financial support from her family. She labours sincerely to augment family income and retain her dignity as a self-respecting daughter of a respectable family. But Chacko along with the rest refuses her any help except allowing her the smallest possible space in their Ayemenem household. It is their compulsion and not will to accommodate Ammu and her kids. Pappachi is as aloof as ever. He never bestows fatherly affection on Ammu or his grandchildren. All he can see is that Ammu has revolted against family tradition and that her children belong to someone outside the community. No reconciliation is ever possible. The idea to forgive his daughter on emotional grounds is unimaginable.

Pappachi is as firm as a lifeless stone. Mammachi is as immune as ever.

By the time Pappachi dies, Mammachi has become habituated to his beatings and rusticity behind closed doors. While Ammu is too distanced mentally to be affected by his death, Chacko is too mature to get emotional anyway. Baby Koachamma is too cool to react. She has adjusted to her spinsterhood and is very content with her own self. It is invariably his wife Mammachi who feels his absence as intensely as she withstood his violence and dominating presence:

> At Pappachi's funeral, Mammachi cried and her contact lenses slid around her eyes. Ammu told the twins that Mammachi was crying more because she was used to him than because she loved him. She was used to having him slouching around pickle factory, and was used to being beaten from time to time. Ammu said that human beings were creatures of habit, and it was amazing the kind of things they could get used to. You only had to look around you, Ammu said, to see that beatings with brass vases were the least of them.
>
> (*The God of Small Things*, p. 50)

Ammu has made a very apt assessment of her parents' mutual relationship. But the fact is that howsoever, distasteful a man could be, his wife, especially an Indian wife groomed traditionally, would like him to survive her. It is indeed painful for Mammachi to see her husband dead. Ammu, having sour relationships with both her husband and her father, can not judge the level of commitment which Mammachi has towards her irate husband. Ammu looks at the whole life of Mammachi from the gender perspective while Mammachi looks at the death of her husband from the spiritual angle. She does genuinely feel bad for the man who married her even though he tortured her till the last moments of his life. She feels it was his right to assault her and it was her duty to obey him and be tortured by him. Being his wife, she cannot complain. Her status as his wife must remain intact, the rest can be ignored. She has paid the price of being a wife willingly. This is the typical Indian woman's stand before society regarding wife-beatings and domestic violence of various types.

Ammu, being a woman of the modern age, can not digest the idea, because it is inhuman and exploitative in nature. Women are psychologically tamed and nurtured to tolerate injustice to maintain the family peace and continuity at all costs. The hardships of abandoned wives instill fear and women do everything possible to avoid such situations. Ammu too has tried her level best to guard her marriage in the past but she is not as tolerant and lucky as her mother. Her father, however bad, did not compel Mammachi to entertain his superiors for enhancement in his career graph. Ammu's ex-husband did exactly that. It is because of this, that Mammachi is thankful to her husband. Their level of understanding is different from those modern age couples who make serious compromises to meet the challenges of today's competitive world. But then there can never be any justification of Pappachi's rudeness towards his wife and daughter. A man who raises his hand upon his wife and daughter cannot be called civilized. His acts of violence cannot be defended on any ground. The traditional approach adopted by Mammachi is an act of encouraging and sustaining wrong precedence.

It is this trait of Indian women to obey their husband that encouraged Mr. Hollicks to seek Baba's consent for illicit ties with Ammu. Baba, being a drunkard and easy going, does not see any harm in it provided his wife cooperates. His initial fears and hesitation are managed by the impact of wine, offered most probably by Mr. Hollicks. Baba's job would be safe in return, Mr. Hollicks promises. Ammu refuses and lands up at Ayememem.

At her native place she is rebuffed and rebuked for her uprightness. She should have been welcomed and taken under the protective shield of her parental home and surroundings. But her marriage outside the community and now her unattached status cause irritation and bias against her. All through her life, Ammu has failed to gain sympathy and co-operation of her own people.

It is strange that Chacko, who cannot stand his mother's beatings by her father, never feels for Ammu. Mammachi's lifelong sufferings has made her son sympathetic towards her while Ammu's aggressiveness and assertiveness has always irritated him. Ammu has broken the rules. She has married outside the community, she has stood for her integrity, she struggles for her children all alone. She fights with both the worlds simultaneously but there is no one who can feel her pain or sympathise with her. She fights against all odds single handedly. The family is as ruthless towards Ammu as Pappachi has been towards Mammachi all through his life.

What is the most remarkable aspect of the story of Ayemenem household is the role of women and their mutual relationships. There are only three most important characters in the novel. The first is Ammu, then Mammachi and the most powerful and manipulative Baby Koachamma. Ammu is the victim of circumstances, Mammachi a persecuted wife, and Baby Koachamma a slave of her own ideology and a blind follower of her own faith irrespective of its consequences upon her and those around her.

No doubt, Baby Koachamma has outwitted the mother and the daughter simply because these two did not support each other. Mammachi refuses to sympathise or support Ammu because Ammu has got married outside the community. Mammachi refuses to acknowledge the fact that marriage is an important aspect of human life. She is not at all interested in getting Ammu married. Hence Ammu's marriage and that too outside community angers her and Pappachi. Mammachi's approach towards her daughter is highly objectionable. Being a woman herself, she should have supported Ammu in her hours of crisis. On the contrary, she pushes her daughter towards mental and moral degeneration. Her family and Ammu herself do not leave any scope for rectification in conduct or reconciliation with each other. Inflated and bruised ego kills its possessors one by one. The greatest irony of the situation is that those who are not directly or indirectly involved in the tug of war get trapped in it and loose the direction of their lives, especially Estha and Velutha. Velutha is mortally wounded and Estha lives on to carry the burden of Velutha's demise upon his soul.

The recklessness on the part of her family, Ammu's revenge, and machinations by Baby Koachamma to guard her family's name and prestige create an environment of emotional upheaval within Ayemenem household. One notices an abnormal level of obsession with family legacy in this Syrian Christian family. They behave abnormally regarding Ammu's marriage. Resentment towards the decision to marry outside the community is understandable but when this resentment attains such dimension, then it must be taken as an abnormal mental state. Forcing a girl to remain single, and then tormenting her for taking divorce on moral grounds and finally pushing her to death. This is the course of action which Ammu's family takes. Her fate denies her happiness time and again. Her family refuses to get her married and support her after divorce. Her husband refuses to protect her after marriage. Her community refuses to own her after death. She could not be buried according to Christian belief, she has to be cremated:

> The Church refused to bury Ammu. On several counts. So Chacko hired a van to transport the body to the electric crematorium. He had her wrapped in a dirty bed sheet and laid out on a stretcher.
>
> (*The God of Small Things*, p. 162)

She is denied justice even after her death. She is denied proper last rites by her envious brother who has pushed her to death. Property is more dear to him and so is the shameless display of authority as the owner of Ayemenem establishment. His lack of sense of justice has killed his younger sister. But, to her misfortune, he lacks tears and pain for her. He has shed more than sufficient tears upon his daughter's sudden death. He has no sorrow left for his unfortunate dead sister.

The way Baby Koachamma and Mammachi consistently push Ammu to her end reflects a very cool and calculative aspect of women's psyche. They can be as ruthless and inhuman as men if it suits them. Being a woman is no guarantee of nobleness. At times, women can be as remorseless as men towards their victims. The point to be noted here is that it is easier for women to victimize their own gender.

Baby Koachamma couldn't have succeeded in victimizing her nephew for marrying outside the community. She would have done everything possible to appease even a Hindu daughter-in-law, because Baby Koachamma's survival in the house would have depended heavily upon the whims of the daughter-in-law.

Ammu always believed in marriage and dreaded a life of spinsterhood. But her family did not attach any importance to her approach towards life. This is the basic reason of Ammu's rejection by the family. They resent her for her insistence upon marriage. They want her to follow Baby Kochamma. Ammu should not have insisted upon marriage and exposed her family's stand on this issue. Above all, she marries a Hindu. They feel demoralized and angry. She has challenged their authority. She cannot be forgiven. And now, when she is a divorcee with two children, she is a liability too.

Ammu is a weak person due to lack of family support, Mammachi, Pappachi, Baby Koachamma, Chacko all exert pressures upon her to move out of their lives as early as possible. Her troubles are not their botheration.

It is not only the immediate family but the servants too dislike her as they get enough hints to ignore Ammu and her kids. The most trusted and loyal maid Kochu Maria, who looks after the house, rebukes:

> 'Tell your mother to take you to your father's house', she said. "There you can break as many beds as you like. These aren't your beds. This isn't your house".
>
> (*The God of Small Things*, p. 83)

Estha's child play is taken as an offence as Kochu Maria's sleep is getting disturbed by his game. He is playing with his sister before sleeping. It is a normal behaviour of small children. But the bias and bitterness running deep inside, provoke Ayemenem loyalist to rebuke Ammu's innocent son. His mere presence irritates her and his happy mood is all the more provocative. How can children born of inter-community marriage afford to be so happy? They ought to feel sad, humiliated and demoralized for ever. They must feel obliged for every moment of their life under Ayemenem roof. The maid's conduct is directly related to Ammu's status in the family. Kochu Maria is more weighty than Ammu—the daughter of the family. Strange! Objectionable indeed! Moreover, it is both uncivil and inhumane to humiliate innocent children. It is not their fault that their parents are separated.

Even Baby Koachamma is very allergic to the kids and their happiness. Like her maid Kochu Maria, Baby Koachamma too makes fun of Estha before Margaret Koachamma and Sophie Mol. When Chacko ultimately introduces Ammu, Rahel and Estha to them, Baby Koachamma exploits the opportunity to make fun of the child:

> 'Elvis Presley', Baby Koachamma said for revenge. 'I'm afraid we're a little behind the times here'. Everyone looked at Estha and laughed.
>
> (*The God of Small Things*, p. 145)

Actually, it is Ammu who is being shown her place. Margaret Koachamma must not take them seriously. That's all. What is transmitted in the air is received by the servants also along with the rest of the people. Even Mammachi does not miss any opportunity to taunt her daughter regarding her grandchildren's mixed parentage:

> Mammachi said that what her grandchildren suffered from was far worse than inbreeding. She meant having parents who were divorced. As though these were

> the only choices available to people: Inbreeding or Divorce.
>
> (*The God of Small Things*, p. 61)

Small children are being used and also abused every now and then by the elders. The domestic environment in Ayemenem is perpetually tense for Ammu and her children. Even the children are dragged into controversies whenever it suits the elders. The children have no say in it. They are simply used to settle scores:

> A pair of actors trapped in a recondite play with no hint of plot or narrative. Stumbling through their parts, nursing someone else's sorrow. Grieving someone else's grief.
>
> (*The God of Small Things*, p. 191)

Estha and Rahel are under-privileged and discriminated against because of their parentage. They cannot compete with Sophie Mol. Though Sophie Mol is as innocent and lovely as the two, but then she has whole family around her, making fuss over her being the daughter of British mother. Her inter-racial legacy does not pose any problem to Mammachi simply because Sophie is Chacko's daughter. She is superior in many ways. They somehow feel blessed and proud of her. Ammu's children can't be compared with her.

Ammu understands these sentiments and tries to keep her children away from those who look down upon them and demoralize them. Her pain, her frustrations come out abruptly and she punishes them to modulate their behaviour according to the situation. But then children cannot be treated as puppets all the time. They time and again forget the instructions of their mother. They, inadvertently, become the cause of Sophie Mol's death. Sophie's death kills them spiritually. They die bit by bit with each consequent event. They live only to suffer in silence over their past:

> The twins were too young to know that these were only history's henchmen. Sent to square the books and collect the dues

> from those who broke its laws. Impelled by feelings that were primal yet paradoxically wholly impersonal. Feelings of contempt born of inchoate, unacknowledged fear—civilization's fear of nature, men's fear of women, power's fear of powerlessness.
>
> Man's subliminal urge to destroy what he could neither subdue nor deify.
>
> (*The God of Small Things*, p. 308)

The life of Ammu is just an example of millions of women who are crushed under the pressure of patriarchy and orthodoxy. The way Baby Koachamma manipulates Ammu's rashness and irritations, follies and mistakes, emotional outbursts and breakdowns, is a reflection of the inhuman aspect of Indian society. Baby Koachamma is not alone in her evil designs. She has rest of the family and local people's strong support and tacit approval.

The death of Sophie Mol gives them an opportunity to get hold of Ammu and subjugate her for ever. Chacko and Mammachi keep telling Ammu to stay away from Ayemenem house after the Velutha episode:

> Mammachi asked her if she'd been drinking and suggested that she visit Rahel as seldom as possible.
>
> Ammu got up from the table and left without saying a word. Not even goodbye. 'Go and see her off' Chacko said to Rahel.
>
> Rahel pretended she hadn't heard him. She went on with her fish. She thought of the phlegm and nearly retched. She hated her mother then. Hated her.
>
> She never saw her again.
>
> (*The God of Small Things*, p. 161)

The misbehaviour of the elders affect the children too. Ammu's children begin to disobey and ignore her, because of her illness and people's dislike for her. As long as Estha is around, Ammu has control over her children, but once Estha is sent away, Rahel begins to ignore her mother imitating the rest. Mammachi should have been concerned about Ammu's ill-health. Instead, she non-challantly insults Ammu at the dinner table by asking her if she has begun to drink. Mammachi has always been protected by Ammu from Pappachi's anger. She has stood by her mother in the absence of her brother Chacko. But her sincerity is too easily forgotten by Mammachi in favour of her only son and grand daughter Sophie Mol. Poor Ammu is indeed in a pitiable situation.

However, Mammachi is as helpless as Ammu in many ways. She is almost blind. She constantly needs advice and help from her sister-in-law and son Chacko regarding every important issue related to her family and also the pickle factory. Her weakness for her son do not allow her to bother much about Ammu. She has allowed her to stay with them after divorce and support her in the minimum possible way. She expects Ammu to feel obliged for their kindness. Instead, every day Ammu indulges in blame game and spoils everybody's peace of mind and family harmony. What Mammachi cannot forgive is Ammu's scandalous relationship with a servant of the family. It is Vellya Paapen, father of Velutha, who informs Mammachi about the two:

> He had seen it there. Every night. Rocking on the water. Empty. Waiting for the lovers to return. For hours it waited. Sometimes they only emerged through the long grass at dawn. Vellya Paapen had seen them with his own eye. Others had seen them too. The whole village knew. It was only a matter of time before Mammachi found out. So Vellya Paapen had come to tell Mammachi himself. As a Paravan and a man with mortgaged body parts, he considered it his duty.
>
> (*The God of Small Things*, p. 256)

Vellya Paapen keeps talking, finding faults in his blood, his grooming, his fate and his Paravan origin. Out of fear and helplessness he cries standing in the rain of December. Mammachi is equally shocked. She is filled with anger and contempt. Her caste-bias comes to the forefront. She can't stop herself from abusing the poor innocent man who has stood by his conviction and done exactly what a principled man would have done. He speaks the truth. He is honest and firm in his faith that what Ammu and Velutha are doing is wrong. Even if Vellya is a Paravan, an untouchable servant, even then he has his own world to feel proud of and fall back upon for survival and support. He cannot allow Velutha to mortgage his family's reputation. Velutha is taking his family to ruin. The delicacies involved therein are thrown to winds by Velutha's foolhardiness. Velutha or Ammu cannot change the norms of society. No society can allow a servant to marry his master's daughter. In the same way, no master can marry his servant's daughter. These things don't happen in the real world.

It is quite obvious that Mammachi is furious and Vellya Paapen frightened. He is as helpless as Mammachi. The dignity with which Vellya and Ayemenem family have sustained their relationship is totally ruined for ever. The human aspect of mutual goodwill and concern is lost for ever. The faith in master-employee relationship is shattered and is under serious scrutiny. It is Vellya Paapen, who has to bear with tears in his eyes, the first outburst of anger, hate, frustration and sense of betrayal which is torturing an old blind lady. He cannot even console his master's wife. He has lost face, his reputation. He is taken as a traitor:

> Baby Koachamma, walking past the kitchen, heard the commotion. She found Mammachi spitting into the rain, Thoo! Thoo! and Vellya Paapen lying in the slush, wet, weeping, groveling. Offering to kill his son. To tear him limb from limb.
>
> Mammachi was shouting, 'Drunken dog! Drunken Paravan liar!'
>
> (*The God of Small Things*, p. 256)

No wonder, Mammachi is forced by circumstance to hate Ammu more than ever. She is so disgusted and insulted that she becomes almost silent regarding Ammu. She never questions Ammu directly about Velutha and her illicit relationship with him. The loss of prestige and that too by the daughter of such a reputed family is a matter of shame and disgust. She cannot bring herself to question Ammu about it. She is, in fact, ashamed of her own self. She is Ammu's mother. They cannot disown this fact. It is Baby Koachamma who comes forward to handle the situation. She offers an immediate solution:

> Baby Koachamma put her heavy arm around Mammachi. It must be true, she said in a quiet voice. 'She's quits capable of it. And so is he. Vellya Paapen would not lie about something like this.'
>
> (*The God of Small Things*, p. 257)

It is Baby Koachamma who can differentiate between Velutha and Vellya Paapen. Mammachi, because of her old age, is quite unable to realise that father and son are two different individuals having drastically different personality types. Velutha is a reactionary while Vellya stands for tradition and ethics. What is morally wrong for Vellya, has no meaning for Velutha. Velutha is too resentful of his social standing to realise the futility of his actions. Revolutions don't occur in a day and that too by amoral ways. Weakness of character may lead to devastation, not victory either at personal level or social. Velutha and Ammu are going to illogical levels to defy the society. Both Ammu and Velutha are guilty of damaging the social harmony and family reputation of their respective families. Their irresponsible actions have ruined the lives of many people and they too lose their lives. Baby Koachamma is too willing to cash in on the situation to exploit both Ammu and Velutha for insulting her in the past:

> Baby Koachamma recognized at once the immense potential of the situation, but immediately anointed her thoughts with unctuous oils: She bloomed. She saw it as

> God's way of punishing Ammu for her sins and simultaneously avenging her (Baby Koachamma's) humiliation at the hands of Velutha and the men in the march—the Modalali Mariakutty taunts, the forced flag-waving. She set sail at once. A ship of goodness ploughing through a sea of sin.
>
> (*The God of Small Things*, p. 257)

It is human nature to feel hurt when people are offended unnecessarily. Baby Koachamma-Ammu-Velutha relationship has never seen good days. There is always an air of hostility between them. Since Velutha-Ammu share emotional tie, their bias against Baby Koachamma is obvious. Baby Koachamma is a puritan. She cannot allow such laxities in her surroundings. Once she gets sufficient proof against Ammu, she grabs the opportunity to take her revenge. She has two objectives in her mind. First, to take revenge on Velutha for insulting her in public and, second, showing Ammu her place. What gives her success is her apparent commitment and sincerity towards her own family and its prestige. She hides her own insult but highlights the family cause to punish them.

Even Velutha is not a very pious soul. He cultivates Ammu to defy the snobbery and the sense of superiority that Syrian Christian family display in their everyday routine. An element of revolt is always present in him. He is temperamentally an independent man who aspires to rise high in social ladder. His naxal connections, his education create mental environment which is not in conformity with the hard realities of rural life in the Indian social context. The traditional approach towards women and the untouchables force people to oppose Ammu and Velutha. They are rebels. Ammu—an unconventional woman, Velutha—a reactionary. They are pitted against Baby Koachamma who is a traditionalist and a staunch catholic whose world revolves around the Bible, family and the legacy. No wonder Baby Koachamma warns Mammachi to take precautionary measures before it is too late:

> 'He must go', she said. 'Tonight. Before it goes any further. Before we are completely ruined'.
>
> (*The God of Small Things*, p. 257)

There are many factors that regulate and modulate human behaviour. Lack of foresight on the part of Ammu, Velutha, Chacko, Mammachi, Pappachi cause their doom. It is Baby Koachamma who survives them all only to lead an abnormal life at the cost of Ammu and Velutha. Even Baby Koachamma becomes a mental case due to her loneliness. She behaves like a sixteen year old who is very look-conscious. She has begun to wear a lot of jewellery of Rahel's grandmother. Since Chacko too has settled in Canada, there is no one left to compete with her:

> Like a young bride who couldn't believe her good fortune.
>
> She's living her life backwards, Rahel thought.
>
> (*The God of Small Things*, p. 22)

It is a curiously apt observation. Indeed Baby Koachamma is living her life backwards. As a young woman she had renounced the material world, and now, as an old one, she seemed to embrace it. She is an abnormal person by the time Estha is re-returned. Each character of *The God of Small Things* suffers for his/her past deeds.

The fall of Velutha from a favoured and dependable man into a traitor has not occurred due to his own doings. Ammu has dragged an innocent and sincere worker into her trap. Velutha, not mature enough, commits an unpardonable sin. He could have emerged as a very promising person from the political point of view. His hold over his caste-people, his ability in the management of the pickle factory, his zeal to bring revolution even in the limited sphere, all could not be channelized properly. He is put to death.

In fact, Velutha's potentiality as a political force has been felt by Comrade Pillai, who feels threatened by his dynamism, his confidence, his restlessness to do something different. The hidden sharpness of temperament has been noticed by Pillai and also by his own father. Velutha's fearlessness, the open display of defiance towards social obligations and family reputation give his enemies a chance to retaliate and crush him. His father is right when he repeatedly asks Velutha if he is blinded in his attraction. He can't see the reason of his father's objections.

Velutha's myopic vision kills him and ruins the lives of two innocent children. These two kids loved Velutha more than anything. Their feelings towards Velutha are as pure as pearl. They do not understand politics. They do not follow instructions to stay away from an untouchable. All they know is that they love their Velutha who is their only friend in the most unfriendly surrounding. They play with him and feel protected, safe and above all very-very secure emotionally. Their world revolves around Velutha who is their friend, philosopher and guide. He gives them fatherly affection and emotional security. Their small world of happiness exists around him. His caste, his background just don't matter. What matters is his affection, his sincerity and his physical presence. "It is Velutha who offers Estha and his sister the love and play which a father or a male relative ought to have provided." (Jaya Prasad, 2003, p. 114)

Velutha feels insulted because of the bias among the touchables against his caste-identity. This alienation from the touchables is killing him from within. He is always treated differently. His father being an elderly person is very cool about these things. But Velutha, being young and full of energy cannot digest the fact that it is just a method of denying him his rightful place in society. Caste bias kills and seals the progress of individuals in the social ladder. The stagnation is suffocating and too demoralizing for him to tolerate. He joins the Marxist party to find a way out. He derives some peace of mind and purpose in his life. His education with the help of Mammachi has been fruitful in making him a politically and socially conscious man. But he is unable to assess his own society and its deep rooted bias against untouchables. The bias and mistrust is mutual and threatening:

> History in live performance. If they hurt Velutha more than they intended to, it was only because any kinship, any connection between themselves and him, any implications that if nothing else, at least biologically he was a fellow creature—had been severed long ago. They were not arresting a man, they were exorcizing fear. They had no instrument to calibrate how much punishment he could take. No means of gauging how much or how permanently they had damaged him.
>
> Unlike the custom of rampaging religious mobs or conquering armies running riot, that morning in the Heart of Darkness the posse of Touchable Policemen acted with economy, not frenzy. Efficiency, not anarchy. Responsibility, not hysteria.
>
> After all, they were not battling an epidemic. They were merely inoculating a community against an outbreak.
>
> (*The God of Small Things*, p. 309)

What the twins did not understand then, they come to realise later in life. It was not only Velutha, the person, who has been eliminated. Rather, the urge to improve, to move ahead, to be identified as humans was crushed by the local police. Baby Koachamma's cunning moves and cold-blooded maneuverings compel Inspector Mathew to act in haste, without giving much time to investigate the issue cool headedly. Baby Koachamma is more revengeful than Velutha had expected. She is underestimated by Velutha and Ammu. Velutha's indifference towards Koachamma and Ammu's defiance of her family prestige and delicacies involved, kill a promising life.

Velutha's enthusiasm and zeal to bring about social change go waste due to lack of foresight and sense of reasoning. Personal life of politically ambitious people do matter even today. People of dubious character may win elections but cannot earn goodwill and respect in society. This is the main cause of Velutha's failure. He should not have allowed himself to be used by Ammu. His weakness of character is in contradiction to his otherwise strong personality.

His involvement with Ammu cannot be justified simply, because of his caste background. Even if he were a Brahmin, Chacko's stand would have been the same. Velutha should not have allowed Ammu to use him as her prey. She should have been refused point blank keeping in view the open heartedness with which Mammachi has been helping his progress right from childhood. She is a broken lady harassed by her husband, neglected for years by her son and insulted by the most trusted servant. He has sinned against Mammachi more than anybody else. He should have exhibited firmness of character. His lack of wisdom, lack of sense of loyalty towards Chacko and Mammachi and his fatal attraction to a upper caste woman's physical beauty blurs his vision, his sense of right and wrong. A person should not be hypnotized either by beauty or glamour. One who does, pays for it sooner or latter.

Ammu is a frustrated woman. She is rejected by her family and wants to take revenge. She even feels jealous of Estha-Rahel-Velutha combination. The three have created a world of their own. They are rejected by the society and feel a sense of unity in isolation. Their pain, agony are the same. They need someone who will not reject them and resent their presence, one who can be trusted. Velutha, on humanitarian grounds, provides all the emotional and social support to the fatherless children. Ammu notices their mutual interactions and almost snatches him away. She finds an easy prey. Velutha is literally dragged away from the children by their mother and then is eliminated by the grandaunt Baby Koachamma.

There is only a void left never to be filled in the lives of Estha and Rahel. They are made tools to eliminate their only support, their emotional anchor, their Velutha. It is only the children who suffer most due to his death. They are unable to forgive themselves:

> A pair of actors trapped in a recondite
> play with no hint of plot or narrative.

> Stumbling through their parts, nursing someone else's sorrow. Grieving someone else's grief.
>
> (*The God of Small Things*, p. 191)

What Ammu's family deny her, she does the same to her children. Velutha is trapped by one and all. He is as helpless and defenceless as the two children. The irony of the situation is that his support system, i.e. his own party has not been able to mobilize itself for fear of severe retaliation from the upper caste people. His caste-men are threatened to remain silent and aloof. It is a question of an upper caste woman's integrity, a family's social reputation. The machinations of Baby Koachamma forced everyone to take a stand against Velutha. He must die. And, it is Estha and Rahel who are expected to give the final blow. Poor kids:

> 'You're not the Sinners. You're the Sinned Against. You were only children. You had no control. You are the victims, not the perpetrators.'
>
> (*The God of Small Things*, p. 191)

Man cannot live in isolation. Society is a controlling agent of human actions and provides sustenance too. When ethics is challenged beyond redemption, social retaliation takes place. Velutha should have questioned Ammu's confidence and sincerity by asking her to accept him in public view, instead of expecting his company in the darkness of the night. She did lack such confidence initially. And he falls prey to her beauty. As a result, two lives are lost and two survive to curse themselves all through their lives for not being able to protect Velutha and defend Ammu:

> Esthappen and Rahel both knew that there were several perpetrators (Besides themselves) that day. But only one victim. And he had blood-red nails and a brown lead on his back that made the monsoons come on time. He left behind a hole in the Universe through which darkness poured

> like liquid tar. Through which their mother followed without even turning to wave goodbye. She left them behind, spinning in the dark, with no moorings, in a place with no foundation.
>
> (*The God of Small Things*, p. 193)

Had Velutha listened to his father's advice, he might have been alive, providing all possible moral and social support to Estha and Rahel, the way Mammachi and Chacko did for him. But his lack of foresight and Ammu's fatal attraction lead to their premature demise. It is only Estha and Rahel who suffer most. Illicit relationship can never gain respectability and recognition in any society. All the goodness and merit of Velutha's personality go waste due to Ammu and Baby Koachamma. Even Chacko cannot save him although Velutha was indispensable for his factory, because his own sister is involved with him. The situation is too embarrassing for him to defend Velutha. With the demise of Velutha, the pickle factory dies too. Chacko leaves for Canada.

Social influence, money power, the skill with which Ayemenem House manages its factory and personal lives all were being watched keenly and people were on the look out for an opportunity to harm them. The Ammu-Velutha episode provides the much awaited opportunity to Comrade Pillai and Velutha's enemies. They hit with vengeance as they are jealous of both Chacko's family and Velutha.

Being a man, Velutha should have succeeded in outwitting Baby Koachamma. But a woman of shrewd moves outwits Velutha, because of the infightings among men. Class and caste conflicts against egalitarian values, commercial factors, political interests—all destroy the peace and happiness of the Ayemenem house. The sin of rejecting their daughter simply because she has married a Hindu, the ill-treatment to her and her children—these are very strange and abnormal way of reacting. They push Ammu to the wall. She is left with no option other than to die and get rid of all her troubles. Ammu's only fault has been her illicit relationship with her servant. Otherwise she has been a hard-working simple lady. Her values were rightly placed till she commits the blunder of her life. She is a single parent of her two children. She has no future. It is not only a story of a struggling single divorcee but also a story of a man-woman relationship against the highly rigid and inflexible social pattern of life. One can fight with one's enemies but one cannot fight with rules that direct the social life.

The complicated social pattern traps Ammu in its web. One can easily understand the tensions and mental pressures Ammu has felt in the Indian society. She has misunderstood herself, her people and the situation. When men have to surrender before the rigidity of tradition, Ammu is a woman after all. Her being a Christian is of no help.

Thoughtless behaviour of Ammu's biased family leads them to their doom. Their mistakes and rigidity of mind, destroy them completely. They fail to support a genuinely needy and helpless daughter who is pleading for help. They prefer to play in the hands of those who are willing to grab the opportunity to wipe them out completely. They, however, do not succeed in their motive as Rahel has survived after all. Even Chacko has survived. Baby Koachamma is still alive and leading life on her own terms. It is Ammu, Velutha and the Pickle factory that died. The rest have survived somehow. They have lost their land, their people, their happiness and got scattered in different parts of the world.

The God of Small Things is a very realistic and sympathetic commentary upon the life of an unfortunate woman Ammu. She is crushed under the social and family values and principles. Abnormal expectations of her parents to remain spinster, unreasonable demands by her husband, allergic reactions of her aunt, resentment of her brother, her fatal attractions for Velutha, innocence of her twin children, financial crunch, indifference of society in general towards her very existence, all have distorted a very sincere, honest, principled, and exceptionally beautiful and self-righteous lady into a norm breaker and a rebel. Ammu's tragic end, which is shrouded in mystery, is a testimony to the inhuman approach towards women in the traditional Indian society. Ammu and

Velutha are products of contradictions found in the Indian society. Ammu's end is regrettable. Life of a beautiful, intelligent and principled young woman is all the more difficult as there is always the possibility that the relatives of such a woman might try to misuse her much against her wishes. Marriage is no guarantee of security. Successful and secure life of a dependent woman is a matter of sheer good fortune and luck. Unfortunately, Ammu, with all possible goodness of personality and temperament, is not so lucky. Her struggle begins with her husband's follies and ends with her family's rejection. Her ignominious death is her final destination.

4

A Comparative Study of Nigerian and Indian English Women Novelists

The Nigerian women writers have been struggling to make a mark in the literary world with a specific motive. Their thrust has been on women and children, the most neglected section of the literary world. Issues related to war, poverty, social turmoil and political upheavals have been given more importance by the other Nigerian writers. The impact of war and its impact upon women and children have drawn the attention of women writers. War and politics, clash of egos among men and their whimsical decisions did not allow much space to women and their opinion. The role of women in the nation-building process, their contribution in the maintenance of family tradition, peace and silent co-operation in keeping African culture intact, inspite of outside influences and domestic compulsions to deviate due to economic hardships, have been neglected for long.

African women, in general, are very forthcoming, courageous, hard-working, forgiving and affectionate in nature, as is evident from their literary works.

The most remarkable trait of the African women, which is reflected in their literature, is that they have a deep sense of commitment towards social life and issues related to their own gender. They work with a sense of empathy. Their commitment to social issues is commendable. The latest example of their social awareness and commitment to social issues is the contribution of noted environmentalist and Noble Laureate (2004) Wangari Muta Maathai from Kenya.

The people of India feel closer to African culture. The legacy of Gandhi has brought the two cultures on one platform, both philosophically and politically. Both the cultures share same value system and understand the problems faced by their people due to the challenges of the modern age. The President of India A.P.J. Abdul Kalam conferred upon Prof. Wangari Muta Maathai the prestigious Jawaharlal Nehru Award for International Understanding, 2005. Prof. Maathai is basically working against global warming, that is, she is working for environmental protection projects. Appreciating her efforts Mr. Kalam said,

> Prof. Maathai has evolved a movement with 600 community networks across Kenya and branches into 20 countries resulting in the plantation of over 31 million trees. Her mission has to spread to all parts of the planet. The award is in recognition of her persistent and courageous struggle for democracy, human rights and environmental conservation.
>
> (*The Hindu,* March, 23, 2007)

The hard earned prestige of Prof. Maathai is laudable. Being a woman is a challenge in itself. Prof. Maathai must have undergone personal and social hardships to reach this stage in life. Her concern for environment, human rights and other issues related to man and the world is remarkable. This shows women can do much more than they themselves can perceive they can. No doubt Prof. Maathai is the pride of Kenya and not a liability. Prof. Maathai stands above all bias and prejudices against feminine gender across the world. She creates more oxygen than she inhales in a day. Accepting the award, Prof. Maathai said she has always been inspired by Mahatma Gandhi and Pandit Jawaharlal Nehru. She has imbibed their values and belief in social service. "Instead of using their position to enrich themselves, these leaders used their power to promote the cause of justice, equity and peace" (*The Hindu*, March 23, 2007).

No doubt, Prof. Maathai is bringing Africans and Indians even closer on principles. A deep sense of pride is evident in their women who fight against adversities but do not plead for mercy and do not blame anyone about anything. They know how to overcome past mistakes and move ahead with full of positivism and courage.

The most remarkable contribution of Prof. Maathai is that of intellectual input and insight which she provides regarding various issues affecting human world, especially issues related to women development and utilization of human and natural resources. Women like Prof. Maathai, provide unique vision and wider understanding of problems of modern age and their solutions.

Similarly, another important Black woman from Africa, whose heroic deeds inspire and motivate people even today, is the anti-slavery heroine of Jamaica the legendary Nanny of 18th century who fought against the British army 'according to the Jamaican folklore'. Being a woman did not deter her from proclaiming her defiance towards the invaders who were far superior to her in every possible way. She declared:

> There's no way I'm going to belong to someone else. I'm going to live freely and I'm also going to help others live freely, and if anyone comes up here and tries to take my home or this land I've created for myself, I'm going to fight for it.
>
> (David Smith, *The Hindu*, March 19, 2007)

It is the spiritual strength of being a woman, a mother which is the motivation behind such bold declaration during that phase of history.

Niomi Mclean-Daley, the singer born of a British mother and a Jamaican father is greatly influenced by this anti-slavery heroine of eighteenth century Jamaica. Ms Niomi has paid tribute to the memory of Nanny by making a TV film on her. Applauding Nanny she says,

> What we would call human rights now, she took and fought to the death for. Women usually seem to take the caring, loving motherly role like Florence Nightingale, but she decided,
>
> 'No, I'm going to be on the front line, I'm going to get all these soldiers together, teach them the art of battle and show them how to fight in a war'.
>
> You wouldn't expect that from a woman. If you dig into black history there are lots and lots of black men that are prominent figures but not so many women.
>
> (David Smith, *The Hindu*, March 19, 2007)

The problem faced by women the world over is more or less the same. Just like Estha and Rahel of *The God of Small Things*, Niomi Mclean-Daley is also a product of broken family. Her father left her Scottish mother with 12 children. One can easily understand the difficulties faced by her mother and Niomi, being the eldest. No wonder she began her rapping career in her teens. This jolt did not deter Niomi from achieving success. She was "the first solo black women to win the prestigious Mercury music prize" (David Smith, *The Hindu*, March 19, 2007).

Her introduction to the legend of Nanny has made her proud of her Jamaican background. Niomi is more humane, confident and sensitive towards women, children and especially towards black history and their sufferings. Nanny's contributions, her sacrifice, her leadership, her bravery all have added a golden chapter to women's struggle for emancipation along with that of African struggle for independence and dignity of African culture. Nanny struggled for the sanctity of African land and dignity. She has given an identity to African women. Nanny is symbol of motherly affection, of bravery, of foresight and fearless leadership. As Niomi puts it, "I found the men had the most respect and passion for her". She further adds,

> Maybe she reminded them a little bit of their mum, because she was quite a fighter and survivor and very courageous. She was very, very important in the abolition movement and paved the way to the end of slavery in the Caribbean. Other people on other islands heard of the Maroons on Jamaica and did the same thing.
>
> (David Smith, *The Hindu*, March 19, 2007)

Ms. Niomi is quick to notice the gender game in the very concept of slavery practiced by the whites in those days. She highlights the notorious contribution of a famous slave owner who became famous due to his theory of 'divide and rule'. He was Willie Lynch.

> The power to enslave the people and divide them: make the darker-skin slaves work in the fields and do the hardest work, and the lighter-skin slaves work in the house and get a bit better treatment. It set men against women. I think that as black people we are still living that law. There is a lot of segregation among black people and not a lot of unity.
>
> (David Smith, *The Hindu*, March 19, 2007)

Niomi further elaborates how gender game worked among blacks. The white owners interfered with the family lives of the slaves and did everything possible to disturb their mental peace. Concept of family was not at all recognized as far as slaves were concerned. In the words of Ms. Niomi,

> There's stuff in the family and home which is also a result of slavery. Men were not allowed to be fathers but were used to breed to create more slaves. It is something that—not with everyone—is common in the black community,

> especially in our generation: the fathers are not always there. We're not that far away from slavery and that way of living, where man is literally just a tool to reproduce.
>
> (David Smith, *The Hindu*, March 19, 2007)

The historical background of gender equation in African context is indeed painful. However, the tendency to create a family and then leave it on its fate is a universal phenomenon among masculine gender. The difficulty in managing a home irritates men and they have developed the traits of escapists and do not realise the mental and emotional jolt which is suffered by the children of such families. Children from broken families grow up too fast and live with sad memories which haunt them all through.

The hardships faced by African women are no less than those faced by men. They have suffered on equal terms from times immemorial. Their tormentors have changed but they continue to suffer even today. There are still problems like over population, poverty, due to lack of sufficient resources as well as under-utilization of resources. The women are still struggling to protect their home, their identity, their family from modern age problems which are unique in nature. The challenges of modern age are typical in nature and are posing threat to the traditional culture and slow paced life of African society. Women are coping with all these and many more with guts and determination. Just like Nanny of 18th century, each African mother is fighting to keep her world intact from evil influences like diseases, poverty, illiteracy, malnutrition, lack of cooperation from husbands and the daily chores. Above all, against all odds, they are hoping for the best. They are making positive contributions in most adverse circumstances which are both natural to some extent and man made to a larger extent. African women are above all forgiving and reconciliatory. They neither lament nor accuse. They simply try to rectify the wrong committed by history to make this world a better place for both the gender. It is this aspect of African women which is reflected in the writings of almost all women writers of African sub-continent.

This spirit of positive thinking against all adversities is reflected best in the women writers of the African continent, especially those from the Nigerian literary world. Women writers from Nigeria are making great contribution to issues related to women and their impact upon children and men. They are struggling to keep the original flavour of tradition intact while creating a distinct identity of their own. Their main concern is that the basic structure of family life must not get damaged. At the same time, women should not be made to suffer any further. They must assert themselves and try to overcome their mental and physical limitations. They should be allowed to graduate into socially enlightened and financially secure members of their respective families. They must have the ability to exercise their rights as humans and do justice to themselves as well. In other words, they no longer want to remain as dormant members of their society, rather they want their share of active participation in social, political, financial and all other possible spheres of life where women can make use of their potentials. Above all, they are against any kind of confrontations with the masculine gender. They are basically peace loving home makers.

Life history of the most important Nigerian women writer, Buchi Emecheta (b. 1944) is itself an example of struggle and perseverance. As Catherine Obianuju Acholonu states,

> As a black woman and a student in London, Buchi's socio-economic problems mounted when, as a mother of five, she was separated from her husband. But she continued to struggle and made a first degree in sociology. She worked as a teacher, a librarian and a community worker before she was appointed Senior Research Fellow in the department of English and Literary Studies at the University of Caliber, Nigeria in 1980. She is as at the time of writing this, a member

> of the Advisory Council to the British Home Secretary on race and equality, and serves on the Arts Council of Great Britain. Emecheta has since been seriously involved in the question of women's rights for African and black women generally.
>
> (Acholonu, 1988, p. 216)

Buchi Emecheta's personal experiences as a woman or, to be more specific, as a black woman must have helped her in giving her insight into women's problems in general. She does not hesitate in highlighting issues affecting women and tries to negotiate with the patriarchal psyche to generate consensus in favour of the women of the African origin.

Writing about the contributions of Buchi Emecheta, Catherine Obianuju Acholonu writes, "with the emergence of her highly sociological novel *The Joys of Motherhood*, Emecheta was able to capture, for all times, the attention of readers and scholars of African literature and to direct these to the plight of the African women" (Acholonu, 1988, p. 217).

What Buchi Emecheta is doing is trying to create awareness about woman's mental stress and pressures that she withstands single handedly to survive on her own. Even though a woman is under the roof of her husband, that is not enough. For, she must have a number of children and she must give birth to more sons than daughters. She must not be barren, must not mother only female child, must be willing to accept co-wives, must not create any problem with either her husband or co-wives. In other words, she must behave like an obedient, loyal and trusted servant of her husband and in-laws.

The Joys of Motherhood (1979) is a masterpiece in this regard. It presents a vivid picture of contemporary African society where women are treated as commodity and machines for child birth and care. It is, in fact, dehumanization of women against which Buchi Emecheta has waged a war on the intellectual front. She feels a sense of commitment to women of Nigeria and the African race. She is struggling to establish the African women as a race of living vibrant class of humans who deserve to exercise all those rights which are availed by their men. They have waited long enough. *The Joys of Motherhood* is a strong protest as well as declaration of emergence of women as a strong force in Nigerian/African socio-political scene.

In *The Joys of Motherhood* Emecheta exposes the dehumanizing effects of polygamy in an urban town where the man, Naife, a domestic servant of white people, who is unable to feed himself and his immediate family, adds to his burden by claiming the wife of his dead brother. This situation inflicts misery and deprivation on the two women specially on the first wife Nnu Ego who has more mouths to feed but no source of livelihood. It leads to economic disaster and the dehumanization of those involved. Their existence is thus degenerated to that of rats in holes. But even here, the man who has been emasculated and reduced by the nature of his job to a state of docility and weakness still insists on exerting his authority on the woman even though she has assumed his fatherly role in the family.

The point which the author makes is that traditional society with its permissiveness and liberty to the men folk entrenches chauvinism and irresponsibility in the men. Thus a great majority of Emecheta's male characters are irresponsible, unfeeling and inhuman especially in dealing with their women-folk. It is the irresponsibility of Agbadi that brings about his first wife's death when she collapses on hearing of her husband "giving pleasure to another woman in the same court-yard where she slept" (Acholonu, 1988, p. 220) .

> Emecheta bemoans the ruthlessness of the traditional system in which a woman exists only to give pleasure to the man, bear his children, wash his clothes and eventually receive his punches. She explores this state of affairs which eventually corrodes the woman's ego, depriving her of every human dignity and reducing her to the state of utter hopelessness. This she explores fully in

> *The Joys of Motherhood* and even more succinctly in *Second Class Citizen.*
>
> (Acholonu, 1988, p. 220)

It is believed that the *Second Class Citizen* is biographical to a certain degree. The main female character of this novel becomes dependent upon the British Social Security Officers. Circumstances force her to "lose her job, her studies, her self-respect—in order to become assimilated with the ditch dwellers" (Acholonu, 1988, p. 220). The irony is that onces she joins the ditch dwellers after leaving her British husband, she feels relieved. She breaks the grip of masculine gender after joining the third class citizens. She begins to feel at home, identifies with other ditch dwellers with whom she is to live for rest of her life. "Here she is accepted by most white people who have been deprived of dignity and in every effect every social inhibition", observes Catherine O. Acholonu (1988) in her article *Buchi Emecheta.*

The racial bias and confrontations with the west and within African society have been a cause of worry for African women. From Ama Ata Aidoo to Niomi all have realized the hard facts facing African women. They have had to put up with racial bias and gender bias on various fronts. But they have faced these problems with a sense of faith in themselves and their inner urge to move ahead and get what is due to them. They don't intend to snatch away what belongs to others. Rather, they are all determined to claim only their own share of space in the social and economic sphere. What belongs to them must come to them. Buchi Emecheta definitely deserves appreciation for giving a graphic description of the various facets of women's problems in her novels.

The urge to win freedom and the hesitation in women to break away from tradition is best reflected in Buchi Emecheta's *The Joys of Motherhood.* Tradition stands against woman's independent identity as an individual. She has no right to interact with society without any reference to men. Through the characterization of Nnu Ego and Adamu, Buchi Emecheta highlights the dilemma of African women. Nnu Ego feels exploited, deprived, cheated, harassed by her husband and tradition. She wants some peace, some space and degree of freedom to make herself realise that she too is a human and deserves some basic human rights to exercise her free will. But she is also fearful of breaking the norms, laid down by ancestors. It is better to suffocate and die rather than cherish freedom even in dreams. It is better to die pleading for mercy than revolt. Nnu Ego reflects lack of courage and will to assert herself as an individual against male dominance and authority over women. She is hesitant to do what is supposed to be her right. She fails to assert herself. She fails to create some space for herself where she is free from all obligations towards family and husband, tradition and society without reducing herself to a prostitute. She dies of shock. Adamu, the other wife, is just the opposite. She does exactly what Nnu Ego has always feared, that is, she revolts against tradition to assert herself as an individual. Her crusade begins from her own family, her husband.

> When she realizes that her husband and the system behind him are indifferent to her and her female children, she decides to fight for her freedom and emancipation. To gain economic power she takes to promiscuity. As a harlot she would make enough money to train her children and give them the freedom and security she herself had been deprived of Adaku, Emecheta's ideal woman thus becomes in the words of Eustace Palmer, the forerunner of women's liberation in Africa.
>
> (Acholonu, 1988, p. 221)

Buchi Emecheta has her own arguments to present against the institution of marriage. She finds every solution of women's problems in the dissolution of the institution of marriage itself. She believes a free woman is in better position than a domesticated one. There is a strange sense of repulsion towards the institution of marriage. Duties of motherhood and housewives are seen as slavery. The domestic violence and dominance of husband are acting as deterrents in reaching an amicable settlement of the gender clashes and ego clashes within the four walls the world over. Buchi Emecheta believes marriage is "a legalized way of committing assault and getting away with it" (Emecheta, 1988, p. 221).

Buchi Emecheta's stand on this issue has been critically analysed by Acholonu in the best possible manner. She states:

> Hers is a crusade poised to debunk the myths of superiority of man over woman and the sacredness of the marriage institution. In doing this Buchi Emecheta oversteps bounds in several ways. Her portrayal of her male characters in exaggerated states of idiocy, irresponsibility and insensitivity reduces the plausibility and reliability of her point of view. The amount of pessimism and bitterness which filter through her narration often make the author incapable of treating other thematic issues that would have given the desired finish to her vision, and these in turn affect the reader-response to her works.
>
> (Acholonu, 1988, p. 222)

The personal experiences of Buchi Emecheta have biased her views, feels Catherine Acholonu. According to Acholonu, Buchi Emecheta is giving a very biased picture of the African male population. Emecheta's personal experiences have dominated over her writings. It seems as if almost all the African women are persecuted and unhappy. However, the reality is that Buchi Emecheta is talking about a particular geographical area, i.e. the Midwestern Igboland.

Even female readers might disagree with Emecheta's style of writing. Her opinions are bold and provocative. This is the greatest irony of Buchi Emecheta's style of presentation. She is a revolutionary out of frustration and finds reprieve in absolute rejection of tradition and culture. What she fails to realise is that no body is free and no one can enjoy absolute freedom, not even men. Society has its own forces and agencies to control human behaviour. The family is one such agency. Culture is another. Tradition is the toughest form of control which regulates the social and family live. Gender-bias is part of certain cultural tradition and this has made her bitter and her resentment is reflected in her characterization and presentation of events.

However, Buchi Emecheta's sincerity towards women's problems and their solution cannot be challenged. She is very sensitive towards problems faced by ordinary women who are crushed under the pressures from all sides. The insensitivity of society towards women and children has made her insensitive towards men and marriage. The concept of family, tradition, culture etc. irritates her. For her, they are liabilities upon women alone while men move around free. But then it is also a fact that negative experiences generate negativity in the attitudes of innocent victims, and hence Buchi Emecheta must be forgiven for her toughness of attitudes towards masculine gender.

But then, Buchi Emecheta's reckless attitude towards society goes against her moral responsibilities as a writer. According to Chinua Achebe:

> The writer cannot expect to be excused from the task of re-education and regeneration that must be done. In fact he should march right in front.
>
> (*James*, 1986, p. 9)

Achebe recognizes that this process commits the writer to identifying and celebrating those particular activities of daily life which enables his society both to recognize and be proud of itself.

Discussing the role and significance of literary figures in their respective societies, Chinua Achebe writes in *The Novelist as a Teacher*: "I think it is part of my business as a writer to teach. ..." (*James*, 1986, p. 9)

Obviously, Buchi Emecheta appears to be doing just half of her duty towards her society and her gender. She identifies the problems in the right perspective but deviates and fails utterly in providing a civilized way of handling the problems. She calls for absolute rejection of men and social bindings imposed by male members. What is reflected in her writings is strong and bold rejoinder and protest against atrocities upon women. She has succeeded in identifying the problem areas. She must be appreciated for boldly and fearlessly speaking out her mind. Her honesty must be appreciated. At least, she is not a hypocrite. She is honest and yet a little deviated. She has lost her way in the middle of her journey. She just doesn't know which way will lead her to her utopia.

Although Buchi Emecheta has succeeded in making a mark in literary world, her opinions and bias against men is not being whole heartedly accepted by her own gender which feels embarrassed at her rejoinders. Still, she has succeeded in producing novels based upon exploitation of women and made a mark of her own. People may disagree with her solutions presented to counter male dominance in women's lives but no one can doubt her merit and her sincerity of purpose.

It is Arundhati Roy who seems to accompany her in exposing the male psychology of subjugating women under religious, social and other pressures. Arundhati Roy too exposes her society but avoids suggesting solutions. Buchi Emecheta is alone in her defiance of the most respected medium of social stability and order that is 'the institution of marriage'. No one seems to defy its authority however torturous it may turn out to be.

Discussing the works of Buchi Emecheta, Helen Chukwuma remarks,

> Emecheta's feministic stance is seen in the females' reactions to these situations. Her characters adopt a positivistic view in crisis, and do not just fold their arms in tears and self-pity. Rather, they think, plan, execute and concretize.
>
> (Chukwuma, 1989, p. 4)

This feature is common in almost all Nigerian female writers especially Flora Nwapa and Zaynab Alkali. It appears from their works that they do not appreciate aggressiveness in women. They do react against male dominance but retain their feminine gentleness and save their home and family from burning down due to family feuds especially between husband and wives.

Helen Chukwuma has rightly observed that the true test of the woman continues to be the marriage institution. In this closed arena every married woman is to fight for her survival as an individual. The marriage paradox lies in the fact that it is both sublimating and subsuming. Through it a woman attains a status acclaimed by society and fulfils her biological need of procreation and companionship. However, through it, a woman's secondary status is emphasized and too easily she is lost in anonymity to the benefit and enhancement of the householders.

It is against this image and compulsion of a woman's domesticated life that Buchi Emecheta writes with all conviction.

> She strongly feels that the female, even in face of an oppressive system of deep rooted norms and practices and belief in female subordination, must live and assert herself. In her novels, Buchi Emecheta gives success to her female characters in their search for self assertions. (Chukwuma, 1989, p. 5)

It is not that only marriage is the target of her attacks. Buchi Emecheta critically analyses the role of women as mothers, their contributions in lives of their children and also attacks at its futility. She feels that motherhood is sheer waste of emotions and time as children hardly ever give returns to their mothers. Women are left to cry on their fate in old age even though they give birth to dozens of children, feed them and earn for them. Children are seen as another source of exploitation, both emotional and financial. Emecheta's attitude regarding children is best highlighted through the character of

Nnu Ego. Nnu Ego speaks out Emecheta's prejudice against motherhood and mother-child relationship:

> She had children, nine in all—how was she to know that by the time her children grew up the values of her country, her people and her tribe would have changed so drastically, to the extent where a woman with many children could face a lonely old age, and may be a miserable death all alone, just like a barren woman? She was not even certain that worries over her children would not send her to her grave before her chi was ready for her.
>
> (Emecheta, *The Joys of Motherhood*, 1979, p. 219)

Nnu Ego's situation is very similar to that of Rukmani of *Nectar in a Sieve* by Kamala Markandaya. Rukmani too is left alone even though she has given birth to five sons and a daughter. All leave her one by one. Only her daughter stays back with her to care for her by the end of the novel. She has been abandoned by her husband for being barren.

Thus, we see that whether it is India or Nigeria, the situations and hardships of women's lives are more or less similar. Birth of a son is essential for both the culture. Both Indian and African society is unsympathetic towards barren women. It is equally insensitive towards those women who have only female child. A sensitive writer like Buchi Emecheta who has led a separated life with a large family to maintain, is no doubt filled with bias, bitterness and anxiety over women's plight and men's negligence.

Obviously her presentation of male characters is greatly criticized. Oladele Taiwo remarks:

> The novelist has done what she knows best how to do. She has created a world of women where for the most part, attempt to portray male characters in unfavourable light may be an intentional device to make

> it back on men because of the image of women in the novels written by men. For example, most male characters in the Ditch are social misfits. Pa Palagada in The Slave Girl is a terror to the slaves. Nnaife in Joys of Motherhood and Francis in Second Class Citizen are irresponsible heads of families who are mostly insensitive to the needs of their wives and children. Chike in The Bride Price is probably the only acceptable important male character in these novels. But he is tainted with slave ancestry, which places some doubt on the validity of his actions.
>
> (Taiwo, 1989, p. 10)

The abnormal temperament of male characters mars the literary creativity of Buchi Emecheta. She has failed to do justice to her male characters. This failure cannot be unintentional. It appears that her personal experiences as a separated woman and a black woman has influenced her imagination.

Even Eustace Palmer believes:

> It is possible to argue that there are elements of distortions and exaggeration in Emecheta's works especially in her presentation of males, most of whom turn out to be little better than monsters.
>
> (Palmer, 1989, p. 10)

However, Helen Chukwuma does not agree with these critics. According to Chukwuma:

> Buchi Emecheta's male characterization is neither exaggerated nor contrived for the purpose of demeaning the male. The truth of the matter is that this is a realistic portrayal of men and events. The quaintness of this is that the truth had never been told before; that writers have

> not been so bold as to dip their heads in their autobiography and spread out all the hidden linen to public view. Buchi looked and portrayed life as she saw it, as she lived it and as she saw others live it at the place and time. It is no exaggeration, it is the truth. The bitter truth.
>
> (Chukwuma, 1989, p. 11)

What Buchi Emecheta is doing is just trying to prick the conscience of all with the hope that this might bring positive change in the attitudes of men towards women, marriage and motherhood.

The positivism behind Buchi Emecheta's negative portrayal of male characters can be understood in this light. She tries to find a way out. There is strong determination to stand on her own against oppositions and criticism and yet spread awareness among readers about women's plight. Emecheta seems to dislike and discourages show of emotion over women's predicaments and limitations in a patriarchal society. Rather, women must muster courage and their self-esteem should motivate them to work hard and earn their rightful place in home and outside.

The compulsions of married life give vast scope for torture and deprivation which Emecheta decries and denounces. Children and their grooming demands life-time involvement and commitment from a woman more than a man. Since children are more emotionally inclined towards their mother, some women feel oppressed and exploited as they spend their entire life in fulfilling various needs of children. The predicament of Nnu-ego is an apt example to stress the point. No wonder feminists term marriage as exploitative institution. What Emecheta fails to realise that 'a mother's duty is unique and exceptional in nature' which cannot be equated with other worldly engagements. It is not exploitation but a rare privilege bestowed to women by nature.

But then, it is not only Buchi Emecheta who cries for relief from duties of motherhood, womanhood, economic dependence, cultural and moral bindings towards family and men. Even Shashi Deshpande feels depressed by the traditional role of women in traditional society. The character sketch of Indu in *Roots and Shadows* is partly like that of Emecheta's heroines. Even Indu dislikes giving birth to children as this may hamper her personal growth in professional field. She needs time to decide whether she wants to have a child or not. Her husband is an ideal man for her as he has given all possible freedom to a married woman. Hence, Indu is the ideal character from Emecheta's point of view. What Emecheta imagines has come true in Indian milieu as women in African society cannot afford to avail the option of not becoming mother.

As far as the institution of marriage is concerned, characterization of Indu is quite different to those created by Buchi Emecheta. Shashi Deshpande's characters are liberal yet conservative in a sense that though they want all possible freedom from the institution of marriage, yet they do not want to break away from it altogether as advocated by Emecheta in her works.

Indian female writers denounce women's role as totally domesticated. What they want is social security from marriage and equitable distribution of duties and responsibilities in marriage and domestic life. They are refusing to accept their subjugated position within the four walls and outside. They want marriage but not its limitations as far as their own personal growth is concerned. Buchi Emecheta finds dissolution of marriage as the solution of women's plight as subjugated beings in domestic life, while Indian women writers seem to negotiate their way through this very institution without damaging its spirit and soul.

Keeping these aspects in view, Shashi Deshpande, writes primarily about the middle class educated women. She depicts their intellectual, moral and psychological growth after independence. Shashi Deshpande has made a 'woman's mind' the subject matter of her literary endeavour.

Just like the African women, the clash of egos, the compulsions to carry on with the age-old traditions, to cope with the present and at the same time the urge to exercise one's own rights as an individual is pulling the modern Indian women into different directions. All these factors are playing an important role in re-shaping and re-defining women's role and position in fast changing African and Indian societies.

The limitations of traditional backgrounds and the opportunities of modernity are both attractive and challenging for the captives of age-old traditions. Tradition demands compliance. Modernity provides multiple options and opportunities but none without a price. As far as Indian women are concerned, they want the security of traditional set-up and the freedom of modern age. In order to create a world where they can retain goodness of the past and attain freshness of the present, women are making experiments and looking for alternatives and better options. However, in their eagerness and honest efforts to enhance their stature, they are faced with multiple problems and hardships.

Shashi Deshpande has opted to catch this very spirit of modern Indian woman who wants to come forward to help herself without waiting for anyone else. Shashi Deshpande writes about women who are educated and enlightened. They are intelligent, self-respecting women who know where they stand and how to help themselves. They don't want to plead for mercy, pity. They expect co-operation from their men on equal footing. They want to work hard and rise in life. Modern women want to be treated as responsible members of their society who must be taken seriously. They expect to be treated equally irrespective of their gender. They strongly feel that intellect and talent are gender-free attributes.

Shashi Deshpande is a very keen observer and she writes with all sincerity and devotion. She is very receptive towards the contradictions found in the life of specifically modern Indian woman who is upwardly mobile. Shabana Azmi the actor and, an epitome of modern Indian womanhood, finds it difficult to "fix an identity" to herself. She states:

> It's free flowing; at different times, different aspects of the personality get heightened.
>
> (*The Hindu*, Magazine, p. 5, Sunday, March 18, 2007)

The compulsions of modernization have made life both easier as well as tougher; easier due to liberalization and tougher, because only technically trained and knowledgeable people are able to exploit the wide range of opportunities that are available. Ironically, most of the youths in India are still semi-educated and untrained. They dream high, but lack the ability to convert those dreams into realities. Mini's cousins of *Roots and Shadows* come under this very category of young people, who are in no-man's land. They envy Indu, the central character of *Roots and Shadows*. Indu is a go-getter. She is aware, agile, enlightened. She knows how to cope with the world outside and grab a job, her cousins lack foresight and courage. They lament over their failure and feel defeated and demoralized before her. There is subdued sense of resentment and bitterness towards Indu. She is a woman and yet more successful than men. Though they are mature enough to accept this fact that she has been better in studies, the sense of being defeated by a girl of the family is hurting their egos. Since, they are civilized men of modern age, they do not make a public scene out of jealousy and underplay their suppressed resentments. But Indu can perceive this wave of negativity in their bearings. She tries to modulate her own conduct and statements so as to mollify and pacify them:

> But now there was actual hostility, positive unfriendliness in his tone. It was not difficult to guess why. His dingy striped pyjamas, his drooping month, they all told the same story. A failure? I hesitated to use the word; but yes, if success meant having a certain income, a certain way of life, both of Kaka's elder sons were failure. And I by that standard I was a success.
>
> (*Roots and Shadows*, p. 37)

The gender clashes within the family is more painful and annoying than those faced outside. In fact, women do not get reprieve anywhere. The case of Indu and Sumant and rest of her cousins is a sheer case of competitiveness in career and since she happens to be a woman, she feels guilty and apologetic. Being the daughter of the family, Indu is expected to maintain the grace of her brothers inspite of their open display of irritations to her successful career. It would be indecent to argue with a brother. Indu is aware of the sentimental values attached to the brother-sister relationships in Indian Hindu families. The religious and social compulsions do not allow arrogance and defiance towards brothers from the female members of the household. The socio-religious restrictions of patriarchy save the tender threads of sibling relationship from breaking down altogether.

Indian women, however advanced, are basically religious and god fearing. They are hesitant to totally denounce the traditions and hence try to adopt middle path on sensitive issues. Too much of sentimentalization as well as too much practicality is avoided. It is because of this balanced approach of Indian society that this culture has survived for so long and is still going strong. It is both flexible and rigid.

Indu symbolizes modernity while Mini stands for tradition. The character of Awa in *The Stillborn* by Zaynab Alkali is closer to traditional Indian approach towards women. Both Awa and Mini comply silently in order to buy peace and solve the immediate problems of their marriage. They just don't bother about the men they marry. What matters for them is marriage, not the man. Mini repeatedly asserts that for her marriage is important not the man:

> But Mini, will any man do? Doesn't it matter who he is?
>
> (*Roots and Shadows*, p. 126)

Mini's response is:

> Yes, any man who says 'yes'. You don't know what it has been like. Watching Kaka and Hemant and even Madhav Kaka running after eligible men. And then, sending the horoscope and having it come back with the message, "It doesn't match". And if horoscope matched, there was the meeting to be arranged. And

> mother and Atya slogging in the kitchen the whole day. And all those people coming.... And staring and asking questions. And if we heard they were old fashioned people, I would dress up in an old fashioned manner and they would say, "she's not modern enough". And if I dressed up well because....
>
> (*Roots and Shadows*, p. 126)

Her approach is in accordance with the accepted ways of the world. The girl gets mentally exhausted and her family is made to succumb under social harassment to accept an unworthy groom. The natural corollary: submission by the defeated and harassed family:

> Oh, I don't know. And I don't care. He will look after me. And no one can say to me, "How old are you?" And not married yet. "What a pity!" I'm tired Indu. I don't care what kind of a man he is. Once we are married, and he becomes my husband none of his flaws will matter.
>
> (*Roots and Shadows*, p. 126)

Mini's submission before the hard realities that she has no better option is directly co-related to her family's helplessness before the unjustified demands of society. It is their forebearance that they swallow this bitter option without much display of pain. But Indu is desperate to get Mini out of this depressing alliance till the last moment. Even Kaka feels the same way:

> Who can guarantee who's the right man? After all, we can do only so much. The rest depends on the girl's luck.
>
> (*Roots and Shadows*, p. 131)

Just like Mini, even Faku of *The Stillborn* has surrendered her future before the harsh realities of her life. She too is willing to get married for all practical reasons. Her priorities are also very similar to that of Mini's. Since, she is a Muslim, she is willing to accept her secondary status in marriage. For her too, marriage matters, not the man:

> The point was that once she married, living alone with her mother was over. They would no longer have to work their fingers sore to feed themselves or mend the leaking roof, because someone else would be responsible.
>
> (*The Stillborn*, p. 46)

Both Mini and Faku are too practical to sentimentalize the issue of their marriage. They are, in fact, helpless before the pressing circumstances and lack the will to fight back. There could be many reasons behind this sense of defeat and mental exhaustion. They have adopted a very practical approach towards their present crisis and refuse to give it a serious thought. Their maiden status is proving to be a great hurdle for them and their family. They want to somehow get over it by accepting whoever is willing and get on with life.

It is this spirit to survive against odds, that has sustained women till date. They have this capacity to swallow insults, crisis and hardships with an inner strength to survive. Their practical sense prevents them from breaking down. They keep their emotions well under control, suppress their expectations before the hard realities of life and become defiant towards their own likes and dislikes. Women are, in fact, emotionally more stable and non-complaining. Even if they suffer, they do not seem to nurse any grudge against anyone.

The Stillborn is Zaynab Alkali's first novel. She comes from Northern Nigeria. The novel has been granted the prestigious Association of Nigerian Authors (ANA) award for such fine and balanced depiction of African society and women. Like Shashi Deshpande, Zaynab Alkali too tries to strike a balance between tradition and modernity. For both the authors, marriage is the main issue to be discussed. Both argue for more space to women for their individual growth within the institution of marriage. Both the authors refuse to see marriage as an evil institution unlike Buchi Emecheta and Flora Nwapa. For Zaynab Alkali marriage is the main issue in a women's life and its modification is being advocated by her. She does not find any future in spinsterhood and divorce too is no solution. According to her marriage is not an evil, rather it is a necessary evil and for the betterment of women, the institution of marriage must survive.

Flora Nwapa, on the other hand, advocates economic independence as more crucial for women's emancipation. Men are looked upon as a tool for procreation and nothing else. The rudeness with which Nwapa rebukes masculine gender might be the result of her observations of suffering of common women of Igbo community. She has written almost all her novels based upon the issue of childlessness in Igbo society. The pathetic conditions of women facing the problem of infertility in her community has inspired her to create such hard hitting novels. Buchi Emecheta and Flora Nwapa are not apologetic about their frankness of opinion and bias against masculine gender. They reflect genuine concerns towards the pains of childless women in African society. People are particularly very rude and ruthless towards the human limitations and hardships of childless women.

> It was a curse not to have children. It was regarded as a failure.
>
> (*Efuru*, p. 165)

The mental agony and trauma of a woman can be well understood by these emotional outpourings.

Infertility is a highly sensitive issue the world over. Especially in traditional African and Indian societies, marriage without children is a curse. Even Indu, who is upwardly mobile is made to feel the heat of annoyance of her elders because of her lack of interest in motherhood. Rukmani in *Nectar in a Sieve* has to work very hard to cure herself of this stigma of childlessness. After much efforts and goodwill of Kenny, the British doctor, who visits her village regularly, she becomes mother. But then her beautiful daughter is thrown out of her husband's house due to infertility. Her plight is very similar to those experienced by *Efuru*. Ira is also very beautiful, excellent in domestic works, obedient and loyal to her in-laws and dear to her husband. But these qualities cannot save her from being treated as evil influence upon her husband due to her infertility.

Kamala Markandaya also deals with the issue of infertility and its consequence for Indian women in *Nectar in a Sieve* with all possible sensitivity along with the problems of old age, generation gap and economic hardships of village people, the problems of unemployment, lack of faith in marriage and other issues related to women of rural background. Zaynab Alkali and Kamala Markandaya appear to stand on the same platform regarding marriage, family, kinship, social interactions and motherhood. Both the writers advocate for better understanding between husband and wife. They cannot imagine a women's life without marriage. Unmarried status is considered insecure, uncertain and unacceptable for decent living. Li and Indu are progressive. Mini, Ira, Faku and Awa are traditional. All are representative of their own respective societies and its limitations with which they fight and survive.

The problems faced by Ira in *Nectar in a Sieve* are very similar to those faced by common African and Nigerian women. The forceful writings of Flora Nwapa, Buchi Emecheta and even Zaynab Alkali highlight the exploitative tendencies of African society towards women. In both the societies, women are made responsible for all the misfortunes that befall a family. At psychological level, African and Indian people treat women with the same kind of prejudice and malice.

Flora Nwapa tries to find out a respectable way out of the state of infertility in a woman's life. She tries to suggest that women must overcome their complex of barrenness and get involved in social work in order to make positive use of their lives. Women must learn to fight back the misfortune of childlessness and overcome this crisis in most practical way. Lamentations will not generate goodwill, sympathy or compassion. Rather, it may provoke people even further. Women must learn to face this challenge with fortitude and find a decent solution of their pain. Women must not sit back and cry for mercy. Instead, they should move ahead and add meaning to their lives by making valuable contributions in society thereby making a mark of their own.

About Flora Nwapa, Dr. Yemi I. Majola writes:

> Nwapa exposes the woman's situation within traditional and contemporary societies, especially her role as wife and mother. She focuses on the importance attached to having children and thereby stresses the unenviable lot of infertile or barren women within the community. She examines the necessity for economic independence through determination and hard work, a sine qua non for self-fulfilment and freedom of action for a woman.
>
> (Majola, 1989, p. 22)

It is very clear that Flora Nwapa wants economic independence for women so that they can fight against most of their problems. She also stress the point that women need to groom themselves keeping in mind the varied nature of problems they face due to their subjugation in male dominated society. Lack of education, financial dependence, traditional social set-up, mental barriers all act as hurdles in women's growth as an accomplished human being. Just like Ira in *Nectar in a Sieve* Efuru is also rejected (twice) by her husbands. She is beautiful but barren. Her fate in domestic world is sealed. She will have to return. And Efuru returns like Ira. But while Efuru dedicates her life to the service of humanity, Ira decides to sell her body to fight starvation. She is forced to adopt unethical means due to lack of employment through rightful means in a small and remote village. Her parents Rukmani and Nathan do try to stop her but her answer that she cannot let her younger brothers die of starvation make them fall silent. Ira is the eldest and feels a sense of responsibility towards her family. Her maternal instinct forces her to tread the path followed by her neighbour Kunti.

While Flora Nwapa provides a decent way of leading a life of deserted barren woman, Kamala Markandaya has made evil dominate the good. Ira's decline should have been avoided. But then literature is a mirror of society. And Ira's life is symbolic of millions of women who are forced to adopt unethical means to sustain themselves and to maintain their families. Lazy husbands, drunkards and characterless people push innocent and economically weak, emotionally immature women towards these forbidden paths.

Life of Ammu is another example of isolated women. Ammu's case is more tragic than those of Efuru and Mini. Mini is saved by her wisdom to adjust with the circumstance and marry the most affordable fellow. But Ammu is denied marriage altogether by her own parents. She is forced to flee and marry the first man who proposes to her. She too has no option. She gets married, has two children but she is pushed out of marriage because of her firmness of nature. She refuses to entertain her husband's boss with her beauty. She is beaten by her drunk husband and thrown out of marriage.

Flora Nwapa stands with Arundhati Roy in rejecting bad husbands. Both believe, no husband is better than bad husband. Ammu after initial hesitation, seeks divorce and returns to Kerala for better future and secure life. But her efforts to re-establish herself fail due to her family's lack of sympathy for her. Amaka's depiction in *One is Enough* is quite different from Ammu's. Amaka even succeeds in having children from another man after break-up with her husband. While Ammu is unable to acknowledge Velutha in public view as her man, Amaka boldly prefers to refuse Father Mclaid's offer to marry her. She is so bold and confident that she declines to marry the father of her two children. Since she has earlier been thrown out of marriage because of her infertility, Amaka has become defiant towards social and moral bindings. Where Ammu fails, Amaka succeeds. She leads life on her own terms. African women when decide to reject, they reject men completely. There is no middle path for them, at least this is what is reflected in the novels of Flora Nwapa and Buchi Emecheta.

There is striking resemblance between Zaynab Alkali's *The Stillborn* and Kamala Markandaya's *Nectar in a Sieve*. Both are based upon the village society of their respective cultures. The village life and its limitations are similar in nature. The problems of unemployment, lack of basic amenities and lack of educational institutions for higher studies, poverty, suffocatingly close-knit societies which almost throttle the individuality of people are strikingly similar. The gender clash, mutual bias and adulations running parallel within family and village community, all are similar in nature. The agonies of an ordinary village woman, whether of Nigeria or India, who has to maintain large family primarily upon agriculture are too identical to mention.

The struggles of Rukmani of *Nectar in a Sieve* and Mama of *The Stillborn* are examples of the similarity of portrayal of village life and economy. The only difference between these two is that Rukmani, coming from a Hindu family, exercises equal right in every sphere of domestic life while Mama in *The Stillborn* is just a silent spectator of events and people within the four-walls. She has to obey and follow instructions. She is denied the right to speak out her mind. She is a dormant member of her family while Rukmani is most active and is fully involved in the decision making processes. Nathan, her husband, never forgets to seek her advice on important issues. But this cannot be said about Mama in *The Stillborn* as Baba is too dominating and too involved in monitoring children's activities himself to allow his wife to have any say. However, both the mother figures are the axis of their respective families. Mama's silence do not relieve her of her moral responsibilities to provide food for sustenance even after Baba's death. Sule disappears and Li escapes to the town to complete her studies. It is Awa and Mama who have to shoulder family responsibilities and arrange food for the rest. Mama works harder on her fields for better harvest just like Rukmani. Both women fight against adversities of their surroundings and try to sustain their families in great economic crisis. They are typical village women who have no ambitions. All they want is progress in family life. Children must grow up, marry and have children of their own so that the family line does not stop abruptly. All they want is all-round growth of their children. Mother-figures in both the cases are gentle, mild-natural and very caring. They neither complain nor expect much from their husbands. They are mature ladies, well aware of harsh realities of village society and hence do not complain about family life and family income.

However, in recent years, even village women who are considered ignorant, naive and innocent are beginning to evaluate their own contributions and also lack of recognition of their labour within the household. According to a report published in *The Hindu* dated March 11, 2007, women farmers who gathered at a function marking International Women's Day at Malpura in Tonk district of Rajasthan highlighted their daily struggle for recognition and equality despite playing a crucial role in the state's agrarian economy.

The village women are not a liability. In reality, they are the most important support system on which the village society exists and survives. They provide labour force for agriculture and domestic works, build-up finance and groom the children. Their contributions are unmatched. "With most men working as migrant labourers, women play a significant role in storage, handling, processing and marketing of farm produce even after the harvest. Besides, they have to brace themselves against the heat and dust and walk for miles to collect food and water for their families" ('Women farmers tell tales of struggle for equality', *The Hindu*, March 11, 2007).

There is a sea-change in the attitudes of today's Indian village women. They are no more ignorant and naive, cut-off from the mainstream. They are very much part of the Indian economic, social and also political systems. Women are voters too and they can change the fortunes of various political parties at local and national levels. There is more awareness among them than previous years. Indian village women are becoming more conscious of their status and rights as citizens and want recognition and due share in economy and social spheres.

There is a sense of pride and also a realization that they are making valuable contribution towards their family welfare, and hence they are no more a perpetually demoralized lot. Village women are not only sustaining their family, they are providing food to the whole of the nation. A village woman, Janku Devi, rightly states:

But my place in my family is unmatched as
I am the one who does all the farm work.
(*The Hindu*, March 11, 2007)

Another dimension of Indian village life is brought to the fore by Arundhati Roy. She writes fearlessly making most of the broad-mindedness of Indian secular temper. She enjoys greater literary freedom in India than Zaynab Alkali in Nigerian society. Zaynab has to keep in mind the local issues and the sentiments involved therein while Arundhati Roy has only one worry, and that is to give expression to her feelings and observation with utmost accuracy and precision. She has nothing else to worry about. Indian masses have matured much beyond expectations. The general opinion is always supportive towards creativity and only extreme vulgarity evokes strong reactions. Generally, people and government in India allow independence of expression and action.

It is this urge to express onself that compels Velutha to revolt, Ammu to retaliate. But the problem here is that those who are reacting are two weak people coming from weaker background against the most powerful people of their locality. Caste-politics overpowers Velutha and outwits Ammu. It is Baby Koachamma and Comrade Pillai who make most of the situation. The mob psychology to identify the culprit and punish on whim without any logic and compassion leads to Velutha's death. He has challenged the established norms of society. He has forgotten that he is an untouchable. His caste-people have been granted the right to live only to serve other people who are higher in caste-ladder. He, being an untouchable, is not permitted to decide his destiny. He has committed unpardonable sin. Hence, all the reactionary elements join together to punish Velutha. Ammu and her children Estha and Rahel get punished too for getting too close to Velutha, the untouchable.

Various factors combine together in just the exact proportion to create much needed environment for Velutha's exit. Velutha is victimized by one and all. Everybody exploits him and dumps him. His caste people cannot defend him because of his illicit relationship with the divorced daughter of their master. They watch with helplessness the desperate Velutha treading a dangerous path. He thinks he can outwit his folks by underplaying his involvement with Ammu. However, one who fails to take the right stand at the right moment, cannot expect right kind of reaction from others. People watch both the rebels with baited breath, for they know this combination will cause havoc some day. They simply bid time till both become victims of a very well laid-out plot. Both die prematurely.

The Stillborn has no such sensitive issue to deal with. The writer plays safe by following the basic rules of her society and does not try to evoke unnecessary upheaval within the community by going to extreme in the name of reality. Literature is a mirror of society in which the writer himself lives. Usually, those literary creations that create disharmony, bitterness and bias against any section of society or any phase of history are not welcomed. Zaynab Alkali is very conscious of her responsibilities towards her people, her culture and her pride as a Nigerian who happens to write about her culture for the outside world. The sense of protectiveness and self-explanatory tone of Zaynab Alkali is testimony of her thoughtfulness and her reservations.

Arundhati Roy dwells upon the ugliness of Indian society, while Zaynab Alkali tries to bandage the injured portions of Nigerian culture. She tries to find a solution while Arundhati Roy tries to prick the conscience of the people against their whimsical decisions and violent manifestations. Zaynab Alkali tries to console, advice and find a way out without demanding any vital change within the system. Arundhati Roy wants to knock at the conscience of the people. She attacks the duel standards adopted by the Indian society towards male and female progeny. Ammu is punished for going against the established rules of caste-ridden society. But Chacko, her brother, can do the same without any guilt. Mammaçhi pays the tribal women for their secret services to Chacko. His acts do not evoke adverse reactions but Ammu's do. The false pride of Ayemenem family and the tension created due to Ammu-Velutha involvement speaks of contradictions in the thinking of the people. Centuries of suppression and subjugation of the low caste people have instilled fear in their oppressors now. The upper castes fear retaliation by the low caste people. The suppressed hatred is the demon that always scares the high caste people. They just don't want that demon to come out in the open and retaliate. On the other hand, the low caste people are still, to a certain extent, fearful of those they serve. Arundhati Roy is full of repulsion and contempt at this unequal and unjust social equation. She writes with missionary zeal rather than for literary satisfaction. Her approach towards her own society is thus not as soft and conciliatory as Zaynab Alkali's.

Zaynab Alkali is accommodative and forgiving towards the limitations, weaknesses, hardships and lack of awareness she finds around her. She loves her nation, her culture, her people too much to talk ill of them, while Arundhati Roy is filled with anger at the ruthlessness with which innocent souls are trapped and tortured in name of tradition, culture, morality and ethics.

The God of Small Things is placed in Kerala. It is the most progressive state of India. Female literacy rate is the highest here. Still the real status of women of Kerala is not beyond reproach. Ammu is typical Kerálite woman who faces all possible problems that can be created to harass a decent woman by those around her. Ammu completes her education that means her matriculation and returns to Ayemenem for good. Her father refuses to invest in her education because she is a girl child. She is not allowed to go out. She awaits her marriage which is never negotiated by her parents. They simply ignore her existence. They want her to remain single just like her aunt Baby Koachamma. Ammu refuses. She marries outside her community to a Hindu. Her marriage fails after few years and she returns to her parents with her twin children Estha and Rahel. Her involvement with untouchable Velutha kills him and eventually her too.

Most of the women in India suffer like Ammu. Their nature of suffering may differ according to their circumstances but the traditional and patriarchal pattern of Indian society does not allow reprieve to anyone, not even males. They have to follow the rules laid down by their ancestors however torturous it might prove to be. It is the rules laid down by the tradition that rule over the people and not the vice-versa.

What one notices in *The Stillborn* is the cool headedness with which Nigerian people resolve their crisis in their personal lives. They do not sentimentalize things. They are more humane and forgiving than average Indians. They value human life more than anything else. They feel sad when tradition is ignored but don't stoop to killing innocent people over differences in ideology and convictions.

The recklessness with which Ammu-Velutha episode is handled by local police can happen only in a very insensitive society. Indians possess the ability to go blind when the ego clash between have's and havenot's takes place. The cold-bloodedness with which the whole system co-operates with Baby Koachamma to get Velutha eliminated and Ammu excluded from the family and community is frightening. She is even refused the last rites by her community. Ammu has failed herself, her children and Velutha too. She is too impulsive, short sighted, reactionary and desperate beyond reason. Her frustration, her recklessness, her honesty, all kill her. She is forced to commit mistakes. She does all that she should not have done. She easily gets provoked. Although she has been very reasonable and honest girl, she is harassed and abandoned by one and all. Ammu commits mistakes but then these mistakes are thrust upon her as any other option is not available at all. Actually, people around her make it impossible for her to keep herself in the right frame of mind:

> Mammachi said it ran in their family. That it came on people suddenly and caught them unawares. Would future generation say, 'There was Ammu—Ammu Jpe. Married a Bengali. Went quite mad. Died young. In a cheap lodge somewhere.'
>
> (*The God of Small Things*, p. 223)

It is not that only insanity ran in the blood of Ammu and her family. There is one more abnormality that go with it and that is the ability to push a normal healthy girl into insanity. The harshness towards Ammu by her own people kill her. They virtually push Ammu to insanity. Her imbalance in nature is not due to her own self, but primarily due to her family's snobbery and selfishness and also hatred towards their own daughter. Ammu has never done anything abnormal in her life. She has been patient, obedient and honest towards her parents yet she is left to serve her family and prepare herself for lifelong spinsterhood. She opts to marry outside her community due to lack of cooperation from her own people. She marries, gets divorce due to her husband's follies and is finally pushed to the wall at her parent's house. She commits unimaginable mistakes later on in her life. There is not much to defend herself. She cannot be defended on moral grounds at least. She has been immoral and her immorality creates problems for herself, Velutha, Ayemenem household and Estha-Rahel.

What Ammu lacks most is the goodwill of one and all. Lack of moral support and sympathy by those who know her, puts lot of pressure on her. All through her life Ammu keeps struggling for sincere support, sympathy and goodwill. The heroine of *The God of Small Things* is a lovely lady, yearning for a helping hand, a sympathetic touch and humane approach towards her and her unlucky children.

The liaison with Velutha becomes the cause of her final debacle. The complicated social system of Indian heterogeneous society does not give much scope to her to extricate herself and her children from the suffocating situation. What Li of Zaynab Alkali's *The Stillborn* gets, Ammu never gets. Li gets enough opportunity to improve herself, her life and those of her people. Li is provided all possible backup support by Awa, her elder sister and brother Sule. Ammu is sabotaged by all, her mother, father, Chacko, Baby Koachamma and even her family maid.

Li's tribal society is very close-knit and agrarian in nature. It is a hilly area where there is no trace of any urban influence. The only trace of western impact is reflected in the hospital run by the Christian Missionary. Rest of the village and its people are in harmony with their tribal heritage and proud of their ethnicity. They worship their own gods and have deep rooted faith in them. The influence of Christianity and Islam have not succeeded in eradicating this fear.

There is same kind of affinity and fear too inherent in Indian Christians regarding their forefather's original religion, i.e. Hinduism. The Syrian Christian family of Ammu claims that they were Brahmins before conversion into Christianity, hence an upper caste woman cannot have any relationship with an untouchable servant. The caste bias and caste conflict take serious turn after Ammu-Velutha relationship comes to light. Ammu is not taken as a Christian lady rather she is more identified as a Brahmin progeny and pushed behind the door and locked up for good.

There is big difference between Ammu's brother Chacko and Sule who is Li's brother of *The Stillborn*. While Chacko asserts himself in the most aggressive manner after his daughter's sudden death, Sule provides all possible moral and social support to Li and Awa as long as he is in the village. Sule is progressive in the sense that he treats his sisters as human beings who must have right to live the way they want, marry in time and have their own family identity. They must not die spinsters. Chacko, though more educated than Sule, is less progressive. He is rather very conservative and traditional in approach. He practices patriarchy and enjoys it every moment of his life at the cost of Ammu and her two innocent, highly vulnerable children. The kids are fatherless and depend heavily upon Chacko for their sustenance. Chacko lacks sensitivity and warmth towards these children simply because they are Ammu's children from a Hindu father. Sule, on the other hand, is very sensitive and sympathetic person. He is very watchful of his sisters' future prospects and warns them in time to think about their marriage. He gives right kind of advices to both the sisters even though he is more close to Li. Chacko lacks sincerity towards Ammu. He hates Ammu for her marriage, he hates her for her assertiveness, he hates her for her divorced status, he hates her for her dependence upon Ayemenem household after divorce. He just doesn't want her to identify herself with them after her unsuccessful marriage with a Hindu. It seems she has committed sin by getting married. Chacko, Mammachi, Pappachi and Baby Koachamma, all wanted her to remain single all through her life. Since, Ammu has refused to lead a single life and go ahead and marry the first man who proposes to her, her family snaps off it's ties with her. They just refuse to turn up for her marriage. Ammu has seen all these and still maintain her cool. She has been pulling on with them as discretely as possible, yet what Ammu undergoes under Ayemenem household is a sad story of endless suffering.

Li is much luckier than Ammu. There cannot be any comparison to Ammu's pain. Li has been lucky in many ways. She always had a well wisher to provide a shoulder to weep on. When Li is single, she has Awa, Sule, younger siblings and her, friend Faku to confide to. They are there to help her, console her guide her and correct her. For Ammu there is none. She has to do all these duties by herself. She has to console herself, guide herself and again muster courage to face the world again with new hope and expectation of some miracle some day. She waits for good days to come but dies alone in a room at a strange place among strangers. An innocent life is wasted due to inflated egos of her own people who keep torturing her till she is dead. Her family and the society at large did not allow Ammu to survive.

A victim of social harassment is turned into culprit and then reduced to ashes. Family pressure and social compulsions can push a needy woman to unnatural end. Even then, there is no guarantee of reprieve to the deceased soul from social criticism, humiliation and satire. Ammu is the best example of such harsh treatment. She fails to win the confidence of her husband. She invariably selects a weak person as her companion. One is unable to defend her in the day light, the other stands by her only as a shadow and not as a reality. Both the men, her husband and Velutha, are very weak people. They have their own handicaps which they cannot shake off and hence can not extend absolute support to Ammu. Both lack confidence in the right sense of the term. The husband has the audacity to assault her when she refuses to oblige his boss, but he cannot take a stand before his boss against his indecent proposals regarding Ammu. As a husband, Ammu's interest and pride is not guarded by him. He prefers to push her into obliging a debauch, much against her wishes. He is desparate to save his job but shamelessly immune towards his pride as a husband of a beautiful and intelligent woman. He should have objected to the designs of his boss and preferred to kick off the job, instead he kicks Ammu out of his life. Strange! A man who lacks guts, cannot withstand the pressures of immoral world.

As far as Li is concerned, even she is abandoned by Habu. But this separation is not official. Rather, she is just left to cry on her fate without bothering to relieve her from torturous marriage alliance. Habu too is not an ideal husband either. He drinks heavily and has relationship with another lady. Li is totally ignorant of this and feels hurt when he neglects her. Habu is very similar to that of Ammu's husband. Both have striking resemblance with each other. This shows that men exhibit certain universal traits of deceit in marriage. They have that ability to ditch their married partners without any sense of guilt or remorse. They marry at will and walk out of marriage at their own convenience. Even though Habu does not push Li into another man's arms like Ammu's husband, yet indirectly he is responsible for all those years of loneliness and social pressures to re-marry a rich business man back home. Poor Li is teased and taunted to succumb before group pressure to accept someone who is highly unacceptable to her.

The tendency to pressurize exceptional women to accept unsuitable match is most cruel type of injustice inflicted upon innocent women. They are made to feel that those who refuse to oblige nasty, resourceful people are fools. And that, it is only money that matters. Young innocent girls are psychologically tortured and pressurized to agree for mis-matched marriages to benefit the relatives and friend circles. Li has to face all these during her stay in her village after separating from Habu. The involvement of Habu with city woman becomes a source of torture for Li who is a young and committed wife. She does not want to dissolve her marriage. Li is desperate to save her marriage like Ammu, who tolerates a drunkard husband despite his violence for the sake of her own future and those of her children.

Women all over the world try hard first to get approval in marriage, then work even harder to sustain the marriage and finally become aggressive to retain their marriage. They become desperate to guard the future of their families and children against all odds. Ammu and Li, Awa or Faku are no exceptions.

The role of mother in *The Stillborn* is dormant while Mammachi of *The God of Small Things* is quite an active figure even though she is playing secondary role before Pappachi and later in the presence of her son Chacko. Mammachi is always playing the second lead and acts as buffer between her husband and society and latter between workers and Chacko. Mammachi is more mature than her son. However, the character sketch of Li's mother is that of a silent and caged individual who has no right to even express her feelings without formal permission of her boss, that is, her husband. She can't even interact with her own son and daughters for fear of rebuff from her husband. She is treated more as a child-bearing machine rather than a human being. Each and every action of her is monitored by her husband. Mammachi is in a better position. She has to remain subdued only before her husband.

The patriarchal influence is best reflected in the characters of Li's parents where father is all powerful and domineering while mother is dominated over in every aspect of human life. It seems even her thoughts are being scrutinized by her husband and she dare not think anything that goes against the wishes of her husband, or else! There has been tension between father and son. Rest of the family is there to play their respective roles including the mother who has to be present of course but who has no right to say anything. As usual she is a silent spectator. She can be present, but she has no right to interfere or assert herself as a mother or as a wife. This is the greatest predicament of Li's mother. Even Mammachi has to tolerate the beatings of her husband, his mental tortures and his abuses, because she happens to be his wife. It is her primary duty to be ill-treated and suffer silently for the future of her family. This is a small price women the world over pay for being married. Married status demands subjugation of ego and women willingly suppress their egos for they want social and religious security out of marriage.

There is striking resemblance between Indian and Nigerian society. Both are similar in many ways. Besides, socio-economic similarities, the psychological impact of male dominance upon female characters are also the same. The women in both the societies are fearful and docile before masculine gender. They dare not challenge the notoriety of male members and do everything possible to stay away from their place of dominance and activities. This discretion by the women is a precaution to protect themselves from any kind of allegation from the opposite gender. This shows that men have the habit of abusing women on trivial issues. Women are, in fact, fearful of physical and mental torture which their husbands inflict upon them to make them realise their inferior status in society and domestic life. Mammachi gets beaten up on daily basis just to remind her of her subjugation before her husband:

> He had always been a jealous man, so he greatly resented the attention his wife was suddenly getting. He slouched around the compound in his immaculately tailored suits, weaving sullen circles around mounds of red chillies and freshly powdered yellow turmeric, watching Mammachi supervise the buying, the weighing, the salting and drying, of limes and tender mangoes. Every night he beat her with a brass flower vase. The beating weren't new. What was new was only the frequency with which they took place. One night Pappachi broke the bow of

> Mammachi's violin and threw it in the river.
>
> (*The God of Small Things*, p. 48)

Men can be as jealous as women. Hard labour and dedication with which Mammachi is running her cottage industry of pickles is untolerable to Pappachi. Her success goes against his male ego. He hates her for her success. He hates her for her dedication towards her work. He dislikes her success as an individual. It is an abnormal tendency to feel jealous of one's own wife, but then most of the husbands suffer from this peculiarity. They feel threatened by their wives. Notwithstanding the dedication of women towards their family, their men begin to feel jealous of their talent and developed personalities.

Mammachi is struggling to keep her house in shape financially atleast. The financial crisis has forced her to use her culinary skill commercially. But Pappachi is biased and feels sidelined and also neglected. He dislikes her identity of a successful working woman. Pappachi beats her to satisfy his ego. He even adopts cheap methods to defame her as a negligent wife who is too busy to spare time for her old dependent husband:

> In the evenings, when he knew visitors were expected, he would sit on the verandah and saw buttons that weren't missing onto his shirts, to create the impression that Mammachi neglected him. To some small degree he did succeed in corroding Ayemenem's view of working wives.
>
> (*The God of Small Things*, p. 48)

It seems as if psychologically and socially Pappachi is loosing grounds before Mammachi. At least Pappachi feels that way. He is fearful of being washed out of the memories of Ayemenem social circle due to his wife's expanding influence. He tries hard to re-establish himself in the public view by moving around in the town in his car.

> He bought the sky blue Plymouth from an old Englishman in Munnar. He became a familiar sight in Ayemenem, coasting importantly down the narrow road in his wide car, looking outwardly elegant but sweating freely inside his woolen suits. He wouldn't allow Mammachi or anyone else in the family to use it, or even sit in it. Plymouth was Pappachi's revenge.
>
> (*The God of Small Things*, p. 48)

His fascination for British lifestyle does not allow him to behave like an educated Indian gentleman. He keeps imitating the British people who are caged in his memories. His behaviour pattern reflects abnormal state of mind. His obsession for everything associated with foreigners is proof enough of his slave mentality. He is more British than a Britisher. This is the main cause of his frustration. He cannot establish normal healthy rapport with his wife who is Indian in every sense of the term. There is no contradiction in Mammachi's personality. Hence, she is at peace with herself. But Pappachi is a dissatisfied soul, dissatisfied of being an Indian, living in an Indian village, suffocated by a thoroughly Indian wife. He is fighting not with Mammachi, the woman, but with her goodness and her merits. His ego is unable to digest her merit, her talent, her versatile personality. His wife cannot have a personality so developed. She cannot prosper under his shadow. It is highly unconventional. He is fighting to re-establish himself against her emerging personality as a successful woman, financially self-reliant and socially established on her own account. This is highly humiliating situation for a husband. Pappachi cannot digest it so easily. She seems to ignore his importance in her life. She must not forget her actual status. Plymouth is a medium to remind her of her real position before her husband and the onlookers.

Indian society gives higher status to a woman once she graduates into motherhood after marriage. Her children too protect her and establish her in society. Mammachi enjoys Chacko's support and protection from Pappachi's assaults. Her son is there to protect his mother and discipline his irate father, whereas Li's brother Sule is unable to do much for his mother. He understands her predicaments but cannot do much to improve her status within the family. She doesn't even talk to her children freely. She spends her time mostly within her hut, separated from rest of the children and family activities.

Mama in *The Stillborn* is left to attend her youngest child while Awa is ordered to manage the daily routine of the family. Mama is virtually ordered to stay away. She does as instructed by her husband. She hardly does anything on her own initiative.

Even after Baba's death, Mama's routine hasn't changed. She stays aloof from her family but with a difference. She goes to the field to toil on the land for good harvest. She has to run a big house full of children, old couple and young daughter Awa, whose husband has become a drunkard. Practically she is faced with the similar kind of problems that are being faced by Mammachi. Both have to arrange finance to run the house. As Awa describes:

> You know now where the money goes. I wouldn't have known how to cope without Mama. We live on the proceeds of her farm. The woman would go to the farm at cockcrow and won't come back until the chickens have gone to roost.
>
> (*The Stillborn*, p. 87)

Women are under great stress and strain the world over. Be it Nigeria or India, Christian or Muslim, the religious identity and cultural differences do not change the circumstances in which women struggle to survive. These novels highlight the pain, the agony of being women and their limitations related with their status as married, unmarried, widowed, divorcee or abandoned wives.

Ammu's struggle begins with Pappachi's refusal to allow her to continue with her education after her matriculation. She is ordered virtually to stay at home and help Mammachi in housekeeping. Ammu obeys with the hope that one day she will be getting married like an average Indian girl. But her eighteenth birthday passes by without any notice being taken by her family. Ammu is surprised at their coldness. She is rather shocked and her hopes of any parental support and concerns towards her and her future fade away. Their silence is more effective than their rudeness of conduct and harshness of speech. Ammu must do something desperate to extricate herself from the grip of Ayemenem house. Ammu finds a way to escape. She does succeed in her plans to get married and settle down in life. But then, misfortune chase her there too. Her exceptional beauty and intelligence prove to be a deadly combination for her. The reason lies in her own lack of determination to fight back the evil forces that try to disturb her otherwise peaceful life.

As far as the characterization of Li is concerned, Li proves to be more strong both mentally and socially when compared to Ammu. Li is more determined to fight back and she struggles in right direction with clear perceptions. She is not a confused soul. She is clear in her motives and also very persuasive. She refuses to kneel down before difficulties. Either at home or with her husband, Li is always thoughtful and analytical. She tries to study the situation in which she is placed. She identifies her goal and also those who may cause problems for her in future. She deals with them with a firm mind and does not allow emotion to disturb her mind. She obeys her father only to disobey him. Ammu too fights back but her style of retaliation and those of Li are very different. Ammu has to return to Ayemenem after divorce and even then she is not forgiven. She is taken as a necessary evil who has nowhere else to go. Due to social compulsions Ammu is allowed to stay in Ayemenem house. Her father, just like Baba, maintains stoic silence which is both intentional and humiliating for her. She is being made to realise that her presence is highly irritating and unwelcome. But then Ammu retaliates in most disgusting manner while Li never does anything that damages family prestige the way Ammu does via Velutha. Li grows up into a very dignified and serious woman who has deep understanding of social values, norms and ethics.

Her each and every move is monitored by her grandfather who keeps guiding her. He provides her with valuable advices and prevents her from committing blunders. Ammu has no such support. She is ridiculed, harassed, taunted, taxed unnecessarily and forced to adopt aggressive stance to defend herself and her children in her father's house. Li faces problems from outside world, which she is able to resolve with the help of her friends and family members, especially Awa and her landlady in the town. There is Faku who is more wise and experienced than Li. She advices Li to keep cool and suffer silently as her crying may provoke people to harass her more. Li is lucky to have so many well wishers who constantly provide advices and moral support to her. Li uses her time and energy to consolidate herself so that she can win back her husband and her lost pride. Since, Li has been left to cry on her fate, she has become as vulnerable as Ammu. But she is given protection and shelter by her own people, which is unfortunately not available to Ammu. The ruthlessness with which Ammu is dealt with by her parents, aunt and brother is quite unnatural.

There is striking resemblance between Pappachi of *The God of Small Things* and Baba of *The Stillborn*. Both the fathers behave in identical manner towards their rebellious daughters. Li is rejected by her own father and never reclaimed by him even during his last days. Pappachi too refuses to accept Ammu back. Ammu's struggle and tears don't rattle him. In fact, he derives satisfaction out of her misfortune. Chacko laughs at her troubles and Mammachl is too cold and aloof to get moved by Ammu's pain and tears. For her it is only Chacko and his interests that matters. Ammu must not pose any challenge to Chacko.

The father-figures all over the world react in a typical manner. The cultural differences do not have any bearing upon their mindset regarding their children. The urge to control the lives of their children is universal. Children must obey their parents, especially their father. They dare not disobey or manipulate their orders and instructions. Concessions are granted to the male heirs but no such liberty is allowed to the daughters. If the tradition is challenged by a girl child, she faces harsh reactions universally.

Be it Nigeria or India, people do not appreciate disobedience by a girl child. For, there are many negative forces active in society who might try to influence young and inexperienced girls. Parents are, thus, very cautious of such elements and exert extra influence upon female child to control her mobility. Sometimes excessive caution misfires. It leads to confrontation and mistrust among father and children. Sule and Li object to their father's restrictions because of his excessive control over their lives. They feel suffocated and want to get out of the psychological pressure which they feel every moment of their lives. They strongly feel they must revolt if they want to survive and retain their sanity. Ammu, Li and Sule react against their respective fathers and make their family suffer. In the process they suffer too.

What one notices here is that while Ammu's struggle turn her almost insane and fatalistic, Li and Sule gain maturity with each experience. They become more and more reasonable and sober down much beyond expectations. They begin to empathies with their fathers who has been a villain earlier. This change occurs with the passage of time. By the time Li and Sule understand their father's worries and anxieties for them and their siblings, it is too late. Their father is no more. He dies yearning to see his son by his side. He had become apologetic for his ruthlessness of attitude with which he virtually ruled over his family. He is guilty of stretching his gender superiority a bit too far. He wants his son back. However, he is not so thoughtful of Li. Even then, Li is more forthcoming in forgiving her father. She maintains a safe distance from him keeping in mind his reservations against her. He never forgives her for her defiance but he is careful not to indulge in any kind of emotional drama. Both maintain safe distance from each other, refusing to change stand. Li is more sensitive and understands her father's psychology much better now that she herself has graduated into adulthood and gained better understanding of people and situations.

It is a misfortune that Ammu never attains such maturity of mind and action. She indulges in emotional outbursts on every trivial issue and spoils her mental peace and also of those who are tolerating her inspite of such strong reservations. The lack of communication and warmth between Ammu and her family is mutual. Due to the clash of interest between Chacko and Ammu, people at home compel her to become desperate. The humane touch is found lacking in this Indian family. It seems Ammu might have survived in Nigerian society.

Ammu's family lacks honesty towards Ammu and her children. They are constantly made to feel that they are a liability upon them and must relieve them of their forced presence as early as possible. They know too well, Ammu is a divorced lady, young and beautiful. She needs social protection and presence of guardians till her children become mature enough to take care of her. The rudeness and insensitivity of Mammachi and Chacko is abnormal even by Indian standards. The Syrian Christian pride of the family is more precious than the life of an innocent woman. They simply push her to the wall and Ammu unable to cope with so much of pressures from all sides makes desperate attempts to seek help and support from Velutha—an untouchable. This proves fatal not only for her but for Velutha as well. They are doomed for ever. Estha and Rahel become orphans and bear the burdens of three deaths upon their conscience till the end. Li is lucky to be a member of benign family. Ammu has paid heavily for being a part of orthodox insolent family.

As far as condition of children in both the countries are concerned, children in Nigerian society are treated with more affection by the relatives and are more valued than in India. Estha and Rahel are not as lucky as Li's daughter who too has to live with her aunt Awa and her grandparents. There is no discrimination between Li's child and her cousins. All are treated with affection inspite of the fact that Li is not always present to take care of her child. Li's marriage to Habu does not make any difference. Her daughter is not treated any differently nor is made to feel unlucky and unwanted by the larger family. Children are not made to suffer due to differences between the guardians. Poor Estha and Rahel! They are treated like slaves and demoralized like anything. They are too small and too innocent to understand the family politics of the adults but they are made to suffer. They must not escape mental torture, ragging and humiliations before outsiders simply, because they are innocent children. Children who live under the relative's roof for sustenance and support must pay back the debt by allowing themselves to be humiliated at free will.

The Stillborn (1984) depicts African culture and psychology of its people in best possible manner. The casual dialogues and conversations throw sufficient light upon the psyche and situation in which the women have to survive. They emulate what is systematically drilled into their innocent minds by their elders.

One can easily notice the uniformity in approach towards women in Indian and Nigerian society. The systematic indoctrination of a sense of subjugation and compliance among women towards men is done with a motive to avert any retaliation by women against authoritativeness of masculine gender. This type of arrangement is made full-proof by inflicting physical injuries upon those who try to defy or challenge this arrangement. The result of revolt is then publicized and propagated like a new faith in order to covertly support and further strengthen the existing order by generating fear and horror among the rest of the population. By robbing the dignity of the women and prestige of her family a warning is sent to those who show potential to threaten the established norms and practices. Ammu in *The God of Small Things* and Li in *The Stillborn* are examples of such social harassments and mental torture.

There is very slow change in attitude towards women in both the societies. Their difficulties are not taken notice of. They are made to feel that what they are getting should be considered enough. The fear of losing out whatever little they have is preventing them from asserting themselves further as most of the women are not self-reliant. They depend on their families which may throw them out if they oppose unjust treatment meted out to them.

The greatest handicap of women is their inability to survive as an individual on their own. The practical difficulties are not much but the psychological barriers and handicaps prevent them from adopting aggressive postures against their tormentors. The emotional void which troubles them when left alone, compels them to voluntarily accept their subjugation before the men. The characters such as Faku, Awa, Li and Ammu reflect this delimma of woman's mind. They want freedom from male authoritarianism but also hanker for a man's presence in their lives. Women need the presence of men primarily for emotional reasons. The way Awa, Li and Faku yearn for a male companion, the way they lose their men without any fault of theirs and the way they reclaim them after overcoming their struggles and crisis of all kinds is nothing but depiction of mental weakness and obsession for male company.

Moreover, the social environment changes drastically whenever a woman begins to live without male presence. It is another method of showing women their subjugation and subordination. This weakness is inherent in feminine gender the world over. The inability of not being able to cope with life without a man forces them to adopt conciliatory postures. The urge to make their life a complete one, in order to complete the family structure of husband, wife and children, women make adjustments of worst kinds and justify them.

The way women themselves ignore their health and education due to overeagerness to grab a man before their young age is over is regrettable. Striving for education and self-reliance cannot be signs of lack of culture and feminity. But undue importance is given to marriage rather than education. There is an undercurrent of nervousness among women for marriage and they do not give much value to self-improvement and education. They use religion and tradition more than men to meet their objective. In fact, it is they who seem to misuse religion and culture more than men in perpetuating gender-disparity. It is conventional and convenient to blame masculine gender for every problem, but women too are not faultless.

There cannot be any logic behind such desperation except the assumption that women are a vulnerable lot and need masculine protection of all kinds from all quarters. Compromise in marriage is a price women pay for all the advantages and liberties they hope to get in return.

A persual of the novels shows that the Nigerians are extremely broad-minded and large hearted people who allow their daughters to become co-wives. Instead of keeping a small family and educating their children, they follow their old tradition mindlessly. Many lives suffer due to lack of resources to meet the demands of decent life. Mutual commitments are short lived and children are forced to suffer in the process.

The problems faced by Nigerian women are not very different from what Indian women face. The gender disparity along with overpopulation, poverty, illiteracy, and obstacles in self-reliance are such problems which are identical in nature. In order to highlight these issues in the world of literature, African and Indian women writers are making great efforts. They are making sincere attempts to make their complex society appear simpler and understandable. There's an attempt to spread awareness about the basic facts and realities of social lives specially in the context of women's status within traditional patriarchal social structure. The task has been challenging and demands impartiality in depiction despite loyalty towards one's own nation and culture.

Under such pressing circumstances women writers of both India and Africa are doing commendable job by coming forward and extending valuable insight into the problems related to women and children. They are trying hard to re-define man-woman relationship and carrying out their joint responsibilities towards self, family, children and nation building process.

Conclusion

5

Indian and Nigerian writers have been very conscious of their cultural heritage and its preservation. They have displayed a strong sense of social commitment in their literary creations. The social fallouts of colonial rule in both the countries have been depicted by almost all Indian and Nigerian literary personalities right from the initial years of development of English literature in their respective countries. Even though the early literary works of both the countries reflect the influence of Western style of writing, the nationalistic temper is dominant and explicit in them.

Right from the very beginning, Nigerians have always displayed strong resentment over social evils, political instability and poor economy, exploitation of their natural resources, mismanagement of human resources by the monopolistic tendencies of their leaders after the fall of colonialism. Writers and social activists from Oloudah Equiano to Ken Saro-Wiwa have been very conscious of their African identity and have made significant contributions through literary creations to bring about social and intellectual awakening in their respective ways.

The contributions of women writers of Nigeria in this regard is remarkable. Right from Flora Nwapa, Buchi Emecheta to Zaynab Alkali all have tried to convince their people for introspection. They have taken the initiative to critically analyse their own society and culture in the context of women and their position in family and society. Buchi Emecheta explores Igbo culture and traditions of bride price and polygamy in her novels. The contributions of Arundhati Roy, Shashi Deshpande and Kamala Markandaya in exploring Indian side of realities related to society and women have provoked serious discussions over the issues related to women's emancipation.

Adopting an introspective style of writing both Indian and Nigerian women writers have dealt with larger issues like cultural conflicts, confrontation between older and younger generation, ideological differences between people and social problems like poverty, illiteracy, communal issues and those related to national interests keeping women's perspective as the centre of their focus. They have never deviated from their focal point, that is, the women and children. Because, it is they who suffer the most in every kind of adversity, whether natural or man-made. The issues related to motherhood, children, housewives' limitations and significance, socialization of feminine gender within family and surrounding, their limitations, economic constraints, spinsterhood, barrenness, isolation, health—both mental and physical etc. have been depicted with all possible sympathy and empathy. According to Ketu H. Katrak:

> Women writers share specific gender concerns in terms of how social and cultural factors appear from a female point of view. Their literary works imaginatively explore several conflicts between tradition (social custom, religion) and modernization.
>
> (Katrak, 1998, p. 232)

Flora Nwapa, Buchi Emecheta and Zaynab Alkali, have been striving hard to spread awareness and enlightenment among Nigerian women in particular and African women in general. The lack of a sense of individuality, lack of education leading to ignorance and self-pity, negligence of health and slave mentality have made their life a miserable one. Women writers are trying to groom them into healthy, educated, socially committed and family oriented citizens of awakened Nigeria/Africa.

The works of Alkali like *The Stillborn* (1984), *The Virtuous Women* (1987), *The Cowwebs* and *Other Stories* (1997) or *Emecheta's In the Ditch* (1972), *Second Class Citizen* (1974), *The Bride Price* (1976), *The Slave Girl* (1977), *The Joys of Motherhood* (1979), *The Family* (1990) and *Kehinde* (1994)—her latest novel, all focus on women and their problems. So is the case with Nwapa who has made considerable effort in spreading awareness regarding women's plights through her writings. Her most significant work in this regard is her first novel *Efuru* which came out in 1966. *Idu* (1970), *Never Again* (1975), *One is Enough* (1981) and *Women are Different* (1986) are hard hitting novels based upon women and their protest against the traditional attitudes of society regarding their rights as women, as human beings.

What most of the women writers seem to stress is that self-development and financial self-reliance do not go against happy family concept prevalent in Nigeria/Africa. According to them, the concept of women's empowerment does not go against the traditional social set up which is essentially patriarchal in nature. The women themselves want a male as the figure-head in the family, however incompetent he might be. For, they feel safe and secure in the traditional way of life. It gives them social safety and secure future.

However, women in Nigerian society want more space within the institution of marriage for self-development and financial security. They want to earn for their own self and for children's well-being. They want to progress, not to break their homes but to rebuild the broken fences or change the damaged ones. They want flexibility in the attitudes of men regarding women. Their horizon is wider than their men can imagine.

Nigerian women writers have been fairly persistent and consistent in their aims and objectives. Their vision is clear and they have been trying hard to mobilize public opinion in favour of women and their emancipation. Time and again, they have tried to convince their society that women do not wish to go against the tradition of Africa. There is a fear that educated women break homes and pollute the innocent minds. It has been attacked by the intellectually enlightened women of Africa. Some African people take the awareness as a war against African identity, culture and men in particular. Male writers like Taban Lo Liyong once said,

> I think I should appeal to us to keep the African household intact at the end of the day otherwise....
>
> (Katrak, 1998, p. 240)

In response to this fear, African women writers have adopted self-explanatory, self-help techniques for women's upliftment. The most important aspect of women's subjugation lies in their own complexities both mental and social. They degrade themselves as secondary elements within family and society. They are gripped with slave mentality and a kind of inferiority complex. They feel guilty in asserting themselves. They seem to suffer from a mental block which prevents them from seeking help or attention in the hours of personal crisis. Womanhood fills them with a sense of insecurity. Their pain and suffering have become their identity. It is this psychology of a sense of subjugation, delight in deprivation and lack of confidence to assert for one's own rights as an individual against which the women writers have been writing for so long with a deep sense of moral binding and obligation.

Women like Nwapa, Alkali, Emecheta, Lauretta Ngcobo, Carol Boyce Davies, Zulu Sofola, Tess Onwuene, Mobel Segun, Ifeoma Okoye, Miriam Tlali and Molara Ogundipe Leslie are very vocal and fearless in their reactions, rejoinders and retaliate with equal force in denouncing baseless allegations upon women regarding their emancipation. They strive for balance in man-woman relationship without causing any drastic change in African social life.

African/Nigerian women writers strive for equal status to women of not only the privileged class but also to the women of working class. They include men too in their consideration. For, they too have suffered racism, colonialism and imperialism as much as women. Although, they are primarily concerned with the well-being of African women and children but these writers are not immune towards the hardships faced by their men on social, financial and political fronts. Hence their approach towards problems faced by African/Nigerian people as such is more holistic and humane than their own men who doubt their intentions and resent their progress. It is the greatest irony of African society that it lacks faith in their well meaning, committed female population.

The question of doubt, misconception and suspicion upon women population have been a common phenomena. Whether India or Nigeria, women as such are considered to be inferior mentally and physically. They are considered immature and reckless. Hence men fear giving freedom and power into their hands.

It is this lack of faith in feminine gender that has been attacked by women writers, intellectuals, social thinkers from time to time. Special mention must be made of some prominent female writers besides Nwapa, Alkali and Emecheta who have made considerable effort in eradication of doubts and misconceptions regarding women. They are South African Nadine Gordimer Ellen Kuzwayo and Miriam Tlali, Dominican Jean Rhys, Tsitsi Dangarembga of Zimbabwe, Bessie Head from Botswana, Ama Ata Aidoo and Efua Southerland from Ghana, Micere Mago from Kenya, Lorna Goodison, Erna Brodher, Liver Senior from Jamaica and Merle Hodge from Trinidad.

As far as Indian approach to women's problems is concerned, it has been highlighted from time to time by social thinkers, intellectuals, political leaders and the general people who have been conscious of their secondary status within the family and outside. Many reform movements have been launched in the past for the eradication of social evils and bias regarding feminine gender.

A.S. Altekar in his book *The Position of Women In Hindu Civilization* has rightly observed:

> One of the best ways to understand the spirit of a civilization and to appreciate its excellences and realize its limitations is to study the history of the position and status of women in it.
>
> (Altekar, 2005, p. 1)

The study undertaken here, of Nigerian woman novelists and Indian English women novelists, shows that a lot still needs to be done for the cause of women in Africa and India. Ideas eulogized do not percolate down to the ground. This is the truth that all women writers and not just Alkali and Roy have endeavoured to expose.

"The ideology of social change is the creative force behind" the works of not only Alkali and Roy but almost all literary figures all over the world.

(Prasad, 1997, p. 5)

The concerns of Indian English women writers cannot be much different from their Nigerian counterparts as their respective countries share a number of socio-economic and political characteristics. Besides coping with native patriarchal ideology women of Nigeria and India bore the brunt of colonialism too. Hence, their sufferings are more or less identical in nature.

In fact, in India the history of the female perspective goes back to the Vedic Age. According to the orthodox tradition itself as recorded in the 'Sarvankramanika', there were as many as twenty women among the seers or authors of Rigveda. It is not that Indian women waited for the Renaissance to be awakened by the social reformists of 18th century India to find their voice. "There has been...in the Indian culture a healthy tradition of the female perspective on graver issues too apart from the mundane." (Jaya Prasad, 2006, pp. 37-38). What Indian English women writers are doing is to carry this tradition further with courage, conviction and a great deal of creativity.

Though Indian English women writers have not been lacking in creative virtuosity or literary dexterity, in India issues relating to women are quite vast and of bewildering complexity, because of variations between different regions, between rural and urban areas, between classes and also between different religions, ethnic and caste groups:

> Indian women writers, however, have more than met the challenge. They have been sharp enough to grasp the complex ground realities and communicate and articulate the same in their works. Far from being evasive or cursory, the women writers have analyzed the caste, community, class, rural and urban angles in the lives of women threadbare. Not only have they alluded to the predicaments of conventional life but also to the problems inherent in unconventional solutions to tide over crisis.
>
> (Jaya Prasad, 2006, p. 40)

To sum up, the present work on women writers of Nigeria and India is motivated by "the concept of human rights" which is "inextricably linked with the concept of human dignity".

(Kumar, 2004, p. 15)

In the introductory chapter the literary effort of Kamala Markandaya and Shashi Deshpande for the cause of women has been highlighted. Markandaya specializes in depicting the struggles of women coming either from rural areas or the lowest strata of society in novels such as *Nectar in a Sieve* (1954), *A Silence of Desire* (1960), *A Handful of Rice* (1966) and *Two Virgins* (1973). She has also focused on the tensions that women experience while trying to come to terms with alien culture as evident in *Some Inner Fury* (1956), *Possession* (1963), *The Coffer Dams* (1963), *The Nowhere Man* (1972), *The Golden Honeycomb* (1977) and *Shalimar* (1982).

In the works of Shashi Deshpande the anguish of middle class educated woman comes out. In works like *Moving On* (2004) Deshpande portrays a female protagonist who changes the notion of 'what is right' and 'what is wrong'. She is unapologetic about her conduct and is not ashamed of arguing with her long time admirer who had all along held her in awe. Shashi Deshpande boldly states:

> We don't reject the ideals, but we know we can't approximate to these pictures of ideal womanhood. And we will not bear any guilt that we cannot do so.
>
> (Shashi Despande in Jaya Prasad, 2006, p. 44)

In fact, Deshpande is not the only one to challenge Indian society in expecting Indian women to practice idealism or propriety all the time when the ground realities are very different. Women are as much 'human' as the men and they are as capable or incapable as the men. Hence they too can go as far as men can go in any matter.

The practice of idealism must be a matter of choice and not collective coercion. Moreover deviation from the norm must not lead to victimization or persecution as long as this aberration does not prove to be life threatening for others. This is the line of thinking that has been adopted by most of the Indian women writers specially in the context of Indian women.

All the elements that became full blown issues in Arundhati Roy's novel have been present in different proportions in the works of the senior women writers of Indian English. Be it the problems of the lower strata women, the East-West encounter, the lonely spinsters, the beaten wife, the neglected children, the relationship of brothers and sisters, extra-marital affairs, the unwelcome family members, pre-independent India, post-independent political scene and its effect on individual lives and families.... The list, in fact, could go on.

Roy's excellence, however, lies in the fact that she highlights these issues and the horrow unleashed by them on helpless men, women and children with extraordinary urgency and even audacity. This thesis discusses in detail a host of complicated issues that Roy has dealt with in her highly disturbing novel *The God of Small Things*. As already stated before, in India women's issues are of bewildering variety because of caste, class, community, tradition, region and political reasons. This complexity of issues and the web that it creates for women and children comes out graphically and chillingly in *The God of Small Things*.

The thesis makes a detailed comparative analysis of women writers of Nigeria and India namely, Zaynab Alkali, Buchi Emecheta, Flora Nwapa, Kamala Markandaya, Shashi Deshpande and Arundhati Roy. Special mention has been made of the works of Zaynab Alkali's *The Stillborn* and Arundhati Roy's *The God of Small Things*. After going through their respective works it is difficult to decide who has done greater justice to her milieu in general and to the cause of women in particular. Each writer has highlighted the cultural peculiarities of her country and how it enslaves or entraps women. These novelists show the defining characteristics of Nigerian and Indian society, that is, 'tribe' and 'caste' and how these "immutable and watertight" institutions suffocate and stifle women with their dogmatism.

(Kumar, 2005, p. 7)

The Stillborn was published in 1984 and *The God of Small Things* in 1997. This means both the works came out in the twentieth century. The twenty-first century is now getting close to completing its first decade. It was imagined that life would become easier for women with time. Great advances have indeed been made in India in the matter of women as far as legal provisions are concerned. Women have been given inheritance rights by amending the Hindu Succession Act in September 2005. Even in the context of live-in-relationships provision has been made for monetary compensation in case of refusal to keep the promise of marriage by the male partner. In some states women have been given job reservations. The 'girl child' is being fussed over by the government like never before, alarmed as it is over female infanticide.

There is, thus, a determined effort by the government, the judiciary and the legislature to give reprieve to the female population. It is true that a lot still needs to be done, because policies take a lot of time to make an impact on the ground. Yet the hope remains of a better future for women, because

Indian society is at last showing the willingness to change its attitude towards women. The same holds true for the women of Nigeria also. In both the countries, society is slowly but surely changing to give women a better present and a bright future.

Bibliography

Achebe, Chinua (1975) *Morning Yet on Creation Day*, London: Heinemann Educational.

—— (1986) "The Writer as Teacher" in Trevor James (ed.), *English Literature from the Third World*, Essex: Longman York Press.

Acholonu, Catherine Obianuju (1988) Buchi Emecheta in *Yemi Ogunbiyi* (ed.), *Perspectives on Nigerian Literature: 1700 to The Present*, Vol. Two, Lagos: Guardian Books Nigeria Limited.

——(1989) Buchi Emecheta in *The Guardian Literary Series, The Guardian*, Saturday, January 25, 1989.

Alkali Zaynab (1984) *The Stillborn*, Lagos: Longman Nigeria Present Edition 1996.

—— (1986), *The Virtuous Women*, Ikeja: Longman Nigeria.

——(1997) *The Cobwebs and Other Stories*, Lagos: Malthouse Press Ltd.

Altekar, A.S. (2005) *The Position of Women in Hindu Civilization*, Delhi: Motilal Banarsidas, First published: 1938

Bhasin, Kamla (2000) *Understanding Gender*, New Delhi: Kali for Women.

Chukwuma, Helen (1989) Buchi Emecheta in Henrietta C. Otokunefor and Obiageli C. Nwodo (ed.), *Nigerian Female Writers: A Critical Perspective*, Lagos: Malthouse Press Ltd.

Desai, Neera & Usha Thakkar (2004) *Women in Indian Society*, New Delhi: National Book Trust, First published: 2001.

Deshpande, Shashi (1981) *The Dark Holds No Terrors*, New Delhi: Vikas Publishing House.

—— (1982) *If I Die Today*, New Delhi: Vikas Publishing House.

——(1983) *Come Up and Be Dead*, New Delhi: Vikas Publishing House.

—— (1985) *The Dilemma of Women Writers* in *Literary Criterion*, Vol. 20, No. 1, pp. 33-36.

——(1983) *Roots and Shadows*, Bombay: Sangam Books.

——(1988) *That Long Silence*, London: Virago

——(1992) *Binding Vines*, London: Virago.

——(1996) *A Matter of Time*, Delhi: Penguin Books.

Emecheta, Buchi (1972) *The Ditch*, London: Barrie and Jenkins.

——(1975) *Second Class Citizen*, New York: George Braziller.

—— (1976) *The Bride Price*, New York: George Braziller.

—— (1979) *The Slave Girl*, London: Allison and Busby.

——(1979) *The Joys of Motherhood*, London: Allison and Busby.

—— (1980) *The Moonlight Bride*, Oxford University Press, (Masquerade Books).

——(1980) *The Wrestling March*, Oxford University Press, (Masquerade Books).

——(1981) *Destination Biafra*, London: Allison and Busby.

——(1981) *Naira Power*, London: Macmillan.

——(1981) *Double Yoke*, London: Ogwugu Afor.

——(1983) *The Rape of Shavi*, London: Ogwugu Afor.

Garba, Ismail Bala (2006) 'Of Real Freedom and Gender, Equality: A Re-appraisal of Zaynab Alkali's *The Stillborn*,' in *JENDA: A Journal of Culture and African Women Studies*: Issue 8.

Guerian, Wilfred L. et al. (1999) *A Handbook of Critical Approaches to Literature,* Oxford: Oxford University Press, First published: 1966.

Indra Mohan, J.M.G. (ed.) (2004) Shashi Deshpande, Delhi: Atlantic Publishers and Distributors.

Iyengar, K.R. Srinivasa (1994) *Indian Writing in English*, New Delhi: Sterling Publishers Private Limited.

Jain, Jasbir (2003) *Gendered Realities, Human Spaces,* Jaipur: Rawat Publications.

James, Trevor (1986) *English Literature from the Third World,* Essex: Longman York Press.

Kapur, Mita (2007) *In Conversation* in *The Hindu,* March 18.

Katrak, Ketu H. (1998) *Post-Colonial Women Writers and Feminism* in Bruce King (ed.) *New National and Post-Colonial Literatures,* Oxford: Clarendon Press, First published: 1996.

Khan, Fawzia Afzal (1993) *Cultural Imperialism and the Indo-English Novel,* Pennsylvania: The Pennsylvania State Univ. Press.

Killam, G.D. (ed.) (1984) *The Writings of East and Central Africa,* London: Heimemann.

King, Bruce (ed.) (1998) *New National and Post-Colonial Literatures,* Oxford: Clarendon Press, First published: 1996.

Kirkman, Bill (2007) *Africa in a Historical Context* in *The Hindu,* March 11.

Kumar, Sangeet (2004) *Human Rights and the Indian Constitution* in *Journal of Applied Research in Social Sciences and Humanities,* Vol. XIV & XV. 2003-2004.

——(2005) *Changing Role of The Caste System: A Critique,* Jaipur: Rawat Publications.

Majola, Dr. Yemi I. (1989) *Flora Nwapa* in Henrietta C. Otokunefor and Obiageli C. Nwodo (ed.) *Nigerian Female Writers: A Critical Perspective,* Lagos: Malthouse Press Limited.

Markandaya, Kamala (1954) *Nectar in a Sieve,* New York: John Day.

—— (1956) *Some Inner Fury,* New York: John Day.

—— (1960) *A Silence of Desire,* New York: John Day.

—— (1963) *Possession,* New York: John Day.

—— (1966) *Handful of Rice,* New York: John Day.

—— (1969) *The Coffer Dams,* New York: John Day.

—— (1972) *The Nowhere Man,* New York: John Day.

—— (1973) *Two Virgins,* New York: John Day.

—— (1977) *The Golden Honeycomb,* New York: Thomas Y. Crowell.

—— (1982) *Pleasure City,* London: Chatto and Windus.

Miller, Jane Eldridge (ed.) (2003) *Who's Who in Contemporary Women's Writing,* London: Routledge.

Mukherjee, Meenakshi (1971) *The Twice Born Fiction,* New Delhi: Heinemann.

Mukherjee, Prabhati (1978) *Hindu Women,* Hyderabad: Orient Longman.

Naik, M.K. (1992) *A History of Indian English Literature,* New Delhi: Sahitya Akademi, First published: 1982.

Niven, C.R. (1958) *The Land and People of West Africa,* London: Adam & Charles Black.

Nwapa, Flora (1966) *Efuru,* London: Heinemann.

—— (1970) *Idu,* London: Heinemann.

—— (1971) *This is Lagos and Other Stories,* Enugu: Nwamife.

—— (1972) *Emeka-driver's Guard,* London: Univ. of London Press.

—— (1979) *Mummy Water,* Enugu: Flora Nwapa Books.

—— (1980) *Miracle Kittens,* Enugu: Flora Nwapa Books.

—— (1980) *Wives at War and Other Stories,* Enugu: Tana Press.

—— (1982) *One is Enough,* Enugu: Tana Press.

—— (1984) *Never Again,* Enugu: Tana Press.

——(1986) *Women are Different,* Enugu: Tana Press.

Ogunbiyi, Jemi (ed.) (1988) *Perspective on Nigerian Literature: 1700 to The Present,* Vol. II, Lagos: Guardian Books Nigeria Ltd.

Otokunefor, Henrietta C. and Obiageli C. Nwodo (eds.) (1989) *Nigerian Female Writers A Critical Perspective,* Lagos: Malthouse Press Limited.

Parameswaran, Uma (2000) *Kamala Markandaya,* Jaipur: Rawat Pub.

Palmer, Eustace (1989) *Buchi Emecheta* in Henrietta C. Otokunefor and Obigeli C. Nwodo (eds.) *Nigerian Female Writers: A Critical Perspective,* Lagos: Malthouse Press Limited.

Prabhu, H. Pandharinath (2000) *Hindu Social Organization,* Mumbai: Popular Prakashan, First published: 1940.

Prasad, Jaya (2003) *The Younger Generation and the Caste System: A Study of Defiance in Indian English Novel* in The Lucknow Journal of English Studies, Vol-II, pp. 111-118.

—— (2006) *Myth and the Indian Novel in English: A Critical Study,* Unpublished Thesis, Patna University, Patna.

Prasad, Shaileshwar Sati (1997) *The Insulted and the Injured,* Patna: Janaki Prakashan.

Roy, Arundhati (1997) *The God of Small Things,* New Delhi: India.

Ray, Mohit K. (ed.) (2003) *Studies in Commonwealth Literature,* New Delhi: Atlantic.

Smith, David (2007) *Journey In The Footsteps of Anti-Slavery Heroine* in *The Hindu,* March 19.

Soyinka, Wole (1996) *The Open Sore of a Continent,* New York: Oxford University Press.

Taiwo, Oladele (1989) *Buchi Emecheta* in Henrietta C. Otokunefor and Obigeli C. Nwodo (eds.) *Nigerian Female Writers: A Critical Perspective,* Lagos: Malthouse Press Limited.

Trivedi, Harish and Meenakshi Mukherjee (eds.) (1996) *Interrogating Post-Colonialism,* Shimla: Indian Institute of Advanced Study, Rashtrapati Nivas.

Wieringa, Saskia (ed.) (1997) *Subversive Women,* New Delhi: Kali for Women, First published: 1995.